Sparks Fly

The Holliday Girls

Sparks Fly

Santa Maybe

Sparks Fly

A Holliday Girls Novel

HAZEL HENRY

HarperCollins Children's Books,
a division of HarperCollins Publishers,
195 Broadway, New York, NY 10007

HarperCollins Publishers, Macken House,
39/40 Mayor Street Upper, Dublin 1, D01 C9W8, Ireland

Avon a is an imprint of HarperCollins Publishers.

Sparks Fly

harpercollins.com

ISBN 978-0-06-347454-3

Typography by Julia Feingold
26 27 28 29 30 LBC 5 4 3 2 1
First Edition

Sparks Fly

ONE

Daisy

LATE-AFTERNOON RAYS OF SUN stream through the sliding glass doors and splash across the faux marble island (don't tell my mom I admitted it's fake) as I dance absent-mindedly into the kitchen, earbuds blasting. Beyond our backyard, and the neighbor's yard, and across the street from them, you can see about one centimeter of the Atlantic Ocean, twinkling in summer light. Well, it's the Sage Port Bay, actually. But according to Sage Port, Rhode Island Realty, our home is considered "ocean view" because of this very glimpse.

I swing open the fridge door, prowling for a LaCroix at the same time that I'm trying to perfect a very specific hip roll I learned on TikTok. I've been in party mode for a while now: The last weeks of school before summer break are always one languorous stretch of warm days, hitching rides around town with whoever has a driver's license (not me), every class full of pointless filler activities and extra-credit projects no one cares about. I've been especially bouncy and happy as May morphed into the early days of June—I can't quite put my finger on why, but I suppose you could say I've been party-moding-for-two, because Georgia is the one who graduated this spring; I'm only finishing my sophomore year.

My older sister has her future all planned out—Duke University with her boyfriend, Rhys, then Yale Law, then marriage (to Rhys, obviously), then two children with great manners and healthy teeth—so I guess to her, finishing high school is just one more check mark on the neatly arranged little list in her brain, not a cause for mindless celebration. It almost seems like she's signing yearbooks and hugging old friends and trading copies of the last school newspaper of the year on autopilot; a pretty smile plastered on her face.

It's Georgia who should be experiencing senioritis. But it's *Georgia*, so she's mostly experiencing her floral planner, which has "Georgia Holliday's Personal Itinerary and Visioning" penned carefully on the inner cover. I mean, you don't even have to read what's *in* the planner, you can tell by how clean the handwriting is, every page filled with meetings, to-do lists, and personal goals. It makes me tired just thinking about that planner. Tired and maybe a *tiny* bit envious, if I'm being honest. It would be nice to have any idea what I'm doing with my life. Then again, Izzy Reynolds, our grief therapist, would probably say it's my sister's way of dealing with loss.

"We all have our own methods of coping, Daisy," she'd say, in that tone where I can tell she's implying something about *me*, but I'm not sure what. It's true that when Dad died I was pretty messed up for the rest of eighth grade. I barely went to class for a while, and my grades plummeted. But that seems like an average response to something as shocking and horrible as what happened to us. One day, Dad was here, larger than life. Everybody loved Mitch Holliday, down to our dentist and the postman.

Then *snap*, he was gone. Crazy. How can that not screw you up mentally?

Also, maybe I wasn't meant for advanced algebra.

But it's been almost three years since then, and there are entire days, even weeks, that go by when I forget to miss Dad. And that's sad in a whole different way.

Still, it's been nice to not be thinking about grief too much and have a bounce in my step lately. It's probably because this summer we're finally going back to Laurel Lake! We grew up going to my mom's lake house up in the Catskills every year—it was a Holliday family tradition—but after Dad's death, we stopped going. It was always such a happy place for all of us. So I know that even if we have to deal with some hard memories, Izzy would say it'll be very *therapeutic* for us to return, and I can't wait.

I mean, I *think* that's why I've been in such a good mood.

There could be other reasons.

My phone pings with a text from my friend Owen Adams.

Owen:

Daze, Project Invisible Shopper is near completion!

He's referring to a remote-control shopping cart he's been working on in his garage, in case that wasn't obvious.

Daisy:

Ready for a test run? Just make sure no Shaws employees catch you.

Because he's building it with a stolen shopping cart.

Owen:

Should I take it for a ride at Jenna's later?

Daisy:

I'm sure it'll be a real hit. Some guys impress all the chicks with their new cars, but not you, my friend. You're an original.

Owen:

I need to put something in it. Like a parade float. Like maybe a giant inflatable clown?

Daisy:

Adams, why.

Owen:

So it looks like the clown is driving the cart.

Daisy:

No, I get it, but like why . . . do you have to be so YOU?

Owen:

😱 Ok so that's a no to the clown? Maybe something less disruptive, like an inflatable cow?

I laugh.

Daisy:

Where are you going to find an inflatable cow in the next hour?

Owen:

The army probably keeps some in reserve somewhere. Maybe I can phone a local base.

This is classic Owen. Just utter batshit, but always so funny. It is highly possible he is really going to bring this thing to the party later tonight, but my bets are on it not working, left abandoned on Jenna Greenberg's lawn.

Daisy:

Just please don't get yourself arrested. This is our last chance to hang before I leave.

Owen:

Oh dang. June 19th. That's tomorrow isn't it. What time do you leave in the morning?

Daisy:

IDK. Early. You won't be awake. And hopefully, you also won't be in jail.

Owen:

That's the beauty of a remote-control cart, Daze. They'll never catch me.

Daisy:

Don't you have to be within thirty feet to operate it?

Owen:

Details details.

Daisy:

Well I gotta go. But don't forget, Owen. The squeaky wheel gets . . . increased amount of attention from its father.

It's a very stupid running joke we have, where we purposefully butcher common idioms like "the squeaky wheel gets the grease."

Owen laughs at my message.

Owen:

And every cloud has a . . . shape outlined by something brighter than the cloudy part of the cloud.

Daisy:

Lol.

Owen:

Later, Daze.

I shiver, realizing I've been texting while standing with the fridge door open. I shove my phone back in my pocket and I'm in the midst of an angry boxing match with our semi-broken ice machine when someone tugs my ponytail, and I scream.

Frozen chunks go flying out of the machine's open mouth, scattering and slithering all over the kitchen floor, and I look up into Georgia's face. She's shouting something.

I pull out my earbuds. "What!" I yell, then realize without my music on that I'm yelling, and bring my voice to a normal level. "Sorry, you scared the crap out of me. I didn't hear you coming."

"Yeah, that's because you listen to those at a decibel not designed for our species," Georgia says matter-of-factly.

"I told Scarlet I'd learn this choreo so we can practice at the party later," I explain.

We're meeting at Jenna Greenberg's sister's graduation party in an hour, and Scarlet Diaz and I have a silly little tradition of performing TikTok dances in people's backyards. I realize it sounds cringey, but we're kind of the funny girls in our class, so people expect it.

Georgia has the grace not to roll her blue eyes, though I can feel how tempted she is.

"I was just reminding you to finish packing before you leave," she says, tucking her blond hair behind her ears.

"Yeah, sure. I'm almost done," I say, which isn't exactly the truth, because I haven't started. But that's what the frantic fifteen minutes before we leave is for.

"Okay," she says. "I need you to pack an extra charger, in case the one in the car dies before you find the cabin."

"Oh my god, Georgia, we'll be fine. Mom's been driving up to Laurel Lake her entire life practically, she doesn't even need GPS. And also, Dave will be with us."

If I'm not mistaken, Georgia flinches ever so slightly at the mention of Dave. As in Dave Carmichael, Mom's boyfriend. They've been dating since last fall, but lately it seems like it's getting more serious than any of us expected—least of all Mom. He's going to be joining us for the entire summer up at the lake, which is maybe weird.

But, like, I'm happy for Mom. She's a writer and spends most of her days completely alone. The woman deserves some joy. Though I get the impression Georgia is less enthused. *She's rushing in*, I've heard Georgia say on more than one occasion. *I just don't want her to get blindsided.* And *What do we really know about this guy?* As if he's some potential criminal. He's an aquatic expert who took Mom to the Sage Port Aquarium for their first date. How many of those turn out to be killers? I'd wager zero percent. Georgia's just protective.

"I'm going to be gone by the time you're home from the party tonight, so I want to make sure you have everything in order."

"Georgia." I put my hands on her shoulders, which are, annoyingly, still a couple of inches higher than mine. I am convinced I'm never going to catch up. She got Dad's height genes, and I got Mom's. "We are going to be fine, and we'll see you up at the lake. Just enjoy your weekend in New York with Eden, and please document every single second of it because I'm jealous as heck and I hate you both."

Georgia laughs and gives me a hug. "Okay. Be good tonight. By the way, are you wearing that? Or . . ."

I look down at my cutoff jean shorts, Rolling Stones T-shirt, and no bra. (I very much embrace having small boobs and hope they never grow. Freedom from the constraints of female undergarments and shapewear!) "Yes?"

She sighs. "Whatever. Love you. I'm gonna go say bye to Mom."

"You should probably hit the road if you don't want to end up driving in the dark," I tell her, because I can tell she's dragging her feet.

Her eyes widen. "Oh my god, you're right." *Now who's the good planner?*

"Love you, Georgia. Go!"

I know she's a little nervous, but I can't believe it. She gets to drive—*alone*—in *her own car*—to *New York City*—to see the *best* human in the world (our cousin Eden), and then the two of them get to spend the weekend doing *whatever they want* before driving up to the lake house together. While *I* get to sit in the back seat while Mom and Dave listen to NPR for the entire drive up to Laurel. It's completely and wildly unfair.

But if it means Eden gets to spend the summer with us in the Catskills, I'm all for it. I love her like the sister I never had, which is to say, I love her like the sister I *do* have, but better, because she's more fun. I'm thinking she'll be a good influence on Georgia, and the three of us are going to have the best time.

Besides, we all know this may be the last time it gets to be like this. With Georgia and Eden off to college in the fall, who knows how much life is going to change. Which is why I'm all about seizing the moment and carpe diem-ing the crap out of this summer.

Starting with tonight's party. Technically, it's a graduation party for Jenna's older sister, Holly, but Jenna is allowed to invite a bunch of her own friends, too.

I watch Georgia jog back up the stairs to her bedroom to grab the last of her things. Then I turn back to the mess of melted ice on the kitchen floor.

Someone should really clean up around here.

"So, Owen told you he's coming tonight?" Scarlet says, cocking her head to the side, causing her bike helmet to tilt. Two long black pigtails stick out the bottom of the helmet and hang down her chest. She's waiting for me to get my bike out of the tangle of pedals and wheels in the corner of our garage where I usually leave it.

"Yeah," I grunt, pulling the handlebars to no effect.

"Did he *tell* you that, or was it a text?" Scarlet asks.

"What? I don't know. I don't remember. Probably both?" I've finally dragged my bike out of the heap. "Why?"

She shrugs. "I was just curious."

I look at her. It's hard to read her expression because she wears one of those hardcore helmets with an eye screen. It could double as a welding helmet. "Since when are you so curious about Owen being at parties?" I ask.

Owen's less of a going-out-to-parties kind of friend and more of a let's-do-our-bio-homework-in-front-of-the-TV-together type. Usually, Scarlet and I make our own plans.

"Oh, you know, I wasn't sure if he was in trouble with his parents again or what," Scarlet says.

Which is a fair concern, given that Owen is almost never *not* in trouble for something. He can't help himself; he's got big golden retriever energy. Like, he means well, but if a squirrel crosses his path, forget about it. And the squirrel could be anything from some snide comment Aaron Eckles made in fourth-period English to, well, that stupid idea for a remote-controlled grocery cart he's been building in his garage. It never seems that bad to me, but I know he struggles with grades and gets himself into too many fights that he always claims he didn't start (and for the record, I totally believe him). He's in Principal Carver's office so often he knows the names of all her plants. It's gotten to the point where his parents have been talking about moving him to a more integrative school in Providence, which would probably be great for him but selfishly would suck for me.

I shrug. "I guess not. Or maybe? We'll find out!" I tell her, hopping onto my bike seat and giving the pedal a twirl.

"When does he leave for his camping trip again?" Scarlet asks.

"It's not a *camping* trip," I remind her. "It's thirteen days backpacking around Europe with his grandfather."

Scarlet laughs. "Whatever. I heard the word *backpacking* and my brain went dead."

"Same," I tell her. I start rolling slowly down my sloped driveway, but Scarlet isn't with me. I stop and turn to face her. She's straddling her bike but her feet are down, and now my psychic senses are tingling (though I'm way less talented at reading the minds of friends. The skill is mainly focused on Mom and Georgia).

"So, you guys haven't *talked*," she says slowly. "Since the last day of school? Or . . ."

"Oh my god, Scarlet, no, we haven't *talked*. I don't think. Why? Is there something you're not telling me? Is there something going on with Owen? What's going on with Owen and why aren't you just spitting it out? Do I need to take my helmet back off for this?"

"What! No! Nothing. I don't know anything about it!"

She's not looking at me.

"Anything about *what*?" I prod.

"Anything about anything! I know nothing about you and Owen! At all!"

"Nothing about *me and Owen*? There is no 'me and Owen,'" I say. And then the wheels start turning in my head. "Is there?"

She shrugs. "I didn't say anything, and you didn't hear it from me. But if you *must* know, Daisy, he likes you."

"Whhhhaaaaaat?!" It's a good thing my helmet doesn't have a wind screen thingy like hers, because it would be splattered with the spit that just went flying out of my mouth.

"Oh, come on," Scarlet says, finally placing her feet on the pedals and rolling down the slope to the street. "You can't be *that* shocked."

She starts biking away from me, and I push to catch up. "What the—! Scarlet!" I shout.

Can't be that shocked? Oh yes, I very much can.

My head is spinning, my heart is racing—though maybe that's from how hard I'm pumping the bike pedals. The cool June breeze does little to calm me down or clear my head. I try to make sense of what Scarlet just told me. *Owen. Owen? Really?*

Honestly, it doesn't click. It doesn't make sense. All this time we've been friends and it just . . . never occurred to me.

As we ride through our neighborhood, evening descending over the houses and turning the bay in the distance from a sparkling blue gray to an undulating purple, there is only one conclusion I can draw from all this: my mind-reading skills *fully* suck.

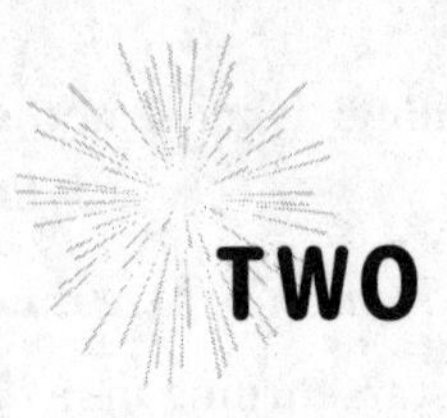

TWO

Georgia

I'M NOT A NERVOUS driver. I'm a careful one.

Clearly this is not a concept New York City drivers understand. By the time I arrive on Eden's block in Tribeca, I have been: screamed at by a hot pretzel vendor, flipped off by a mother jogging with a double-wide stroller, honked at by three taxis plus one produce delivery truck, and nearly run down by a bicyclist with a pizza. My hands are shaking, my heart is pumping, and sweat has gathered in places I really don't enjoy sweat gathering.

But somehow, I'm alive? *No thanks to Dave Carmichael.* I cannot believe he convinced my mom to let me make this drive alone. How dare he point out that I'm a careful driver who could be trusted in the city.

Still, there's pride mixed with the relief that washes over me when I finally spot the seventeen-year-old girl with messy honey-brown bangs and gap teeth practically skipping down the sidewalk toward me, waving her arms.

I roll down the window. "Eden!"

"Georgia!" She comes over to the driver's-side window and

plants a huge smooch on my cheek. "Thank god you're here. We have so much to do!"

"Where do I . . ."

She swings open my door. "Scooch over. I'll drive this into a parking garage. You don't want to leave it on the street. There's a guy who's been shitting on people's bumpers."

"Seriously?" I climb over the gearshift to the passenger seat so Eden can take mine.

"Welcome to the city!" she says by way of an answer, and then she's squealing away from the curb and rumbling us over cobblestoned side streets toward a parking garage that's so well-hidden I'm convinced she's about to drive us straight into the wall of a fancy furniture store.

We drive down into a cement dungeon of sorts and hand my keys over to the valet, leaving with only a flimsy paper ticket promising I'll see my car again. Not to mention the entire summer's worth of clothes and swimsuits I packed, plus the big box of books in the trunk. I have so much to do before college starts.

Daisy was totally right: I left too late, and the sun has already set—but in New York it never gets totally dark, and as I follow Eden to her family's loft a few blocks away, I feel like I'm entering a dreamland where time isn't real. A feeling of lightness fills me. This is the Eden Effect. I always feel like anything's possible when we get together.

Although I guess it could also be the halo effect of realizing I'm here, and not dead on the side of the road.

We say hello to Eden's doorman and ride the elevator to her

floor. The whole time, Eden's going on about our itinerary for the night, involving dinner with her "lame" parents and meeting up with some of her friends at an escape room. Then, before we go into her apartment, she interrupts her own stream of chatter— "Oh, by the way," she says, pausing with her key in the doorknob, "don't tell my mom I helped you park just now!"

"Wait, why?" I ask, trying to read the guilty look on her face.

She shrugs. "Failed the driver's test. Again. She'll kill me."

"Eden, you don't have your *license*?" I hiss, but it's too late. She's opened the door and now I have to mask my shock and act chill—as in, the opposite of my true personality—as her family gathers to greet me with hugs.

Luckily, I'm instantly distracted. Nyla Chu and John Holliday are *not* lame, they're two of the best people on the planet and I'm obsessed with them. But I always get this tiny jolt when I first see Uncle John because he looks so much like Dad. Different builds— Dad was a professional baseball player, tall and muscular, fit even in retirement, while John is an entertainment lawyer and got the scrawnier, lanky genes in the family. Still, my uncle's hazel eyes and light hair, wide smile and tall forehead are so familiar, it takes my breath away for a second, leaving a small ache in my chest.

I hug him fiercely, and Aunt Nyla too. They both ask about Mom and Daisy, and then they drag Eden's younger brother, Jesse, out of his bedroom, where he's apparently been working on "a new set of beats" with headphones so soundproof he'd probably miss it if the microwave he's allowed to have in his room exploded. The kid is a serious hermit; between making music and maintaining his YouTube channel, he rarely sees the sun.

Unsurprisingly, Jesse puts up a serious fight about going out to dinner with the rest of the family. When he finally concedes, we pack into the elevator like sardines, then walk to their favorite French place—where, they tell me, it's *impossible* to get seats and a *miracle* they're squeezing all five of us in, so long as I don't mind squishing into a "four-top."

I nod along happily, truly unsure what the difference is from every other dining experience I've had with them. Everything in New York seems to involve cramming as many people as possible into tiny, ambient-lit, absolutely un-fire-safe venues that they swear are the *best* place to be *ever*, but which definitely have rats in the basement and would look like someone's unkempt storage closet if you turned the lights up.

After we're seated, my aunt and uncle tell me all the things I just *have* to order and *have* to try because *no one makes them better*. I try to remember everything to list in my planner later, but my French is terrible.

Then, as plate after plate arrives at our table, they pepper me with questions about my mom and Dave. I know they're just excited and everybody loves a little gossip, but the questions make me kind of uncomfortable.

Yes, I say. Dave seems kind, Dave seems lovely, Mom seems happy.

But then, she never dated anyone before my dad, because they met in high school. So what does she even know about dating? It's a crazy, predatory world out there and we should really all be encouraging her to go slow.

That launches Aunt Nyla into a story about how *her* dad, who's in his seventies, got scammed by a Russian model on Facebook who somehow got him to hand over his bank account information, address, and Social Security number.

"See?" I say, nodding. "That's exactly my point!"

Though Uncle John points out that it seems quite unlikely that Dave is secretly a Russian model. "What does he do again?"

"He's a professor of water science, I guess," I tell them. "Or as Daisy likes to call him, an aquatic expert."

Eden laughs and proclaims that this isn't a real job. Which only proves my point that you really never know the truth about people.

The food is all as delicious as promised, but at one point Eden literally slaps a piece of bread right out of my hand. "Don't fill up too much! You'll get sleepy, and we need to go *out*!"

Frankly, I would be just as happy to curl up with Aunt Nyla and Uncle John to watch Netflix, but instead I dutifully put the bread back into the basket. When it's time for dessert, Eden insists we both order espressos. I grimace, unable to drink more than one sip, but she downs hers. Before her parents have even finished paying the bill, she grabs my hand and practically shouts, "We're going to meet friends at You'll Never Get Out of Here Alive!"

I experience brief alarm before remembering that's the name of the escape room.

"Home by eleven" is all her dad says, and we're off.

My aunt and uncle trust Eden—when she's with me. They know I'll do my best to keep her in line, even for a whole summer at the lake. She's been a little . . . *wild* these days. They say the country air will be good for her. But I'm pretty sure they're also expecting me to keep an eye on her.

And of course I will. Because I love spending time with Eden.

And also because I never—and I mean *never*—disappoint people.

"Oh no!" I say when we pop up out of the subway nineteen minutes later. We were only accosted once, by a man peddling pamphlets about salvation, which Eden informs me is a reasonable amount of being accosted. I'm still awkwardly carrying around the pamphlet, which features a lot of rainbows and sunlight through clouds, because I am too polite to say no. "I need to call Rhys!"

Eden barely slows. "Now? Why? We're already late!"

I feel a wave of guilt. "I was supposed to tell him when I arrived safely, but I totally forgot."

"What is he, your mom?" Eden asks, turning to face me and crossing her arms. "You guys are long distance anyway. What's another few hours of not talking? He's not your *keeper*, Georgia."

But it's *sweet* that Rhys worries about me and asks me to check in. He's not being controlling—he doesn't care what I do. He just cares that I'm okay, because he loves me. A concept that Eden obviously cannot wrap her head around. I may be young to have a serious boyfriend, but it's really not that unusual. My parents met when they were our age!

Rhys Kingsley and I actually met three years ago—at Laurel Lake, the summer before Dad died. We were both taking lessons at the tennis club. We're in the same grade in school, but he was several leagues better at tennis—and he still wanted to practice together. I found out he lives in Connecticut but not that far from the Rhode Island border, only a half-hour drive from Sage Port. It was all very innocent—by the end of the summer, we finally had our first kiss, but that was enough. We started calling each other every day and seeing each other on weekends when we got the chance. I brought him with me to my high school homecoming dance that fall, and everyone was amazed (including me) that I had this handsome out-of-town boyfriend.

Then that horrible day in October happened, just a few weeks later. The morning I will never forget. Dad was built like an oak tree, the healthiest guy, full of energy and optimism. He spent most of his time coaching the high school baseball team, doing the occasional brand sponsorship, and being the best dad ever. Needless to say, practically everyone in Sage Port was devastated when he got up one morning, went for his typical three-mile jog, and never came home. He was found on the path by the water. By the time they got him to the hospital, he was gone. Heart attack. I was in second-period World History when I got called to the office. My mom was so hysterical over the phone that I couldn't understand what she was saying.

I still can't think about that day without crying.

After that, I'll admit my relationship with Rhys moved quickly. Tragedy has a way of either splitting couples apart or knitting them together tightly, and the latter is what happened for us. He was constantly there for me on the worst days, holding me when I cried and taking me on weekend ski trips with his family. It was what I really needed. Someone on the other end of the phone, someone who had known my dad—well, had met him a handful of times, anyway. Someone solid and reliable, and as driven and ambitious as me. When we first started dating, I don't think either of us had any idea how compatible and *similar* we were, but maybe that was the hand of fate, steering me in the right direction when I needed it most.

As much as I want to hear Rhys's voice right now and tell him about my adventures in solo highway driving, I don't want to be rude. Plus, there's our curfew—I don't want to get us in trouble with Eden's parents.

"Fine," I say. "I'll just text him."

Eden gives me one of her big, gap-toothed smiles. "Great!"

I shoot off a quick text—**Made it to NYC!**—and take a selfie in front of the escape room door. Then I make sure my location is synced on Find My Friends.

Before I've even put my phone back into my pocket, it starts to ring. Rhys.

I'm tempted to answer, but Eden rolls her eyes at the ticket counter, where she's already holding both our passes.

"Come *on*! Call him back later!"

So I silence the ringer, pasting a sociable smile on my face as we allow ourselves to be locked into a room with nine of Eden's best friends, none of whom I've ever met.

I figure, soon I'll be up in Laurel Lake, where I'll have all summer to be with Rhys.

Not to mention our entire future.

One evening offline won't hurt.

THREE

Eden

I DON'T REMEMBER WHOSE idea it was to wear these fake astronaut helmets, but mine's stifling. Our deep space research station is nearly out of power and we've only solved six of the nine puzzles that will unlock the multitiered security system, granting us access to the escape pods.

"Terraformists," a robotic voice says over an intercom, referring to our team name. "You have ten minutes of life-supporting oxygen remaining."

"As opposed to the non-life-supporting oxygen?" my friend Ray asks, throwing his arm around me.

I roll my eyes and poke him in the shoulder. "Honestly, Ray, this is your fault. We all went for your stupid first-letter code theory."

"Excuse me?" He puts a hand to his heart, as if he's been mortally wounded. His curly hair takes on a life of its own as he shakes his head. "It's *so* not my fault if you can't recognize genius for what it is, Eden. The first letters of all the safety directions spell out P-L-A-N-E-T-A-R-Y and you're trying to tell me that's just a wild coincidence? How can it mean nothing?"

"He has a point," says Jackson. "How can it mean nothing, Eden?"

"You guys are ganging up on me," I say, laughing.

"I have a new plan," says Suzanne. "We perform a lifesaving *dance* to communicate with aliens, who will naturally be delighted by our choreo and decide to stage a rescue."

Everyone laughs, except Alex and Isla, who are consumed with a word scramble that the rest of us have given up on.

Well, and except for Georgia—I notice she's not laughing either, she's checking her texts. *Again.* Even though we all agreed there should be zero reception in space—you know, for verisimilitude. (In fact, there really *isn't* very good reception since we're in a soundproofed basement in K-Town.)

I totally get that she doesn't know any of my friends and is probably feeling a little shy, but she could make more of an effort. I'm not saying my cousin's being a killjoy, but something has definitely been bugging her since we got to the escape room.

Finally, someone—okay, it's Isla—basically finishes the three remaining puzzles on her own, and by some miracle, we make it to the escape pods (that is, we get out of the room), with about ninety seconds to spare.

As soon as we take off our space helmets and I hug all my friends goodbye, I turn to Georgia, trying to modulate my annoyance with her.

"Everything okay?"

"What? Yeah, it's just . . ." Georgia trails off, typing again. She's still got her face down over her phone like she's breaking a war code.

"So do you want to get some late-night bibimbap and meet up with Ray and Alex? They were talking about renting a karaoke room."

Georgia looks up, as if startled I'm still here.

We're standing on the sidewalk, neon signs blinking brightly overhead, cars squealing past us, people talking, singing, shouting. It's June in the city, warm but not too hot, and New York is *alive* with activity. Can't she feel that electric buzz?

"Sorry, Eden, what did you say? I'm a little distracted." She holds up her phone and makes a cringey face. "I missed like three calls from Rhys while we were down there and his texts weren't really coming through because of the service, and now . . ."

"Now . . . ?" I prod. I mean, what could be such an emergency?

"Let me just see if I can try him back," she says, already dialing. But the phone rings and rings on the other end. "Darn." She hangs up.

"I'm sure whatever it is, it's fine," I insist, but Georgia seems stressed. "This one karaoke place . . ." I start, but she holds up a hand.

"Eden, it's after ten. We don't have time to do karaoke and still get home by curfew." The lights from the street are turning her pale blond hair a pretty shade of pink.

I sigh. "Fine. Ray always hogs the mic anyway. But we may

as well use up all the time that we have. Hey, I know. Why don't we walk home?"

"Is that safe?" Georgia asks.

"Of course! And I carry my trusty pepper spray with me at all times, just in case. It'll be great. We can grab some tacos and walk through Washington Square Park. Maybe the saxophone guy will be there. You never know. We could accidentally stumble on another Timothée Chalamet lookalike contest or something. And *that* way," I add, "if Rhys calls back again, you'll be able to answer."

I can see the visible wave of relief cross Georgia's face. "Okay," she says, starting to smile. "Thanks, Eden. That sounds great!"

After about ten blocks, I manage to get Georgia laughing at my dumb jokes and weird stories about the friends she just met. We're passing by Madison Square Park, where the Shake Shack still has a line.

"Your friends all seem so great," she says. "I really liked them. That guy Jackson was *so* funny. And Ray seems cool, too. He seems kind of into you, actually." Georgia elbows me.

"Ray? He's gay, babe. But Jackson . . . there *was* something there. For maybe a week. But he was getting clingy, so I had to end it."

"Clingy? What did he do?"

I shrug. "Nothing really. It was more an energy thing. I could, like, *feel* the cling. In his eyes."

"He was giving clingy eyes?" Georgia asks skeptically.

"It's a thing!" I insist, laughing.

Georgia shakes her head. "It is *not* a thing. You're just a chronic heartbreaker."

I roll my eyes. "We're seventeen. We are supposed to be testing the waters, not settling down. And by the way, Alex was *definitely* flirting with you. If you hadn't had your head in your phone the whole time you might've noticed. He's cute!"

Georgia looks at me like I've sprouted two heads and they're both purple. "I have a boyfriend, Eden!"

She sounds so scandalized I can't help but laugh again. It's so easy to rattle her!

Despite the fact that people have always called us "twin cousins," since we were born only a few weeks apart, in many ways Georgia and I are opposites: Georgia is a romantic, loyal, sunny blond who can't hail a cab or navigate a subway to save her life. She's a nature girl at heart; she's been known to talk to bunnies and frogs and, once, she rescued a skunk. Like some sort of real-life Sleeping Beauty.

And I'm, well . . . *not that.* The only animals I speak to are pigeons and cockroaches, and you do not want to know what I tell them.

"Boys can be fun," I tell Georgia now, "but they always reveal themselves to be scum in the end. Even the cute ones. Why wait around to find out?"

Georgia shakes her head. "Are you sure that's really the truth, Eden? Or are you still bitter because you never properly let yourself heal from Leo Goldbaum?" She looks at me meaningfully.

I look away, pretending to be extra concerned about whether we have the walk signal or not. "What happened was, he was a judgy little jerk and I should've seen it coming from a mile away. I won't make that mistake again," I say before marching into the intersection. The idea that I'm not over Leo Goldbaum is ridiculous.

Utterly absurd.

I haven't thought about him in like two whole years. At all. *Barely.*

The thing about Leo Goldbaum is that he really does come off as a decent guy.

Or at least, he did to me. We'd known each other all the way back in middle school, when we were both total babies. He was a nice, curly-haired kid who got insane math scores and busted his chin open doing the worm at Malcolm Levy's bar mitzvah. He let me touch his stitches. At the age of thirteen, this was a serious level of intimacy, so, yeah, I got the idea that maybe he liked me. We smiled at each other at a few more of those bar and bat mitzvahs. Got seated near each other in a handful of classes thanks to our last names. And despite his failing dance skills, he was a great soccer player. You could tell all his teammates were obsessed with him, which can be a very green flag, though I suppose it depends on what the teammates are like. Anyway, he was cute then, in a dweebish, "wanna see all my Boy Scout badges?" kind of way.

Then we both got into Stuyvesant High School. Leo got even cuter. He made varsity soccer as a freshman, which everyone thought was a big deal. His dimples settled more into his face; his curls settled a little more into dark waves.

Okay, fine, he got hot.

I thought he'd forgotten I existed, and then one day in the cafeteria toward the end of that year, he asked me if I wanted to go to a basketball game with him at Barclays. He had courtside tickets to the Nets.

Do I like basketball? Not really. Did I say yes anyway, then tell all my friends we had "net side" tickets? I'm telling you, I know nothing about sports.

And back then, I clearly didn't know much about boys, either.

Still, we had a great time. At the end of the game, he kissed me. It was a good kiss—maybe even a *great* kiss—and after that, we were dating: studying together at the library on Tuesday evenings; going to parties together instead of just running into each other there; texting all summer; me actually going to some of his soccer games sophomore year and holding up signs, like a classic, totally cringey "cheers for her man" girlfriend type.

Ew. I was smitten, and I can admit that, even if I'm not proud of it.

We dated for kind of a long time. Most of sophomore year! There were a few rough patches—red flags along the way that in retrospect I really should have paid more attention to. Like the time he told me I was a little self-absorbed because I hadn't asked him any questions in a full week; I'd only been talking about myself. (Who keeps count of how many questions people ask them? So rude.) Or the time he said I only wanted to go to school dances for the attention, and when I asked him why he thought that, he basically implied that I couldn't possibly be there for the joy of dancing because my moves weren't that good. Ouch! I wasn't sure which was worse, that he was insulting my dance style—mostly of the jump-around-waving-arms-in-the-air-like-you're-steering-a-plane-on-the-runway variety—or that he thought I was both self-centered *and* attention hungry.

Accurate? Maybe, but definitely *not* cool to say.

The biggest red flag—and this one really stung—was when I found out he'd blocked my brother, Jesse, from getting onto varsity soccer team tryouts that August. Obviously, it was the coach's final decision, and extremely rare for anyone to make varsity right off the bat like Leo had, but apparently, he'd been "planting seeds" in the coach's mind that Jesse wasn't a serious player. That even though he showed talent, he didn't have the drive.

Jesse did end up quitting the JV team to "focus on his beats" halfway through the season. So, it's possible Leo was right all along . . . but I didn't like the fact that he was going around saying negative things about my brother. It spoke to this judgy side of him; the part of him that thinks he knows what's best for others.

Still, I was willing to look the other way on all these issues because I was so stupidly dazzled by how handsome and funny and smart and well-liked he was. *Is*.

And who knows what would've happened if it weren't for the disaster that was Becca Johnson's fifteenth birthday party.

That, and everything that came after.

* * *

Georgia's phone rings at the exact moment that we're walking beneath the Washington Square Arch, and we halt our progress so she can answer. Because, of course, it's Rhys! I'm not trying to be a jerk about it; I actually think Rhys is fairly cool. He's been there for Georgia when she really needed it. Also, he's hot, smart, popular, and success driven. Everything Georgia could ever want. But I'm kind of annoyed that he's hijacking our night of independence in the city.

On the other hand, I don't mind sitting on a park bench for a second because my clogs are killing me.

I can tell from Georgia's face that this conversation isn't going well—a lot of "What?!" and "It's not that I'm not happy for you, I'm just surprised!"—and by the time she hangs up, her hands seem a little shaky.

She turns to me. "Wow," she says, letting out a tensely held breath. "Okay, brace yourself."

I nod, wondering what this could be. He didn't just break up with her, did he? If he did, I'll personally murder him. It would be *great* if Georgia started the summer single, but I don't want her starting the summer *heartbroken*, and definitely not because of that guy. My mind is already conjuring a list of fitting responses when Georgia finally spits out the news.

"Rhys got the internship!"

I stare at her. "Huh?"

"You know, the one I was telling you about over dinner? At Bank of America!"

"Bank of America?" I try not to shudder at the boringness of the word *bank*, and mentally replay dinner, but all I remember was some stuff about an online scammer.

Georgia shakes her head in disbelief. "He told me he was applying to a few of these finance internships but didn't really think he'd get one. He said the Bank of America one is the *most* prestigious and the *only* one he'd consider saying yes to."

"So . . . what does this mean?" *And no offense, but why should I care?*

"It means he's going to be living *here*, in New York, for the summer. Instead of up at the lake. He'll still commute up to Laurel for the weekends, but obviously it won't be the same." She rubs her jaw, clearly upset.

"But you're used to long distance at this point. And aren't you guys going to college together in the fall? So what's another couple months apart?" I ask, twisting my ankles, watching my clogs dance around on my toes.

"I know, it's just . . ."

"Not what you'd planned," I fill in.

"Exactly." She sighs. "It's . . . it's okay. It'll be okay. It'll be fine! We'll still get lots of time. Every weekend is, like, two out of every seven days. What does that come to?" She thinks for a second. "Something a little less than thirty percent."

For a moment, I stare at her, in awe of the rapid mind math.

But I know Georgia. And I know how much she dislikes things that weren't part of her plan.

I throw an arm around her shoulders. "It'll be great, babe. You'll have me to distract you! I mean, when I'm not doing the *stupid* wilderness camp thing Dad's *forcing* me to do. Hey! You should join it with me! It's probably not too late—"

"Eden, I'm committed to the lifeguard job at the lake. Assuming I pass the tests," Georgia says. "But you'll be fine. A little time in the woods won't kill you."

"And you know what, Georgia? A little time away from Rhys won't kill you either."

"You're right." She sighs.

While she's mulling on what the summer will look like with seventy percent less Rhys, my own brain strays into the dread I get every time I think of Boundless Horizons, the two-week "outdoor adventure and wilderness survival" program my parents signed me up for. It's exactly the type of activity a person like Leo Goldbaum would *love*—a chance to show off his lifesaving knowledge of deciduous leaf varietals or whatever. Yet another reason we were never meant to be—not that I thought we were.

Don't get me wrong, I'm fully pumped to spend the summer in the Catskills. I was just imagining most of it spent sunning on the beach, barbecuing (or more accurately, consuming the fruits of other people's barbecuing), and bumming around town. Laurel Lake was a fairly rustic place when our parents were younger but it's become much more posh, full of arty Brooklyn expats, with a tennis club, lake beach, ski lifts that go up into the mountains for breathtaking views, and off-road biking—all a couple of miles outside a quaint little village with the best muffin café, cute shops, art galleries, pottery studios, candy stores, ice cream parlors, a bandstand in the town square, canoe and bike rentals, and an old schoolhouse that's been converted into a library. Basically, heaven. That is, if you aren't spending your time hiking, fishing, and camping . . . aka slapping mosquitoes and rubbing sticks together in the woods.

My parents acted like Boundless Horizons was the one condition under which I would be permitted to spend the summer up there, but honestly, I think they were dying for me to leave the city regardless. They think I've been partying too hard, which is ridiculous, because I am actually very well-behaved. Sometimes I try telling them what some of my friends have gotten into, but instead of realizing they have a perfect saint of a New York teenager, they just lose it and worry even more. Between me running loose in the city, and Jesse, who almost never leaves his room, they're longing to set at least one of us straight and turn us into more well-rounded and functional humans.

Whatever. Well-rounded and functional are overrated.

"Hey, let's get a cab. My feet kill," I tell Georgia, slinging my arm through hers so our elbows are linked.

"Mine too," she admits. "Besides, it's 10:46."

"Crap!" I say, leaping up and pulling her with me. We head back out through the arch and prowl around for a cab. Eventually we make our way over to Seventh Ave, where I finally flag one down, and then we're inside, heaving a breath, heading south to Tribeca as the night city streams past our windows.

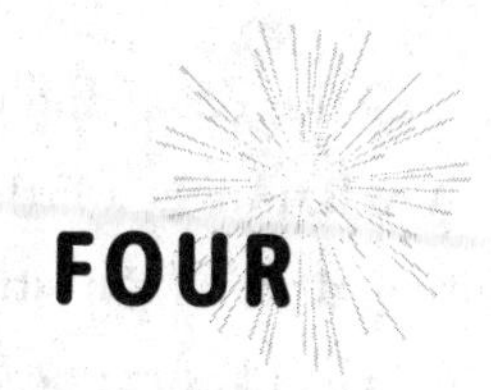

FOUR

Daisy

MY ALARM GOES OFF, playing Avicii's "Wake Me Up," but it's pointless: I'm already wide-eyed, staring at the ceiling. My heart has been racing since last night's party. Is this normal? Should I go to the hospital? Undecided, I roll over and squint at the window. Sunlight falls across the two suitcases sitting open, each with some random clothes and skin care products thrown inside with absolutely no sense of order. *Rude.*

I wrench myself out of bed, throw on a fresh pair of jean shorts, and hunch over the suitcases. I know Mom and Dave will be honking the car horn at me in no time, so without thinking, I start throwing more stuff in. Surely, it's a quantity game, and if I just manage to assemble enough items, I will avoid forgetting anything essential.

Ugh. I really hate packing. So many decisions; so much demand to imagine your future self and what she'll feel like wearing and doing. Probably, a lot of lying on her back staring at ceilings, thinking *Did that really happen?*

I feel a physical need to text Scarlet, but I'm guessing she's sleeping in. Also, there's this equal and opposite force within me that wants to hold on to last night a little longer, keep it mine.

Mom knocks on my door as I'm sitting on top of both bags, trying to zip them up. She pokes her head in and I briefly wonder if she's been dyeing her roots since dating Dave, a sure sign that things really are serious. Somehow, me and Georgia and Eden all got various shades of light hair from our dads, and not our moms (remarkably gray-free) deep brunette or, in Eden's case, the jet-black hair of Aunt Nyla.

Mom surveys my room, hands on her hips. She's wearing khaki shorts, a plain blue tank top, and Tevas. "Wow, sweetie! Are you actually ready, or do my eyes deceive me?" Her expression is a look of true shock.

"I think so," I tell her. "Just need to brush my teeth, and can we stop at a Dunkin' on the way out of town?"

"You know how I feel about you kids having so much caffeine," she says.

"I'll ask Dave. He'll say yes," I tell her.

Right then, I hear Dave in the hall. I can't see his sunny smile, curly hair, and glasses, but I can hear his voice. "I do say yes. I need a coffee, too. Let's hit the road, ladies!"

I smile. Dave has his perks.

He helps me lug my suitcases down the stairs and out the door, and as we're cramming them into the trunk—a true Jenga challenge—Mom waves a postcard at me.

"Daisy, this was on the front stoop for you." She hands it

over, and I try not to blush to the roots of my hair. "Who could it be from?" she asks.

I shrug and get into the back seat of our sedan, slamming the door before she can think to ask any more questions. On the front of the postcard there's a picture of the Sage Port Christmas Parade. I smile to myself as I flip it over. The note on the back is short and sweet, jotted in a messy scrawl I recognize from the many homework assignments we've done side by side over the past two years.

Of course. Incongruous and out of season, his favorite kind of gesture.

The grin on my face physically hurts, and I feel a warm fluttering in my belly. I can picture Owen, his blond hair flopping in front of his eyes, sitting down to write this note. Did he set an alarm to get up early enough to deliver it to my house before I woke up?

We must've pulled out of the driveaway, but I've barely noticed the car moving, lost as I am in my thoughts and memories. . . . A few minutes later, I'm chugging my milky coffee as we merge onto the highway. Mom and Dave put some sort of mind-numbing NPR station on, and the voices form a relaxing, hypnotic background noise.

I lean back against the seat, completely exhausted from this morning's speed-packing effort. And, you know, from barely sleeping all night. Still holding the postcard, I close my eyes for just a minute.

Savoring last night one more time as I leave Sage Port—and Owen—for the whole summer.

You could hear the music pumping out of Jenna Greenberg's backyard from down the street by the time Scarlet and I got there on our bikes, and somehow the neighbors weren't complaining . . . yet. Sage Port's the kind of town where if someone's got a problem, they're likely to knock on your door and tell you to your face. But it's also a town that just loves celebrations. Every holiday is an excuse for Main Street to get a makeover, and the winter lawn decor is truly off the charts.

I was still fully shook by what Scarlet had told me, but I was starting to settle down a little. For one thing, it probably wasn't true. Scarlet had said *he likes you* with such confidence, but that was always her way. Scarlet had the same confidence when she told me that she'd heard Miss Trubaker was postponing our test on ancient Rome last month, but she'd been dead wrong . . . and so was I, on about a third of the exam questions, as a result.

What does Scarlet know? I told myself as we dropped our bikes near the front stoop. *Just be calm. Just be normal.*

And then the door swung open before we could even knock, revealing Owen.

He smiled, and for possibly the first time ever, considering how long I've known him, I was struck by how cute he is, with a grin that's slightly too big for his face, blond hair that's slightly too long and disarrayed, and squinty blue-gray eyes that make him perpetually seem on the brink of laughing or crying. He was wearing a too-big T-shirt that said IT'S NOT CONTAGIOUS, over dusty black jeans.

"Yo, are you the butler?" Scarlet asked as he stepped aside, holding the door for us.

My shoulder brushed past his bicep, and that's when I started basically hyperventilating. *This is crazy*, I kept repeating to myself. *It's just Owen!*

He smirked. "I was literally standing in the front window and saw you guys coming."

I nodded like a broken bobblehead, suddenly devoid of human language.

Thankfully, Scarlet was being normal. "What were you doing inside, loser? Isn't everyone out back?"

He shrugged. "Trying to fix this," he said, holding up what looked like a Game Boy console but was clearly his shopping cart remote-control thingy. I didn't even notice if his contraption was out on the lawn, that's how brainwashed I was by what Scarlet had told me.

Owen likes me. Owen likes me?

Wait, do I like Owen?

The answer wasn't readily available. Owen had never given me that vibe; never given me any sign whatsoever. His attention was always so focused on whatever his latest obsession was . . . who'd believe his brain could even run a separate, concurrent track on which he'd be holding a secret crush? It really didn't seem possible.

And it probably wasn't. I should probably set Scarlet's weird rumor aside and enjoy the last night before everyone departed for their summer camps and vacations.

"Let's party, fools." With that, Scarlet marched ahead of us through the house.

"Come on, Daze," Owen said, putting an arm around my shoulders. "Our leader has commanded we go to the backyard and socialize with the plebes."

Scarlet looked back, tossing one of her long dark braids over her shoulder, and rolled her eyes at us.

Then we all stepped out onto Jenna Greenberg's back porch, from which you could see the rest of the party people spread out around her massive lawn under twinkling fairy lights. Beyond them, her yard sloped down to the bay. There was a "Happy Graduation, Holly" banner drooping between two trees, and I saw Jenna's dad manning the grilling station, flipping burgers, while Jenna's mom was chatting up a couple other parents who'd stayed to hang out.

But I couldn't take in the details of who was there or what music was playing or really anything other than the smell of Owen's T-shirt, freshly washed with his mom's favorite laundry detergent. Why did it smell so good?

In one corner of the yard, people were dancing, and Scarlet beelined for that crew, leaving me and Owen alone. He took his arm off my shoulder, which was both disappointing and also a relief. I needed to get my bearings.

"I'm starving," Owen said, which helped break the spell. "I'm gonna grab a burger. Do you want one?"

I felt like I was going to throw up. "No thanks. I'm gonna chase down Scarlet."

And then I did the cowardly thing and physically *ran away.* I found Scarlet in the dancing crowd. "I can't be alone with him now," I told her. "It's too weird!"

"Well, good, let's practice our choreo," she said.

And for the next hour, I tried to ignore Owen chatting with his other friends, focusing instead on Scarlet and Jenna and our dance moves. After a while, I had loosened up and drunk too much Sprite and was on a sugar high. Just having fun at a party.

But I'd be lying if I didn't say I had one eye on Owen the whole night. There was a moment where I gazed out at the ever-darker yard and couldn't see him, and I panicked. Had he left? Had I screwed up our last evening to hang out for the whole summer by avoiding him out of nervousness?

"I have to pee," I told Scarlet, and left the group to go find him.

But as I was crossing the crowded lawn, someone grabbed my arm. "Daisy!"

I turned—and sighed, realizing who it was. *Here we go again.*

"Hey, Anthony," I said, trying to smile.

Anthony put both his hands in his jeans pockets and tilted his head. "I didn't know you'd be here!" he said. "Owen told me Jenna said it was okay for me to come."

"That's great!" I lied.

Jenna only invited a handful of friends to her sister's graduation party, and Owen knew it was our last night to hang out, and yet he invited Anthony to come, too?

I mean, Anthony is nice enough. There's nothing *wrong* with him, he's just annoying and insecure . . . and kind of in love with me, which is sweet but very one-sided. Owen's always saying, "Are you gonna take pity on Anthony at the dance this weekend?" And I'm always saying, "Absolutely not a chance," and then he gets this look like he feels bad for his friend, and then we move on.

Which, come to think of it, might have been another reason why it never would have occurred to me that Owen could like me, too. I assumed since he was always gently pushing Anthony on me that he couldn't be interested himself.

"Speaking of Owen," I said, "have you seen him around? I, uh, need to tell him something."

"He was just out here," Anthony said. "He went into the kitchen to see if they have any more salsa."

"Cool, thanks."

"Want me to come in with you and help find him?" he asked.

"Actually," I said, "I think Jenna wanted to ask you about something? She's over there." I pointed to the cluster of girls who were now throwing a glow-in-the-dark Frisbee around.

"Really?"

"Yup!" I felt bad, but I was suddenly feeling the urgency of regret. I had already spent way too long ignoring Owen, and if I wanted to find out what was really going on, I had to just talk to him. What if he'd taken my avoidance as a sign to leave?

Was he already on his way home?

Thankfully, Anthony walked away, and I bolted up onto the

porch, pushing past a group of Holly's friends, until I found my way to the kitchen.

The fridge door was open, a pair of legs beneath it.

"Owen?" I basically shouted.

The fridge door closed, and Owen stood there, blue eyes twinkling, holding some hot peppers, limes, and a couple of avocados in his large hands.

"Guac?" he asked with a smile, and all my urgency faded away as I laughed with relief. He hadn't left.

"Thought you'd never ask."

"Great! But I have to warn you," he said, his voice getting serious as I helped him find some cutting boards and a large bowl. "They don't have any cilantro."

"Can't we just use parsley or something?"

Owen practically dropped all the avocados. "Daisy! Parsley's like cilantro's boring cousin who no one invited to the party." He handed me the avocados while he worked on chopping the peppers and juicing the limes.

"Speaking of not inviting people to parties . . . why did you tell Anthony about tonight?"

Owen shrugged. "He called and asked what I was up to later. I said I was meeting you at Jenna's. Once he heard you would be here, he wanted to know if he could tag along."

"You didn't have to say yes," I said as I cut open the avocados, removed the pits, and scooped the insides into the bowl.

Owen shrugged. "I guess I'm a nice guy."

I looked at him. His hair was covering his eyes and he seemed to be concentrating on a special way of chopping the peppers into tiny bits. "Do you *want* me to go out with him?"

Owen glanced over at me in surprise, his knife coming down hard on the cutting board. "Why, do you like him now?"

"Whoa, don't chop off your thumb! And, no, I'm asking because you're always trying to push us together."

"No, I'm not! Why would I care? I want whatever *you* want. He's my friend. I'm a good friend, Daisy, in case you weren't aware."

"Hmm. Okay," I said, not loving his answer. *Why would he care?* "I just feel like giving him hope is pointless."

"I don't think hope is ever pointless. But I hear you." He put down the knife and the pepper and turned to face me fully. "I promise not to keep giving Anthony hope. Swear." He offered a hand to do our signature handshake.

"Wait, I can't." I held up my hands—they were covered in avocado at that point, but that didn't deter Owen. He grabbed my right hand anyway and we did the dumb pinky swear/handshake thing we've done since forever. Then both our hands were covered in green mush.

"Ew!" I said, laughing, and then he was laughing too, and we ran over to the sink, which turned on hard, getting water all over both our shirts. "Oh my god, this is a disaster."

"I beg to disagree."

We got back to work once we'd dried off. "So," I asked him, "are you excited for your trip with Grampa Dan?"

"Excited? I have to leave my phone at home. For two weeks!

And my parents made it pretty clear it was this or some camp where they force you to sleep in the woods for a month and learn about *focus* and *good values* or whatever. So, no, excited wouldn't be the word I'd use. It's like, whatever almost total dread feels like."

I laughed. "Apprehensive? Dubious? Trepidatious?"

"Wow, you are going to absolutely murder the SATs."

"I can't believe I won't be able to get a play-by-play of this adventure over text," I told him, beginning to comprehend the notion that he would not be able to text with me for nearly half a month. That would be the longest time we'd spent not communicating since . . . ever?

He smiled at me, dumping a pile of chopped peppers into the bowl. "Will you miss me?" For some reason, this question caused me to flush to my ears. But before I could answer, he added, "Because don't worry, I have a plan."

"A plan?" I asked as he handed me half a lime and we both started squeezing lime juice into the bowl.

"Yeah. Postcards. I've always wanted to have someone to send postcards to. Although by the time you get them, I will no longer be wherever I sent them from."

"Ooh, that's . . ."

"Deep? Profound? Thoughtful of me?"

"I was gonna say, a challenge for your bad handwriting."

"Also that," he agreed. "I'll send them to the Laurel Lake address."

"If I write back, you won't get anything until you're home, though!"

"Here," he said, handing me a spoon. We started smashing up the guacamole. "That's okay. You don't have to write back. It can be a tragic one-sided conversation."

I smiled. "The best kind."

"Is it?" he asked. He stopped mushing up the guacamole and left his spoon in the bowl.

I shrugged, aware of how close we were standing to each other, of how intensely he was looking at me, scanning my face for an answer. And suddenly, I wondered if he was asking about more than just postcards. I didn't know what to say.

"Daisy . . ." he began. I could feel him take a shaky breath, like he was about to tell me or ask me something important. His hair was falling in front of his eyes, and he brushed it back behind an ear. "I—I . . . *Oh. Ow. Ow!*"

Then he was half shouting, half screaming, covering his right eye. "Crap, I touched my eye, and I still had pepper on my fingers."

"Seriously? Oh no!" I grabbed a paper towel, wetted it in the kitchen sink, and handed it to him. He pushed it against his closed eye and groaned.

"Oh man. It burns like crazy. Am I gonna go blind from this?"

"Okay, okay, calm down," I told him. "You won't go blind. Don't you know you're not supposed to touch your face if you've been cutting hot peppers?"

"No! And I am clearly learning that the hard way right now, Daisy!"

"Come on, follow me." I grabbed him by the shoulders and

steered him out of the kitchen. "Let's just find somewhere for you to sit down for a minute and hold this over your face," I said, handing him a fresh paper towel drenched in ice-cold water. "I'll see if I can find any eye drops."

I led him up the stairs and into the bathroom, closing the door behind us. I didn't need Jenna thinking we were ransacking her family's medicine cabinet, even if that's exactly what I planned to do.

He sat on the closed lid of the toilet holding the wet compress to his eyes and swearing under his breath while I rapidly searched the shelves behind the mirror.

"I see some contact solution. Maybe that will work?"

"Okay," he said. "I trust you."

"As you should," I told him. "Lean back, and just . . . hang on." I had to sort of straddle his legs and drape myself over him. "Now remove the paper towel." He slid it away slowly, and his eye was all red and squinty.

"You have to open your eye more!" I scolded.

"I'm trying!" he said, fluttering his eyelid.

I leaned in and squeezed a few drops of the solution into his eye. "Now blink rapidly, to wash out the pepper's oils," I told him.

He did as I commanded.

"Is it starting to feel a little better?" I asked. "Do you want more drops? Here," I said, mopping his face gently with the wet paper towel. "Is that helping?"

He nodded. "I can't tell if that actually helped, but I think it's calming down a bit," he said, and tried to smile.

I was still leaning over him, straddling his legs, dabbing the corner of his eye. He looked up at me.

"Wow, saved by Nurse Daisy."

"To the rescue," I said.

I started to pull away, but he grabbed the belt loops of my shorts. "Wait," he said.

I sort of fell forward and ended up sitting on his lap, facing him.

"You're really enjoying being the injured patient, aren't you?" I asked, laughing a little. I didn't know what else to do. I was *sitting on Owen's lap* and he was *gazing into my eyes* with this smile on his face that I couldn't quite read. So, I just kept gently dabbing him with the compress.

"I am," he agreed. His hands didn't leave my waist. He still had that smile. "Thanks."

"Anytime." Looking at his face, a little red and blotchy from his reaction to the pepper, but also so familiar, I started to get this . . . I don't know how to describe it. It was this feeling of *knowing.* A feeling of *oh*, deep in my gut.

Like the answer to whether I cared that he liked me, and why, was suddenly so clear. Yes. Because I wanted him to like me.

Because maybe I liked him, too. Maybe this was a whole new thing that had yet to be discovered between us.

"Anytime? Really?" he asked, his voice kind of quieter.

"Yeah, really."

There was this pause—kind of awkward, but heated—where

neither of us moved. And then I felt his thumbs kind of pressing against my hips, and I leaned all the way over him, and our lips touched, and . . .

He kissed me. Or I kissed him? I think it was both?

It was definitely both. Our tongues found each other. I felt his teeth. His lips were soft and full against mine. It was a *real* kiss, our bodies pressed up against each other. It was maybe the hottest kiss I've ever had, actually.

He pulled back a little and so I did too. "Whoa," he said under his breath.

"Yeah." I knew what he meant. We were both reeling.

"Is this really happening?" he whispered.

"I didn't mean for it to happen. . . ."

"You didn't? Wait, did we just do something super insane?" he asked.

A tremor of worry went through my chest. I was wondering the exact same thing. "I mean . . . maybe? I'm not sure. But should we, like, do it again? Just to see?"

"Okay, that's a really good idea," he said.

"Okay, great," I said.

And then we went back to kissing. And it was even hotter than before. His hands moved from my belt loops up to my waist and back, and then one hand found the back of my neck and I thought I was going to completely lose control of myself.

I had to pull away and catch my breath. "This is definitely insane," I told him.

"Insane in a good way or a bad way?"

"I think in a good way," I said, searching his face for some sign of whether this meant as much to him as it did to me. Because it felt like my entire life was changing in this moment.

"Me too," he said.

I grinned, all of a sudden feeling dizzy.

"Daisy . . ." he said.

"Yes, Owen?"

And then there was a rapid knocking on the bathroom door, and I leapt off Owen's lap, and he sort of leaned forward like he was in a new kind of pain. I didn't know what to do and I wasn't thinking straight, so I just flung open the door, which was probably the dumbest response, but it was too late.

Anthony was standing on the other side. "Sorry, I— Oh. You're both in here?" he asked, looking between us.

"Owen got something in his eye," I explained, then pushed right past him and ran down the stairs before I could face what had happened.

"Come on, Scarlet," I told her, finding her near the porch. "We gotta go."

"Now?" she asked, but I was already pulling her around the side yard to the front, where our bikes lay together in the gathering dark.

When I wake up, it's because the car has slowed down. We're pulling off the highway, and immediately turning down a single-lane road surrounded by forest on both sides. My face is smooshed up against the window, which has probably left an imprint across my cheek. We pass a sign for Laurel Lake.

I look down at my hand. I'm still clutching the postcard from Owen, but now it's a little damp and sweaty, the ink already rubbing off a little, onto the inside of my palm.

I reread his note, searching for some sign, some indication of what last night meant to him.

Happy holi-DAZE from the great town of Sage Port. (They don't pay me enough for these puns.) (They don't pay me anything for these puns.) Anyway. I meant what I said! You'll be hearing from me this summer. From all around the world. Well, all around Europe. Though with Grampa Dan you really never know. I'm sure we'll be hanging out in hostels with decent food but for some reason all I can picture is us sleeping in a tent in the hills of Austria, foraging wild berries to survive. Wish me luck.

Love, Owen

PS: Why'd you leave so quickly last night? The guacamole was disappointed you didn't stay to give it a try.

FIVE

Georgia

SINCE EDEN STILL HASN'T gotten her license, I do all the driving on the way to the lake house. Once we get out of the city it isn't so bad, and we have our favorite snacks—watermelon Sour Patch Kids, Reese's Pieces, salsa-flavored SunChips, an Arnold Palmer for me and giant Diet Coke with ice for Eden—plus a well-curated playlist, which I know we'll talk over the entire time.

Eden sits in the passenger seat in her loose black overall shorts and cropped black tank top, like an exact negative of me in my new white eyelet romper that buttons up the back.

(She took one look at me this morning and was like, "You're in a beautiful pee prison! How do you ever go to the bathroom in that?"

"My arms are extremely flexible," I told her, easily reaching behind my back for the buttons.)

Now Eden's munching hard on her Sour Patches and shouting out orders.

"Merge!"

"Watch out for that biker!"

"The exit is coming up!"

I can tell she's a little surly over us driving up today—we were supposed to spend the whole weekend in New York and drive up Sunday afternoon, but once I learned that Rhys would only be at the lake for the weekend, I couldn't stand the idea of us missing each other. So we left early this morning, and I'll have the whole rest of today and tonight with Rhys.

Rhys and I usually hang out every other weekend, but because of various end-of-school-year commitments, it has actually been three weeks apart, and I have this *anxiety* to be in his presence. I always get this feeling when he's away too long. It's the nature of being in a long-distance relationship, I suppose. You end up putting a lot more energy into planning when you'll see each other next, and it just carries a different kind of weight and intensity. Which I *like*, because we never waste any of our time together. It's always full of activities and deep conversations. Neither of us wants to laze around when we could be doing something more meaningful together.

Anyway, he's not the only reason I decided to leave early. I also need to prep for the lifeguard test. More time at the lake this weekend means more time for me to get in that practice I need. I've been swimming at the Y consistently, but I need to do some basic circuit training and sand running, too. Just thinking about training has my body itching to move. Unlike Daisy and Eden, who are slugs, I thrive on constant physical activity. I *hate* relaxing.

"Damn," Eden says, looking at me over the lid of her huge soda. "You merged into the left lane like a demon!"

"I did? Oh, sorry. Guess I'm just eager to get to the lake."

"No, no, don't apologize. It was *fierce*."

When we finally pull up the long dirt driveway to the lake house, any guilt I was feeling about dragging Eden out of bed early this morning dissipates.

The tall evergreens paint stripes of shadow and light across the lawn. The house peeks out between them, its dark brown chipped siding and white shutters so familiar and cozy they bring instant tears to my eyes. I roll down the windows to take in the fresh, summery smell of the lake and the forest.

It looks like we're not far behind Daisy and Mom and Dave—the Subaru's trunk is still sprung open and only half unpacked.

"Come on!" I say to Eden as I kill the engine and our playlist along with it.

With a squeal, she leaps out of the passenger seat and beats me to the front door. Mom, Dave, and Daisy are in various stages of carrying boxes and suitcases and grocery bags around.

"Girls! You're here so early!" my mom exclaims. "Eden, look at you!" She goes in for a hug with one arm, still holding a grocery bag in her other arm, and ruffles Eden's hair. "I love these bangs. You look adorable. I mean adorable and very mature."

"Mom, please don't embarrass her," I say, taking the groceries and heading to the kitchen.

"I don't mind!" Eden calls from the other room. "Please feel free to shower me with praise, Aunt Elena. I'm not picky."

I hear Mom laugh. "Oh, good. Nothing's changed, then."

Daisy comes pounding down the stairs as I'm emerging from the kitchen, having already unpacked all the groceries and disposed of some seriously sketchy-looking three-year-old mayo from the fridge. "Eden!" my sister yelps, throwing herself at our cousin, and they do a little happy jumping hug dance. "Oh my god, I'm so glad you're here!"

Dave comes down the stairs next, sneezing into a Kleenex. "I opened up all the windows," he says to Mom. "This place is fantastic, but it could use a little love, sweetie. And all the dust is activating my allergies."

Mom shrugs. "That's to be expected! It's been empty too long." For a moment, a cloud of sadness passes across her face. And then, just as quickly, it's gone. "Come look at the upstairs den," she says, turning to Eden. "That'll be your room this year, if that's okay! But it's going to need to be put in order. The good news is you can rearrange it however you like!"

Eden follows Mom up the stairs and Daisy trails behind them, leaving me in the living room facing Dave. He stands with his hands in his khaki pockets, hovering behind the old plaid-and-wood couch as if he's afraid I'll bite.

And I can't help feeling glad that he still seems a tiny bit afraid of me. Dave is a perfectly kind man. But he doesn't know our family. He doesn't understand what we've been through, not really. He doesn't know how anything works between us. The Holliday girls don't come with a manual. He's going to have to earn his place in our world, and that takes time. Until then, it's only right that he's a little uncomfortable.

"So—" he begins, but my phone rings.

"Rhys!" I answer, turning away from Dave and stepping back out the front door onto the lawn.

"Baby!" he says. I almost choke with happiness and relief at hearing his warm, deep voice.

"Where are you? What are you up to? Can I come meet you?"

He laughs. "Mateo and I are heading over to the club to knock the ball around a little."

"Oh! Mateo?"

"Yeah, he's staying up here with the fam this summer. I told you that, right?"

I nod, the phone bobbing against my ear. "Yeah, of course." Although I'm not actually sure that he did. Mateo Roman is one of Rhys's close friends, so I know Mateo's parents are divorced and he lives with his mom in Connecticut.

"So . . . wait," I say. "Is he up here all summer or only this weekend?"

"All summer," Rhys answers. "His mom's going to Italy this year to see extended family, and he didn't want to go with her."

"But your internship . . ."

"Yeah, I know. I feel bad, but honestly, I think he's stoked to spend more time with my parents. You remember all that shit that went down with his dad. . . ."

Again, I'm nodding, but honestly, I really don't remember or care. I'm . . . frustrated. My time with Rhys has already been reduced to weekends only. Now I'm going to be sharing his limited attention with Mateo?

Not cool.

But I know Rhys is just being a good friend, and his family is so generous to host Mateo even when Rhys himself can't be there the whole time. Rhys's family is truly the American dream—they're the real-life version of those beautiful, multiracial families you see in movies or luxury car commercials, all gorgeously confident, nurturing, well-traveled, and sincerely smiling.

"When can I see you?" I blurt out, trying to contain the weird mix of eagerness and annoyance in my voice.

"Why don't you come down to the club, too?"

"We can't all three play," I say.

"Bring Daisy or something. We'll play doubles!" Rhys says cheerfully. I can tell that it hasn't even occurred to him that I'm a little upset—which is for the best. I'm being really pouty and immature.

"Doubles sounds great! I'll drag Daisy or my cousin Eden over with me. See you there in twenty minutes?"

"That sounds perfect, babe," he says.

"Yay! I'm so excited to see you. I miss you so much."

"Me too. Love you." Then he hangs up before I can say, "Love you, too."

I look up to notice I've wandered away from the edge of our lawn. It's a short walk through the trees and down a narrow path to get to our part of the lake. It's rocky—no beach area or boat dock—but we can still clamber in up to our knees and then swim out or drag a kayak off the muddy bank. Though I shudder to imagine what state our kayaks are in. Probably home to an entire civilization of spiders, full of spider infrastructure. Spider highways, spider bridges, spider sewage systems.

I stand at the edge of the biggest rock that juts into the water and stare out at the sparkling lake and the opposite shore, still feathered with a morning fog. I take a huge deep breath of the mineral-scented air and feel it rejuvenating me. I hear the distant sound of kids laughing and splashing around, though I can't see anyone. I wonder if it's just an auditory hallucination.

For a moment, a memory of me and Daisy and Eden, all squeeing and splashing and calling out to each other, floods my senses, and there he is. Dad. Standing out there in waist-deep water, tossing us one by one off his shoulders into the blue water.

I blink, and he's gone.

I turn back to the house.

I'm not really surprised when Eden refuses to come with me to the tennis club, instead joining my mom, who needs to run into town for some supplies for the house and offers to take her shopping. That's obviously much more Eden's speed. At least she promises to bring back candy.

So it's Daisy's arm I have to twist. She looks at me skeptically. "You want me to play doubles with you and Rhys and his friend? You realize I am terrible at tennis, right?"

"No you're not!" I say encouragingly. She's exaggerating. She used to play with me when we were younger, but since starting high school she plays JV softball and that's about it.

"Like, almost as terrible at it as you are at lying," Daisy says.

"But fine, I'll go. I need to stretch my legs after sleeping in the car anyway."

It takes her so long to swap her cutoffs for athletic shorts and a sports bra that I've found the rackets and filled our water bottles and am sitting behind the wheel, ready to go, by the time she comes out and hauls herself into the car.

"I still can't believe you didn't take the rest of the weekend to party in the city with Eden," she says, removing a handful of candy wrappers Eden left on the seat.

"I have my priorities," I tell her.

"Oh, I'm aware, Georgia," she says with a smile. She fiddles with her sunglasses and looks out the window at the sun spraying down through the trees. She seems unusually quiet.

"What are you thinking about?" I prod.

"Nothing. Just . . . guacamole, I guess."

"All you ever think about is food, Daisy. How was Jenna and Holly's party last night?"

Daisy shrugs. "It was . . . um. Good. Really good!"

"Anything interesting happen?"

"Depends on what you'd call interesting," she replies. Classic Daisy. She loves to be coy.

"I hope you and Scarlet didn't make a total scene," I tell her.

"*Georgia*, we're not five. And no, we didn't."

After that, Daisy broods and ignores me until we pull up at the club.

We check in and find the boys already out on a court, easily rallying the ball back and forth. Rhys is what my mother would call "a tall drink of water"—his height and build, his dark skin and radiant smile, make him magnetic to look at.

Rhys clocks us as we enter the court and lets the ball sail past him, jogging toward me with a huge smile on his face that wipes away all the angst I was feeling earlier. "Baby," he says, enfolding me in his arms. I can practically feel Daisy's judgment (she hates that he calls me "baby") but I don't care. I fall into Rhys's arms, into the delicious scent of his sea salt and cedar body wash.

His lips find mine and we kiss, and for the whole minute that my eyes are closed and I'm surrounded—the feeling of Rhys, the smell of Rhys, the presence of Rhys—I get this immense sense of peace. Like falling into a hammock on a beautiful day, but better, since I get easily bored lying around in hammocks.

Then I become aware that we're kissing in front of Mateo and Daisy, and I pull away.

Rhys wraps an arm over my shoulders, and with his other hand, he offers my sister a fist bump. "Hey, Daisy! Been a while!"

"Hey, Rhys," she says as Mateo jogs over toward us from the other side of the court. "Who's this?"

"That's Mateo Roman," Rhys says. "My buddy from Connecticut. You'll be seeing him around the club even when I'm not here. This guy is way better than I am. And you know I don't admit that easily," he adds with a laugh.

Mateo smirks. "And you wouldn't admit it at *all* if you weren't forced to by blatant evidence."

"Whatever, dude," Rhys says playfully.

I glance at Mateo, surprised. Rhys isn't being modest—he

really is an incredible tennis player, so Mateo must be impressive. He's quirkier looking than my boyfriend, which matches his quieter, moodier personality. He's tall, too, but thinner than Rhys, and a little more feminine, with an angular nose, wide-set eyes, prominent cheekbones, and messy hair. Cute enough, but there's something about his face—it's impossible to read. Gives me untrustworthy vibes.

Rhys joins Mateo on the far side of the court, and Daisy and I take the closer side. But our attempt at a game is disastrous. Daisy and I both have competitive personalities—our dad was a pro athlete, after all!—but no amount of determination can get us even close to the guys' skills, and it's rather annoying for everyone, them included. Quickly we realize it's best to swap partners. Rhys and I team up against Mateo and Daisy, and that goes much, much better—mostly because Mateo is basically playing for both himself and Daisy.

Letting off a little steam on the court helps my mood . . . as does dreaming up some activities for me and Rhys to do *alone* later. A little swim in the lake. Or a bike ride into town to pick up some sandwiches for a late picnic somewhere private. We have so much to catch up on!

I'm so lost in my fantasy of the rest of our afternoon that I inch up too close on the net and miss the ball on my side completely.

"Baby!" Rhys shouts, exasperated, as I realize the winning point just went to Mateo and Daisy.

"Oops!" I run over to him. "I'll make it up to you, promise.

Why don't we rematch next weekend? I could use a break," I say.

"Yeah, all right. My game's off today, anyway," he says, and his signature smile is back on his face in no time.

"I'm hungry," I announce. "Maybe we should sneak away for some lunch?"

"We just ate an hour ago," he tells me.

"Oh. Well, what do you want to do next? I was thinking we could grab a couple bikes and—"

"I told Mateo I'd show him around Laurel Lake today. You know, all the good spots to hang out. Since he'll be here all week on his own."

Mateo and Daisy cross over to where we're standing. "You act like I can't take care of myself," Mateo says with a laugh.

Rhys rolls his eyes. "You really can't, though. Girls, do you want to come with us?"

"We'd love to! Right, Daisy?"

Daisy shrugs. "Sure, I guess. As long as Eden doesn't get too lonely without us."

"Hang on, I have an idea," I tell them, going into director mode. "Mateo, why don't you drive my car. You can take Daisy to pick up our cousin Eden. She can show you how to get there. And I'll ride with Rhys!" I turn to Mateo. "You're okay with that, right?" It's not exactly a test or anything. But the sooner he understands who takes priority in Rhys's life, the better. It'll just make things a whole lot smoother for the rest of the summer.

Mateo looks back and forth between me and Rhys. "No problem. Where are your keys?"

I dig them out of my bag and toss them to him, and before those two can dwell too much on being ditched, I grab Rhys by the arm and steer him out of the club.

"Finally!" I say cheerfully as we climb into Rhys's car and close the doors. I put my hand on his leg as he starts the engine, and he puts his free hand on mine.

"Oh, Georgia," he says, smiling to himself and shaking his head.

"What?"

"Are you going to be like this all summer?"

"Like what?"

"Jealous of my time with Mateo. Baby. Don't worry, he's not your competition."

I laugh. "I know that!"

He glances at me. "And I know *you*. You get possessive."

"I do not!"

He laughs. "It's okay, I like it. It's cute."

I sigh. He *does* know me. "Fine, you're right. But only because our time together is so precious. I hate having to share your attention."

"There's enough of it to go around," he says.

I take a deep breath, reminding myself that this is true. I don't need to be anxious about my time with Rhys. We have all the time in the world. We have our entire futures together.

But still. Rhys is like a bright light—he's the person everyone looks toward when he walks into a room. He doesn't just *go* to parties in every single social circle at his school, he holds court at them. Groups naturally gather around him, moths to a flame. I can't help but feel jealous and uncertain occasionally.

I am genuinely a naturally confident person. . . . It's just sometimes hard to believe that I'm the one he's chosen to commit himself to, when anyone would die to be with Rhys.

"Feel better?" he asks me.

I love him so much, but sometimes it kills me how well he can read me. I *hate* seeming down or insecure around him. I smile. "Of course, baby. I love you. And by the way, I'm a jerk for not congratulating you sooner. I'm so proud of you for getting the internship. You're gonna *kill* it."

His smile is huge. "Thanks! I'm super excited about it. I really think I'll learn a lot, and obviously it'll open up even better opportunities next summer."

"Right! It's so amazing." Once again, I take in how handsome, accomplished, smart, and kind Rhys is. I quickly forget my momentary annoyance over Mateo and the weekends-only thing, and remember instead how freaking *proud* I am to be this guy's girlfriend.

Together, we are going places.

It's as if he's had the same thought. "And I'm proud of you too. Lifeguarding is no joke. I know that process is rigorous as hell."

"I mean, I don't *quite* have it guaranteed yet. I need to test in," I say sheepishly. "But," I add, "I feel really prepared."

Every year, there are up to twenty teens vying for these spots, and the lake needs, at most, a staff of five or six. They usually only end up with that many qualifiers anyway because the drills and the safety and stamina tests are so grueling. The lake is remarkably calm, but Mr. Bailey, the beach director from the lake association, is originally from Australia, where, word has it, he nearly became a pro surfer back in the day and takes water safety super seriously. You also have to be seventeen. The last summer we were here, I was only fourteen, but I watched the drills and started practicing them on my own. And even though it was three whole years ago, Mr. Bailey told me to come back and test in when I was old enough to qualify.

"You're the fittest and most responsible person I know," Rhys tells me. "You have it in the bag."

He's probably right, but the test-in is on Tuesday—only a few days away . . . an overheated feeling comes over me, like a restless itch.

"You know what? Much as I want to hang out with you and Mateo and the girls, I should do some more training anyway. Can you drop me at the beach?"

He looks at me in surprise. "Are you sure?"

"Yeah. I can jog home from here easily enough."

"Great. And I'm sorry about this. I know we don't have that much time before I head back to the city," he reminds me. As if I'd forgotten!

"Why don't you come by later to say hi to the family and, you know, kiss me good night."

He smiles. "You got it."

He hangs a right instead of continuing toward town like we'd planned, and soon, we're pulling into the dirt lot with the wood-planked path that leads down to the public access beach.

Before getting out of the car, I lean across the console and kiss him slowly, deliberately.

He moans as we kiss, and his hands find my waist. "I really missed you, Georgia."

I sigh into him. "I know. Me too."

"Don't go just yet," he whispers.

"Okay," I whisper back.

He pulls me closer, and I crawl all the way onto his lap. We make out a little more, his hands moving up inside my shirt. I'm conscious of wearing a super unsexy sports bra.

"Maybe we should park somewhere more private," he says.

I pull back a little, hitting my head on the car ceiling. "Not right now. Besides, in this small town even the trees are watching. Let's find some time alone later, okay?"

And then I shimmy back over to the passenger side and open the door. As I grab my gym bag, I lean back inside the car for a minute. "Have fun!" I blow him a kiss, secretly pleased with myself.

Because now I've flipped the tables on him and reminded him just how much *he* wants to get *me* alone.

Leave them wanting more.

Works every time.

I keep a couple of spare swimsuits in my gym bag so it's easy enough to throw one on in one of the wooden stalls in the dingy beachside locker room. Despite it being a Saturday, there are only a couple of families hanging at the beach today, and a few other stragglers sunbathing and reading. The beach feels *almost* private. Probably because it's so early in the season; some schools are still in session, and a lot of folks don't come out to Laurel until the big Fourth of July festival, which is a couple of weeks away.

I start with running across the sand from either end of the beach and back, getting my heart rate up until I'm pouring sweat. Then I wade in and begin my laps. The water is pleasantly cool. Laurel Lake's not huge, but it is surprisingly deep at the center, and holds its cold temperature longer than some. The water won't get truly warm until August.

I feel strong and relaxed as I push myself to faster speeds, lapping the deepest part of the swimming area marked by a series of buoys. I know rest is good for building muscle stamina, though, so I alternate between hard laps and "rest" laps. It's during one of the latter that I notice one of the people on the beach—a teen guy, though I don't recognize him—staring at me. He's got dark hair and warm, sun-kissed brown skin, and he's sitting on a bright red towel in swimming trunks and a loose-fitting tank top, leaning back on his elbows. His face is distinctly pointed in my direction. What else could he be looking at?

I duck my head in and out of the water as I swim, but every time I sneak a peek, he's still watching me. He looks to be around my age, maybe a little younger. He's got a book in his hand, a finger marking the spot.

I keep looking over, wondering if I'll catch him returning to the book, but no—he's got his eyes on me like I'm a fascinating TV show.

I decide it's best to ignore his rude behavior, and refocus myself on perfecting my freestyle stroke.

When I finally feel my body getting exhausted, I turn toward the shore and wade out, cool water dripping down my legs, drop by drop, as a breeze picks up.

I can't help myself, and briefly cast my eyes over to the guy with the book. He can't possibly *still* be watching me, can he?

I breathe a sigh of relief. The red towel is no longer strewn across the sand, and the boy, whoever he was, is gone.

SIX

Eden

SOMEHOW, I END UP riding shotgun in Georgia's car with this guy Mateo driving, and Daisy in the back seat. Rhys meets up with us downtown and we walk around, poking into shops. This is my second shopping trip in one day and I'm not sad about it. But it's a little random—me and Daisy trailing around with Georgia's boyfriend and his friend. I've met Rhys a couple of times and never met Mateo, and they're both a little fratty for my taste, but fun enough. And Laurel is such a cute town. We end up having a silly time trying on hats and getting boba, and then we drive up to one of the mountain lookout points you can get to by car, where Daisy and I snap some selfies fully blocking the view while Mateo jokes around pretending to shove Rhys off the edge of a cliff.

Boys. Sheesh.

By the time the guys drop us off back at the house, the early colors of sunset—fresh peach and pale gold—are starting to filter through the trees. Daisy and I take the rest of our tea and plop into the hammock, which is so crusty from years of neglect it almost snaps in half under us.

We sit facing each other, our knees tucked up under our chins, swaying slowly. "So now that those losers are gone, we need to catch up!" I command.

Daisy laughs. "They're not *losers*, Eden," she says, slapping my knee.

"Okay, fine, they're nice enough. That Mateo guy is kinda cute, actually. Which one do you think is hotter?"

Daisy blushes a little. "Mateo? I mean, I have to say that. Rhys is my sister's boyfriend. But also, Mateo's a bit too . . ."

"Brooding?" I fill in. Other than roughhousing with Rhys, the guy didn't say much all afternoon.

She nods. "Exactly."

"Yeah," I say. "Mateo *is* hot, though. You like a slightly tortured boy, don't you? Maybe we should set you up with him."

Daisy coughs a little on her iced tea. "Stop! I'm not sure he even remembered my name. He kept calling me 'the sister.'"

"I'm pretty sure he called me 'the cousin,' so I wouldn't take it personally."

Daisy shakes her head. "Anyway, he was flirting with *you*."

"He was?" I ask, genuinely surprised. I hadn't noticed anything. I mean, I was sitting shotgun, so I suppose I talked his ear off, but he was only being normal by occasionally replying.

Daisy sighs. "They're always flirting with you, Eden. Guys can't help themselves around you."

"Wow, that is so *not* true," I tell her. "I think you just idolize me because I'm your glamorous city cousin."

"Maybe. Or maybe you're a boy magnet and you're in denial."

I roll my eyes. "Ugh, you sound like your sister right now. Georgia thinks I'm this horrible heartbreaker. You guys really have a bad impression of me."

Daisy smiles. "No, we don't! Anyway, whatever. Let's agree Mateo is annoyingly brooding and hot, and move on."

"Fine. Agreed."

We sway some more in the afternoon quiet.

"So, are you breaking any hearts over there in Sage Port, Daze?"

She studies her iced tea. "Maybe."

"Wait, really?!" I lean forward so quickly we both almost fall out of the hammock. "Tell me everything!"

She laughs, hiding her face with her hand. "No, it's nothing, it's just . . . Okay, first of all, promise me you won't tell Georgia. . . ."

I raise an eyebrow. "Why?"

"Because if it turns out to be nothing, I don't want her breathing down my neck about it."

"You realize she's going to college in like three months. You won't have her around to judge your choices. Not that she would, but I understand how you feel."

Daisy sighs. "I guess that's true. But, like—she knows him, so . . ."

"Knows *who*?! I'm dying from this suspense!"

She laughs. "It's my friend Owen. I really don't know if it's anything or not. I, like, heard a rumor that he had a crush on me, which to be honest I really didn't even believe, but then at a party last night we were making guacamole and then one thing led to another and we kind of . . . kissed."

"Daisy!" I scream, hitting her knees like bongo drums. "That is so cute!" I love watching her go through her little romantic dramas; my younger brother is like a non-emotive rock, so it's fun to play big sister every now and then with Daisy.

"It's probably nothing," she says, squinting into the distance.

"Wait, why? How did you leave things? Did he say he liked you? Do you like *him*?"

Daisy shakes her head. "We didn't really talk about it because I sorta . . . I don't know. Spooked? I basically sprinted out the front door immediately after."

"Oh *noooo*, Daze. You need to stop with the running when things get good!"

"I know, I know," she admits.

"But *was* it? Good, I mean?"

She smiles and blushes all the way to her ears.

"Okay, I take that as an affirmative. Wow, this is so adorable. I love this for you. Should we call him right now and get some clarity?"

Now it's Daisy's turn to spring forward in alarm, shaking the hammock. "No! We are not 'getting clarity.' What if it's all some weird fluke? And anyway, he doesn't have a phone."

I nearly spit out my tea. "Huh? Who doesn't have a phone?"

"Oh, I mean, he has one," she clarifies, "but it was confiscated for the summer. And he's traveling all around Europe. So, he's gonna send me postcards."

"What!" I shout. "This is the plot of a Nicholas Sparks movie."

"Aren't all of those tragic?" Daisy says.

"I have no idea. I don't watch that sappy crap."

She laughs, and then we're both laughing, and then Aunt Elena is calling us to help with dinner.

While Daisy and I help get stuff ready for the grill, Georgia comes back with drenched hair from the beach, her gym bag over her shoulder. She takes a long outdoor shower, seemingly lost in her own world.

Dave is actually a decent chef, as it turns out, and we settle around the table on the enclosed porch for a cozy dinner of barbecue chicken and kale Caesar. You can see glimmers of the lake through the forest, and you can hear it during the pauses in conversation. The hum of insects, the lapping of water. It's insanely peaceful, and a tiny bit scary. I'm not used to the quiet, eerie sounds of the woods.

I'm also surprised by how chilly it gets as the sun sets. In the city the summer temps somehow only seem to get warmer at night, after the heat's been trapped in the pavement all day, but up here the heat of the day dissipates in the breeze, and I wrap my chambray button-down tightly around my chest.

As we're clearing dishes, Rhys comes over again—this time without his friend. He whisks Georgia away for "a drive." Georgia blushes and I'm pretty sure going for a drive is code for "we're one of those couples who have to literally schedule sex or else we'll never get the chance."

But I'm sure Georgia would say I'm jealous.

Yeah, right. I'd rather be having no sex than scheduled sex

with my too-perfect boyfriend. *Yawn.* Besides, I lost my virginity last year to this guy named Sebastian Thompson in his dad's apartment in Brooklyn (while his dad was traveling for work) and let me tell you, the whole thing is overrated. It was over so quickly I could've blinked and missed it, and while it did last, it hurt and felt awkward. I wasn't sure if I was supposed to be rocking my hips like you see in movies and our rhythm was just not matching up; it sort of felt like trying to walk up the down escalator. And Bastian's face was twisted into this weird grimace that made him a lot less cute, so I tried to stare at the walls, but they were covered in his dad's unsettling modern art. All told, I was glad when it was done, and I rode the subway home playing sudoku on my phone to soothe my anxiety.

Bastian and I mostly avoided each other after that. I think he was just as embarrassed about the whole thing as me. Still, it was good to get it over with, so I don't have to go to college not knowing anything.

After Rhys and Georgia drive off to sexland, Daisy and Elena and I curl up in our sweatpants and put on a murder mystery series about a beautiful woman getting murdered on a beautiful beach full of beautiful suspects, and after a few episodes, I'm sleeping peacefully on the coach with my cold feet under Daisy's butt.

I wake up on the pullout couch in the upstairs den with a crick in my neck. The mattress is decent, but I get stiff sleeping in a bed I'm not used to. Sunlight peers cautiously through the blinds and I stretch, happy to remember I'm at the lake with my favorite people in the world (and Dave, who I really don't know) . . . that is, until something occurs to me. Today there's this orientation thingy for the Boundless Horizons program. I'd been hoping to conveniently miss it and just show up tomorrow for day one of the "Journey into the Wilderness Within and Without," as the website calls it.

But now that Georgia forced us to drive up a day early, I know Elena will make me go. She's under strict orders from my parents, so I get it. Elena can be a pushover and probably would not care at all if I played hooky on the whole thing, but she doesn't want to upset my mom and dad, and I don't want to upset *her*, so. Here we are.

Anyway, maybe it'll be fine?

I throw on cute black shorts with my skull-and-crossbones suspenders over a white T-shirt, and slip into my most practical shoes: a pair of neon-yellow rubber platform sandals. (They're waterproof! It doesn't get more practical than that!)

In the kitchen, Daisy and Georgia are already up. Daisy's in her sweats from last night and a giant Fleetwood Mac T-shirt, while Georgia is wearing an emerald-green one-piece bathing suit with a zipper between her boobs, along with white jean shorts.

Our breakfasts, like our outfits, are deeply reflective of our personalities.

Georgia: Greek yogurt with granola, banana, berries, and a tiny drizzle of honey.

Daisy: a giant, gooey apple fritter from Luna's Bakery in town.

Me: a generous bite of everyone else's food and a quantity of Diet Coke that would certainly kill a small dog.

"Wow," Georgia says, eyeing me as I chug my soda. "You *really* don't want to go to orientation, do you?"

I let out a giant Diet Coke burp. "I mean, what is there to get oriented to? We're going to be in nature with nothing to save us. Isn't that the whole point? To make us as *dis*oriented as possible?"

Daisy giggles. "Good luck, Eden. I think you'll need it."

"Thanks?" I slurp my drink. "What are you doing today while I offer myself up as a human sacrifice?"

She sits up straighter. "I think I might apply to work at the club, actually. I saw they need staff at the restaurant when we were there yesterday. I figure, extra cash and free food, seems like it could be a good deal."

"That's an excellent idea, Daisy!" Georgia says, sounding a bit surprised. "I assumed you were just going to spend the whole summer doing nothing."

Daisy rolls her eyes. "Gee, thanks."

"What? It's not an insult!" Georgia insists.

"I think it's a great idea, too," I say. "I wonder if they have guacamole on the menu." I give her a conspiratorial wink.

Daisy just about chokes on her fritter, and Georgia looks between us, puzzled, but doesn't ask. Instead she says, "I'll give you a ride, Eden."

The unspoken rule around here is we're allowed to come and go as we please so long as we don't interrupt Aunt Elena's "flow." She writes all day, and hates driving. Besides, Dave will mostly be taking her car into town as he plans to spend a gajillion hours at the local library. Over dinner last night I politely asked him about what he's working on, but it was a paper that had something to do with molecular biology, so I stopped listening.

The point is: Georgia is in charge of carting us around as much as we need it.

A responsibility she seems fine with, based on the way she's taken over acting like the boss of our schedules. "And then, Daisy," Georgia says, "I can take you to the club later. Though you're going to have to start getting dropped off at the same time as Eden starting tomorrow."

Georgia drags me out the door before I can reconsider making my escape. After all, my best option would be running into the woods and . . . well, being lost in the woods is exactly what I'm trying to avoid.

"So," Georgia says, settling behind the wheel. "What's the address."

I pull out my phone. "It looks like we've just been given these numbers . . . Oh my god," I say, realization dawning. "It's a set of coordinates!"

Georgia laughs hysterically at this.

"Okay, that's enough. It's not safe to drive when you're laughing that hard."

"Sorry, sorry," she gasps. "It's just. You should've seen your face."

I enter the coordinates into the GPS and soon we're pulling up into an abandoned square of gravel on the side of the highway.

"Am I going to get abducted? I'm sharing my location with you in case I die," I tell her.

"I'll come pick you back up in two hours. It's just two hours! You got this," Georgia says, grinning at me in what I sense is a very mocking way as I reluctantly drag my ass out of her car and step out into the glaring sunlight. Squinting, I see a group of people gathered at the other end of the gravel lot, right at the edge of the woods.

I blow my bangs out of my face. Panic starts to rise in my throat. Maybe there's still time to convince my parents to let me out of this?

I turn frantically back to the car and call "No! Wait!" but Georgia is already pulling away.

I wobble over the gravel toward the group of ten or twelve kids my age, gathered in a huddle. Beyond them is a variety of trailheads leading into a tangle of trees and underbrush.

A woman is standing in the center of the huddle talking, but I can't really see who it is or hear what she's saying. Reluctantly, I approach the group. At first, they don't notice, so I loudly clear my throat. The people standing closest to me open up a spot, and I squeeze into the circle as the woman in the center, who, I see now, is holding a clipboard, finishes up a lecture on . . . timeliness.

"Out in the wilderness, tracking time can be a matter of life and death. You're late to the group huddle, you could be face down in a ravine," the woman is saying sternly, her curly hair bouncing as she shakes her head.

"Sheesh," I whisper. And suddenly, everyone's looking at me. "I— Sorry. Sorry." I shuffle my feet, looking down at the gravel.

"And you are . . . let me see," the woman says, scanning her clipboard. "Eden Holliday, is it?"

"Um, yeah, that's me!" I say.

She eyes my outfit silently, though her expression says it all. I don't belong here.

That's okay. I couldn't agree with her more. I scan the group, everyone else in seemingly matching sets of Patagonia and North Face and L.L.Bean. I'm so distracted by the array of truly *pragmatic* (and I mean that in a bad way) shoes, that it takes me a second to realize someone across the circle is trying to get my attention.

We lock eyes, and I gasp.

What are you doing here? he mouths.

Ohhhh god.

I blink, convinced I'm having an anxiety-induced hallucination.

And yet, he's still standing there, in a pair of truly repugnant cargo shorts, a less offensive but highly boring V-neck T-shirt, and a *visor.*

It really is him. Leo. Leo Goldbaum.

I shake my head in confusion, trying to make sense of seeing him here: his dark wavy hair; his tall, tanned forehead. Those twinkling eyes and familiar smirky grin, like we're sharing an inside joke . . .

No, what are YOU doing here? I mouth at him.

"What's that, Miss Holliday? Was there something you wanted to say?" Clipboard Woman asks.

"Who, me? Oh, um, nope. Be on time. Got it." I give a salute. No one laughs.

Jeez, tough crowd.

By the time our fearless curly-haired leader (whose name, I learn, is Judy Jacobs, but we can call her JJ) tells us to stand in formation (which turns out to be a straight line) and hands us each a series of supplies (duffel bag, medical kit, fishing pole and tackle box), I'm about to faint with panic.

Leo Goldbaum, my ex. Leo Goldbaum, the smug soccer-playing asshole I once thought I was in love with, who ruined my sophomore year, is in the same Boundless Horizons program as me? What are even the chances?

Actually, now that I think about it, I remember him saying he spends his summers upstate. And I also recall him bragging about his Boy Scout days. I realize this is probably *exactly* how Leo Goldbaum spends *most* of his summers. I suppose to him it's not even torture, just an excuse to show off his whittling and fire-starting capabilities.

It's only two weeks, it's only two weeks, I remind myself.

"You are responsible for your own individual wilderness pack," JJ tells us. I pick up my bag. Wow. It's a lot heavier than it looks. "Every day," she says, "you show up with everything you might need. No advance preparation required, just your presence and your readiness to meet each day and each task as it comes. Because in the wild, there are no rehearsals. Nature doesn't give advance notice. To be immersed in nature is to be immersed in the needs of the present moment."

No. I can't do this. Fishing poles? Needs of the present moment? My present needs include having to pee from all that Diet Coke, preferably in a bathroom several miles from here.

I try to catch Leo's eye again, but it's impossible when we're standing in a straight line, facing JJ. I feel like I've signed up for army camp or something. Terrified. Am I getting punked? This cannot be real.

But apparently it is, and we spend another forty-five minutes listening to JJ drill into us all sorts of instructions about safety protocols, and how to identify poison ivy and poison sumac and probably some other poisonous things, most of which flies past me because I'm too busy hyperventilating and dropping my fishing pole with a clatter and getting my finger pinched in the tackle box and other nonsense I don't care to recount and will probably black out anyway.

Finally, she has us march out into the woods along one of the dirt paths. *We're just hiking*, I tell myself. *You can hike, Eden. It's like regular walking but with less pavement.*

We follow her on a (thankfully short) trail that leads down to a strip of lake edge, and I notice Leo has moved somehow to the head of the group, practically shoulder to shoulder with JJ. Because *of course*. But at least it gives me space to process for a second.

Ever since what happened sophomore year, I've tried to keep to my own social circles. Of course I see him in the halls, but our high school is really big—if you want to avoid someone, you can do a pretty good job of it. And I was *very* committed.

But as a result, it's been a while since I've really *looked* at Leo.

And it's strange, seeing him out in the world. He seems . . . taller? And more, I don't know. *Real?* In high school, people morph into the role they play in your head sometimes. The jock, the mean girl, the debate team nerd, whatever. But outside—out in the *wild*—it's kind of like seeing him for the first time as a real person.

Deeply disconcerting.

"You have compasses in your bags, and printed trail maps. You will not be relying on GPS," JJ warns, "since reception can be inconsistent out here. And I don't want any of you thinking you can just google your way to success. In fact, if I find any of you relying on your phones, I'll have to confiscate them," she warns.

"Then how can we call Uber Eats?" I ask, trying to make a joke. But again, literally no one laughs.

The unfunniness of this crew is eating away at me and I'm honestly hoping *I* get eaten by one of the vultures that I've noticed circling above us in the sky.

"Eden brings up a relevant topic," JJ says, which I guess is nice of her. "Food. You will eat a proper breakfast every morning before you arrive. There will be no snacks. Each day there will be a starting point and a destination. We will do basic education and drills first, and then you'll be partnered off. You and your partner will find your way to the designated destination, and once there, you will be provided a well-rounded lunch. You will then be tasked with making your way back to the starting point."

I glance over at the lake beside us. In the distance, tree-covered mountains loom. From this far away, it's a pretty scene. But I have no desire to *explore*.

"Anyone who can't swim?" JJ asks.

No one raises their hand. For a moment, I worry JJ is going to make us get in the water, and I feel like an idiot for not even thinking to wear a bathing suit.

Thankfully, JJ just tells us to split off in pairs and find our way back to the trailhead without using the path.

Without using the path? She wants us to literally weed-whack our way through the woods?

I'm going to die of tick bites or poison fill-in-the-blank (why do all the leaves just look the same to me?).

I'm going to pee my pants, too.

When will this nightmare end?

As soon as JJ tells us to find a partner, I look hopefully over at another girl who is standing near me, and wave awkwardly.

But just as I'm walking toward her, Leo intercepts us. "Hey. Eden. Be my partner!"

He says it like a command, and his tone clearly scares off the nice-seeming girl, who gloms on to someone else.

"What? Why do you want to be my partner?" I demand as Leo comes to a stop two feet in front of me.

He appraises me head to foot. "Well, for one thing, I need to know what you're doing here! You're not stalking me, are you?"

"What?!" I nearly scream. "This is the *last* place on earth I want to be right now, and you're the *last person* I want to be here with!"

"Relax, jeez, I was kidding. I just . . . would never in a million years picture you doing Boundless Horizons."

"Yeah, well, you and me both," I mutter angrily, trudging

ahead of him into the woods, determined to get back to that damn parking lot and call Georgia to pick me up. Maybe if I *beg*, I can talk my parents out of making me do this. Surely they don't expect me to spend two whole weeks lost in the woods with only a compass, a fishing rod, and a judgmental ex-boyfriend?

"Eden, wait, wait," Leo says, and I hear him jog through the underbrush to catch up to me. Then I feel his hands land confidently on my shoulders.

His touch sends a surprised buzz through me. He hasn't touched me since . . . since we were going out, more than two years ago. His hands seem bigger now, his voice deeper. His presence more commanding.

I spin around and he drops his hands to his sides. "What?"

"You're going the wrong way. Here," he says, nodding in the right direction. He holds up his compass with that smug grin of his.

"Oh." I follow him reluctantly.

The underbrush is dense and scratchy. I attempt to use my fishing pole to thwart the tangles, but it just gets caught in a bush, and Leo has to wrestle it out for me, laughing.

"So glad to see one of us is having a great time out here," I mutter.

"You need to loosen up, Eden," he says. "It's unsafe to let your emotions take over when you're in the wilderness."

I don't even bother to suppress my eye roll. In fact, if I could remove my eyeballs and physically roll them past him to make a point, I would.

"If you must know, I'm only here because my parents are making me. They think it'll reform me or something."

"Ah," he says. "That makes sense."

"What does? Me needing to be reformed?"

He holds his hands up in surrender. "Dude, no. I meant, it makes sense that you aren't here of your own volition."

Who ways the word *volition*? Ugh, I hate this guy. "Let's just get back to the lot, okay? I have to use the bathroom," I tell him.

To my annoyance, he laughs again. "There's no bathroom at the trailhead."

"What? There's not? Where are we supposed to pee? What is this, torture?"

"Eden, you can pee in the woods."

"What?!"

"Oh my god, calm down."

"Pee in the woods?! Do I look like a total lunatic? Who does that?"

He laughs. "Literally everyone. It's natural."

"Natural? Sure," I say. "Naturally disgusting."

He shakes his head, still laughing. Actually, he's not laughing so much as giggling. It's been a while since I've heard it, and I forgot how he laughs, in this very boyish, giggly way that I used to think was so cute. Now I'm finding it extremely grating.

"Suit yourself," he says with a shrug, and starts marching ahead of me, faster than we were walking before.

"Hey, wait," I shout. Last thing I need is to get left alone to starve, get eaten by vultures, and piss myself to death.

"We're only like five more minutes from the trailhead, right?" I ask. I seem to recall the path down to the water was pretty short.

"Did you miss the lecture about time?" he asks, checking his watch. "The path took us twenty-three minutes. I calculate through the woods at the pace we're going, and uphill, it's likely still half an hour."

I let out a groan.

We grow silent as we walk, and I'm keenly aware of the tension between us. The only thing keeping the awkwardness from killing me completely is my outrage. It's impossible to be around Leo and not think about what a judgmental jerk he is. How cruelly and humiliatingly he treated me. The anger propels me forward.

That and the fear of running into bears. I should have brought my stupid pepper spray! Mental note for next time.

But after about another ten minutes, I realize I'm really not going to make it. I curse the Diet Coke gods for doing this to me. They're usually so kind.

"Okay," I say, breaking our heavy silence.

"Okay what?" he asks.

"Okay *you-know-what*," I hiss.

"Do I? I'm not sure I do," he says, his voice a little singsongy.

"Don't mock me, I'm serious. I need you to stand guard, okay?"

Leo stops walking and turns to stare at me, a look of delight on his face. And then, like I did earlier, he salutes. "At your service," he says.

Then he turns his back. Without looking over at me, he says, "Take about thirty paces, where you can still see me. Squat behind a tree."

I hate this so much. I hate Diet Coke, and I hate fate itself, but most of all, I hate how happy Leo Goldbaum is to be a part of one of the most mortifying experiences of my life.

But nature—just like JJ said—is a powerful thing. And right now, I have no choice but to obey it.

I stomp toward a tree and glance around, desperate to make sure no one else is nearby. Then I pull my suspenders off my shoulders, yank down my shorts, and squat.

Peeing in the woods is actually much harder than I expected, and I nearly fall onto my naked butt in the bushes. I also come dangerously close to peeing on my own heels. Guys have it so much easier; they don't even realize how good they have it. My thighs are shaking from the effort of balancing when I finally finish and stand up.

I'm mortified, but at least I can think more clearly now. As I approach Leo, who is still dutifully facing the other way, I hiss into his ear, "If this ever gets out, you're dead."

Then I shove past him and keep marching through the trees, half hoping we're almost at the trailhead and half hoping I march my way right off a cliff and never have to face Leo Goldbaum again.

SEVEN

Daisy

Dear Owen,

First of all, I hope you apologized to the guac on my behalf. If it makes you feel any better, I'm having a heap of really underwhelming guacamole as we speak, on top of my breakfast burrito from the club. (See that grease stain in the corner? Sorry.) Got a server job here. Today's my first day—I aspire to be one of the world's worst waitresses. Think I have a shot? Anyway, I hope you're having fun backpacking and eating schnitzel or whatever you're doing out there. If you're reading this, it will mean you did not in fact get lost and starve to death in the vast Austrian mountains. So I offer a preemptive congrats.

Daisy

PS: Just me or does that grease stain look eerily like Stalin?

I sit at a faux-iron table on the lake-view terrace with my feet up on an empty seat, rereading the postcard a few times, flipping it over to look at the front, which has a picture of the Laurel Lake Tennis Club as well as the club's logo: a tennis racket with a happy face and waving hands. I got dropped off early since Georgia was eager to get her day started and Eden was, well, a lot less eager but had no choice. (She came home from orientation yesterday and told us all about seeing her ex, Leo Goldbaum. Georgia gently suggested maybe it was a sign it's time for Eden to make peace with Leo once and for all, but Eden was having none of it, and literally begged my mom to let her bail on the whole program. Mom just smiled and shook her head, saying it'll do her good to be out there communing with nature.)

Anyway, I don't mind the extra time to check out the breakfast menu and write to Owen. As I stare at my own handwriting, I try to imagine him receiving this postcard. On the surface, it's friendly banter, not even the slightest bit flirty. But then again, neither was his postcard to me. Just funny and cute and . . . basically normal. And yet, none of this *seems* normal because in normal life we don't write each other postcards. It makes me feel like we're in some old-fashioned love story where he's gone off to war while I stoically take care of the farm.

And I guess the other reason it doesn't feel the same as before is because *I'm* not the same. The Daisy of Before didn't know what it felt like to lean over Owen like that, to feel his hands on my waist, to kiss him for the first time: that crazy rush like going over the drop on a roller coaster.

I tuck the postcard into my paperback to mail later, with the urge to hide it away, keep it private, like a secret message. Even though it's a postcard, so literally the postal workers could all read it if they wanted to, and it would be totally legal.

I flip open the book to my current page—the part where the rebel vampire clan are just making the dangerous crossing into the Kingdom of Gremlins—and take a huge bite of burrito. I should be going down the checklist of my summer reading assignments for ELA rather than finishing book sixteen in a romantasy series where everyone is always marching into battle and having sexual awakenings with different species of magical creatures. But we can't all be perfect.

I'm just at the part where Ronaldo, the vampire army general, confesses his adoration to Sahara, the demigoddess who has snake blood in her veins—which I saw coming from a mile away but is still incredibly titillating because they're on the cusp of battle, naturally, and he may never see her again, and I'm pretty sure Sahara is going to take him back to her war tent so they can be alone after he says *I've been waiting so long to taste the serpent lifeblood in your veins*—when a shadow falls over the page.

"What're you reading?" says a guy's voice.

I squint up, my brain still in the book. Ronaldo the vampire? But no. It's Rhys's friend Mateo, standing just behind my table, smirking down at me and swinging a tennis racket against his leg.

"Oh, nothing," I say, an extreme blush creeping across my face as I flip the book closed so he can't see the sex scene I was about to read.

Only to realize that now he can plainly see the book's title.

He leans closer. "*The Mercy of Thorns* series . . . I feel like I've heard of that."

"Georgia thinks it's trashy. She calls them *The Mercy of Porn* books," I admit, figuring I may as well just own the situation. "But the writing is good."

"Huh, I'll have to check it out sometime." He laughs. Unlike Owen's out-of-control, sometimes-verging-on-maniacal laughter, Mateo's is breathy and low. I notice he's wearing athletic shorts and an oversized light blue T-shirt. He's lanky, but through the shirt you can see the shape of his chest muscles. His shoulders droop as if he really can't be bothered to hold them up all the way.

"Are you here to play with someone," I ask, "or just taking inventory of what the kids are reading these days?"

He shrugs. "Not looking for a partner, sorry."

"Oh, I wasn't offering," I tell him. "I mean, in addition to being way less good at tennis than you—understatement, I know—my shift starts soon. I work here."

"Yeah. Cool." He nods, looking a little bored. Not necessarily bored with *me*, per se, but with, like, reality in general. "I'm doing the advanced clinic. Starts soon. I should be warming up. Just killing time."

"Well, I'm sure Time did something truly awful to deserve it."

"Huh?"

"You know, since you're here to kill it?"

Mateo's eyes twinkle but he doesn't laugh again. Maybe because we both know the joke was terrible. "Anyway, gotta go. See you around, Georgia's Sister. Enjoy those, um, *thorns*." He winks and walks away.

At least, that's what I think he did, though the sun is pretty bright out here right now, so it could have been more of a half squint . . . or a flinch of embarrassment for me.

But I'm pretty sure it was a wink.

The same smiling tennis racket logo with dancing arms adorns the T-shirt that the club restaurant manager, this mom-aged woman named Kristy, hands me at the start of my first training shift fifteen minutes later.

"Here. Throw this over your tank top," Kristy says. "I'll get you a few more because you'll want to wear them for every shift. Oh, and you might want to put that in a braid." She gestures to my long, unruly reddish-blond mane.

I put the shirt on, which nearly comes down to my knees and completely hides my cutoff shorts, then do a quick side braid while she shows me the ropes. I nod along through the ketchup refill tutorial and the cash register practice drills, trying not to drop into an existential apathy like Mateo.

Once we've walked through all the basics, Kristy tells me to shadow Tre, this twentysomething guy who runs the snack kiosk. Tre informs me I have the "lame shift" and I'm never going to make any money because I clock out in the afternoon. It's sunset that's really hopping here at the club, he insists. The bar opens at four p.m. and once cocktails are being poured, tips go up all around. "Even if you're not working the bar, you still make way more. Rising tides lift all ships," Tre explains like a sage.

Things are slow for a while, then get crazy busy as lunchtime approaches. Tre lets me practice working the cash register, which involves a lot less spontaneous math than Kristy made it sound like, since most people charge everything to their club account.

During lunch, I notice when Mateo pops in with a few other tennis players, but he's focused on chatting with another guy in his twenties and doesn't say hi to me. He nods, though, and does that squinty maybe-wink thing again.

By two o'clock, everything slows down to a dribble, and after cleaning up the tables and counters, I'm back into the depths of *The Mercy of Thorns* pretty much until the end of my shift. I text Georgia as I clock out, and while I wait to hear back from her, I wander over to the tennis courts and sit on an empty bench. On the next court over, Mateo is playing against his lunch friend.

A coach hovers nearby, barking out feedback to both of them. "You're muscling it, Sam. Stop muscling it! Easy on the wrist! Stay low through the slice, Mateo. You're popping up too early."

The game seems to be wrapping up because Sam hollers in defeat at a missed ball and Mateo suddenly has a huge grin on his face as he jogs over to the coach to break down her responses. While I'm staring at their huddle, it's as if he's got eyes on the back of his neck—Mateo pops his head up and sees me watching him.

I quickly pretend to be scrolling my phone, but he saunters off the court and takes a seat beside me on the bench.

"What's up, Georgia's Sister?"

I roll my eyes and keep scrolling. "I was just texting Georgia, in fact."

"That's cool," he says. I expect him to get up and go for another game or do some drills or whatever, but he stays right where he is.

"You know, some people might call her 'Daisy's Sister.' Like if they didn't care to learn her actual name." I realize I sound bratty, but honestly, it's kind of annoying that he can't be bothered to remember mine.

"Noted." He doesn't seem to take offense. He's just staring off beyond the courts, at the trees swaying against the bright blue sky. "So, what's it like having Georgia for an older sister?"

I look up at him in surprise. "What do you mean by that?"

He shrugs. "I don't mean anything by it. Just curious."

"Hm. Well, she's a lot to live up to, if that's what you're implying."

He nods thoughtfully, still staring out at those trees. "That makes sense. And what about that other one. The cousin with the hot bangs."

"Eden?" I ask casually. But what I'm thinking is: *I knew it.* He thinks Eden is cute. He wants to know if Eden's single. In fact, I know exactly what his next question is going to be. I'd bet money on it.

"Yeah, that's right. Eden," he says with a slow nod. "Does she have—"

"A boyfriend?" I say too quickly.

He turns to me with a half smile. "I was gonna say, the same last name as you guys?"

"Oh." I blush again. Either I misread him and I was wrong, or I read him right, but he sensed it and pivoted quickly. In which case, that's kind of impressive. "Um, yeah. She's a Holliday, too. Our dads were brothers."

"Were? Pretty sure once you're someone's brother you don't stop."

"Well, my dad did stop. You know, being alive."

"Oh, shit." He puts his palm on his forehead. "I knew that. I just forgot for a second. Sorry. I'm a dickhead."

"No, that's okay. I mean, it's not like I was wearing a sign."

He shakes his head. "Nah, I should've remembered that. I knew that about Georgia. And you're her sister. So, obviously."

"I think the fact that I'm Georgia's little sister has been well-established by this point."

He turns to me, as if uncertain—and actually caring—what my tone is. As if the possibility that I could be annoyed with him has finally crossed his mind. "Georgia who? Oh, you mean Daisy's Sister?"

I roll my eyes again, but I can't help smiling.

He smiles back, and then I hear it: that soft, low laugh. It is, I have to be honest with myself, an extremely sexy laugh.

Before he can say anything else, my phone pings. "Speak of the devil," I say, opening up the text from Georgia. I sigh. "She can't get here for half an hour. She's supposed to pick me up.

Maybe I'll wander back to the kiosk and get a soda."

"Want me to give you a lift? I was gonna head out anyway," Mateo says, standing up and grabbing his tennis bag.

"Oh, I mean—" I pause, oddly nervous all of a sudden. Then I force myself to spit out: "Sure. Yeah. That would be great!"

Mateo drives an old Ford Focus with cords dangling out of the console (the Bluetooth doesn't work, he explains) and sweaty tennis gear thrown in the back. Getting into his car gives me a fluttery, nervous feeling. Sure, he's one of Rhys's best friends, but I barely know him—it's not like I often tag along with Georgia when she hangs with Rhys in Connecticut. Some obscure indie rock comes out of the speakers when he starts the car, which just adds to the air of intimidation.

"I was gonna see if that record store in town is open," he says as we drive along the winding back roads toward the other side of the lake. "We walked by it Saturday but didn't go in. Wanna come? Or I can drop you off first."

"Oh!" I say awkwardly. He's inviting me to hang out? I guess it makes sense. With Rhys in the city, he must be a little bored. "You mean Record Time? Yeah, I think they'd be open. Sure, I'll go. Nothing better to do," I add with a shrug, because I don't want to seem eager.

I don't know if I even *am* eager. I mean, Mateo is cute and, let's face it, a little mysterious. But then, in the back of my mind, there's Owen, and the rumor, and the kiss. Am I making too much of it, or is there something there? How am I supposed to know?

It gets quiet in the car, just the sound of a female singer whisper-whining the lyrics to something angry but also somehow relaxing. "Who is this?" I ask.

"Cat Power," he says. "You don't know her?"

"Oh yeah, no, now I recognize it," I lie.

He asked me to hang out but he's not exactly the world's most active conversationalist. So, I lean back in the passenger seat and just let the trees whiz past our window as the music lulls me into a kind of trance.

We go to Record Time and I try not to seem like I'm just following Mateo around, but I don't really know what to browse for. He holds up a few dusty records and reads the back, then replaces them. We do this for about fifteen or twenty minutes and then he just kind of shrugs.

"Not much I'm into here," he says, and for some reason, I can't help but feel insulted. Like he's saying he finds all of Laurel Lake—people included—lacking.

"Well, it *is* a small town," I say defensively. "The variety of used records is going to be a bit limited."

"It's all good," he says casually, mopping his hair out of his eyes. "Should we just wander around?"

I shrug. "Okay. There's a vintage store that's kind of cool," I tell him.

He simply nods, and now it's my turn to lead as we head out of the store and down the block toward Best Threads. And then it's his turn to stand around while I browse racks of old band T-shirts. For someone apparently into music, he doesn't seem to care for music paraphernalia.

"Nothing interesting for you here, either?" I ask him, trying to act casual. What will break this guy?

"Not really into clothes."

"Okayyy. Should we just head ho—"

"But I could go for a milkshake. The food at the club sucks," he adds.

Even though I only started working there today, and sort of agree with his broad assessment, I still find it a bit rude.

"There's that diner on the corner."

"Yeah," he says.

So, we walk to the diner. On the way, I get a text from Georgia: **where are you?** and I text back that I'm hanging out with Mateo in town. She likes the message. **That's nice of you**, she writes back.

What I don't tell her is that this is the weirdest hangout I've ever been on. I can't help but assume if Mateo had literally anyone other than me to spend time with, he wouldn't be bothering to trail around town with me acting all world-weary.

"Hang on," I say as we walk past a mailbox. "I'm just going to drop something off." I unzip my backpack and pull out my book.

The postcard to Owen goes fluttering out onto the sidewalk, and Mateo bends down to pick it up. "What's this?"

I grab it from him hastily. "Nothing! Just a postcard for my friend."

He raises an eyebrow. "You have a pen pal? That's cute."

I blush, partly wondering if he can psychically intuit my weird, uncertain, maybe-something-maybe-nothing Owen situation, and partly because he sort of just called me cute.

At the diner, we sit at the counter; I get a strawberry milkshake, and he gets a chocolate hazelnut malt.

"My milkshake brings all the boys to the yard," I say, sort of to no one.

If Owen were here, he'd probably respond with something like "my snack-like bod brings attractive prospects to my place of residence," and we would both try to outdo each other by butchering the phrase further.

But Mateo says nothing to this. I clear my throat and look at his order. "I didn't know anyone drank malts," I say, scrambling for any semblance of conversation at this point. "Seems like an old-man order."

Mateo nods and slurps. "They're really good. My dad used to get these for me and him. Got me hooked young. Wanna try?"

I take a sip through his straw, which feels strangely intimate. "Oh wow. Super sweet, but decent. I can see why young Mateo was influenced."

He half grins and shakes his head. "I was influenced by everything my dad said and did. That was before I realized he was a lying dick."

"Oh."

"I'm sure you've heard all about it. Everyone has." He takes another long, contemplative slurp.

"Heard about what?" I drink my strawberry shake, having no idea what he's talking about.

"My dad. The prison thing."

"What!" I nearly choke on a chunk of strawberry.

"My whole town knows. It's such a cliché. Like, do a real crime at least. Then I'd have some respect."

"What did he do?" I ask, starting to sweat slightly. Have I just been casually hanging out with the son of an axe murderer?

"Embezzling, mostly. Boring white-collar crap," he says with a shrug.

I nod, acting like I totally get it, while secretly processing the shock. Call me sheltered, but the only people I know who've had altercations with the law are kids from my town who get caught driving after drinking a couple of beers.

I sneak a look at his profile. "That . . . sucks. I'm sorry. I didn't know."

He nods again. "No worries. Nothing as bad as your dad thing. Did him dying really mess you up?"

Once again, I'm taken aback by the way he can flip from apathy to such an intense, personal question. But I roll with it, happy to have something to talk about at least.

"To be honest, yeah, it did," I tell him. "My grades were destroyed the rest of that year. It was just so hard to feel motivated by anything, you know? And I hated that everybody pitied me. I know they meant well, but it made me feel like even when I was doing okay, I sort of had to pretend to be grieving, or, like, I had to be ashamed of the good days. And I was already ashamed of the bad days." I stir the pink, frothy ice cream in my glass. "Starting high school helped—I could start over. People still knew about it, but it became a thing of the past, not a thing of the present, if that makes sense."

He nods. "It totally does, Daisy." My eyebrows shoot upward. It's the first time he's called me by my actual name. "People love to speculate," he goes on, looking down into his glass. "But they can't possibly get what's going on inside you. And they don't have to know. You don't owe them anything."

"Yeah, that's true." I stare at him. I can tell he's talking about me, but also about himself. I realize that I've been expecting him to be more sociable, to act a certain way, but I really have no idea how he's feeling or what he's going through. Living up here with a friend's family for the summer when that friend isn't even going to be around much says something about his choices—or lack of them.

His malt is almost finished; he put it away fast, but that doesn't surprise me. Tall, active guys built like him can eat about a thousand calories a second. It does surprise me when he says, "These are on me."

"You really don't have to," I say, but he throws a twenty on the counter.

"Yes, I do. You're saving me from feeling like a total loser, and that is very much worth the cost of your milkshake."

"You're not a loser."

At this, he simply shrugs. But then he turns to me and smiles, and it changes his face completely. "I guess I'm not so bad, am I?"

My heart hammers in my chest. Because in this moment, with this hot older guy grinning at me like we're in on some joke together, I can't help but agree. He really isn't so bad. In fact, maybe I'm starting to get him.

I punch him in the arm. "Don't get a big head."

He laughs.

Just then, Georgia texts that she has to pick up Eden, and do I want a ride home now? I show the text to Mateo.

"Tell her we'll pick up The Cousin ourselves. I don't mind playing chauffeur. I love driving. It's a Zen thing."

"Okay," I say, once again going along with his suggestion. Because it seems like he wants to spend more time with me. And maybe I should give him a chance. He's lonely, he needs friends, and I'm lucky. I have Eden and Georgia and my mom and even Dave. And somewhere off in Europe backpacking around with his grampa, I have Owen.

Compared to Mateo, my life is pretty full.

"Let's hit the road, then," he says, picking up my backpack off the hook where I hung it and slinging it over his shoulder, which strikes me as kind of gallant.

"What did the road ever do to you?" I say.

He just looks at me, not getting the joke. "Huh?"

I smile and shake my head. "Never mind."

Mateo drops me and Eden off at the lake house, and Eden invites him to stay and hang out. I'm already a little annoyed—on the way home, Eden got shotgun and I sat in the back. And somehow in the fifteen minutes it took to drive back from the trailhead, Eden and Mateo talked more than I got out of him all afternoon. Though to be fair, it was mostly Eden talking. And cutely blowing her "hot bangs" out of her face. But I could tell he's smitten with her, like everyone is. And even though I know we were just hanging out as friends, and he bought me that milkshake to be nice, and he's two years older than me, it's still disappointing. I can't help but feel a little sidelined as Eden makes Mateo laugh with her hiking horror stories.

Georgia is already back and showered from her day of lifeguard drills and sunbathing by the lake or whatever she's been up to. Now she's throwing sticks into the firepit. Mateo and Eden and I join her and we all sit around the fire she makes, roasting marshmallows before dinner as the sun starts to fall behind the trees. It's fun, and I find myself laughing along with Eden's tales of woe in the woods and mortifying herself in front of her ex-boyfriend.

"You should just call a truce," I tell her, "and put it behind you!"

Georgia shakes her head. "I still think there's an opportunity for you to have it out. Talk about the past. Clear things up. It might give you peace of mind."

Eden rolls her eyes. "Nothing about Leo is going to give me any peace of mind, Georgia."

Mateo chimes in. "I don't know. He sounds like a douche. I say you sabotage him."

We all turn to him. "What?" I ask. This guy is full of surprising opinions.

He shrugs. "Cut his fishing line, put a worm in his sleeping bag, whatever. Make his life hell. Have fun with it."

Eden's eyes light up and she throws her arms around Mateo, which makes my chest constrict. "You're a genius," she says.

Eventually, Mateo stands up and says he should get back for dinner. Georgia walks him to his car, asking him something about whether he's heard from Rhys. I'm bummed that he's leaving—his presence has added an interesting new dynamic to everything—but I'm also a little relieved. It hasn't been *great* watching him and Eden flirt. Not that I should care. Not that I *do* care. What is wrong with me? Why would I care?

But then again, I don't even know where I stand with Owen. And it's not easy being the youngest person in our group. I thought this summer was going to be so escapist and fun, but I'm already feeling left out even while I'm sitting right here. It's an itchy, yearning sensation I can't quite pinpoint. I'm used to feeling a tiny bit behind when it comes to Georgia and Eden. But this is something else.

As I watch the fire flicker and burn down, it occurs to me that it's more than feeling too young or left out. I *want* that feeling of being in love. Or at least in lust.

I want the feeling of being in *something.*

Georgia comes over and nudges my back with her knee. "Mateo agreed to drive you home after work for the rest of the summer! This will be so great. Two birds with one stone. Rhys wanted me to make sure Mateo didn't get too bored alone up here, and we know Mom and Dave will be glued to their laptops, type-type-typing all day, and this way, I don't have to worry about rushing off to get you when my lifeguarding shifts start!"

A mix of emotions washes through me—excitement, curiosity, embarrassment. On the one hand, I'll be spending every single afternoon driving home with Mateo. On the other hand, he's doing it as a favor to my sister, and he's clearly more interested in my cousin than me.

"I don't need babysitting, Georgia," I inform her.

"So, you're saying you'd rather ride your bike to work and back?" she asks.

"Fine, you win. He can drive me," I say, staring back into the dying flames again. On the other side of the firepit, I notice Eden's eyebrows go up as she gives me a questioning look. But she's not the only one with questions. I myself have to wonder what in the world is going on with me right now. Because even though I'm annoyed at the whole situation, I'd be lying if I didn't say I'm also a little bit . . . curious. To see how this all plays out.

EIGHT

Georgia

I LEARN A COUPLE key things during the lifeguard test.

The first is that Australians have very weird nicknaming customs. Mr. Bailey tells us he will respond to any variation of "Truck Cap," "Truckie," "Truck," or "Cappie," but that most people call him "Caps," which has taken on a *captain* implication. And after a few rounds of drills, he's already freely spouting off nicknames for the twenty of us who've showed up for the test. "Sandman" for the guy who trips and face-plants during a relay on the beach. "Leftie" for the one whose freestyle stroke makes him look lopsided. And when the small group I've been partnered with wins the relay, I squeal in glee, leading Mr. Bailey—er, Caps—to shout, "Do I hear a pod of dolphins? Pipe down over there, Dolphin!"

The second is that there's no such thing as overpreparing. I was so confident when I first arrived, but despite my days of practice and self-directed workouts, Caps's militaristic drills leave me weak and breathless. At one point he tells a girl to go sit in the shade and cool off because she looks like she's going to faint or throw up, only to inform her once she's recovered that she can go home—she's been disqualified.

It sends a jolt of uncertainty through me. Deep down, I know the stakes aren't that high. Even if I don't get the job, I can probably find one elsewhere—or take the summer to study and read and prepare for college. But just the idea of not accomplishing what I set out to do, what I *told everyone* I was going to do, makes me queasy.

Still, I don't want Caps to detect my queasiness and ask me to sit out like that other girl, so I grin and force myself to give every exercise a hundred and ten percent.

My legs are more than a little wobbly as I finally walk back up the beach at the end of the test. We gather around Caps and wait for him to make his final decision. He reviews his notes and looks at all our eager faces, then rattles off five names. Four of them are guys. I'm shocked when the fifth is . . . Georgia Holliday.

So surprised, in fact, that I let out a little squee.

"Pipe it down there, Dolphin," Cap says, taking his baseball cap off and re-bending the bill. Then he puts the hat back on and assigns one other girl as an alternate. Everyone else is sent home in dismay, and the six of us remaining get our first schedules and a set of rules.

Despite the full-body fatigue I was experiencing just minutes ago, the relief of landing a spot floods me with a wave of new energy.

And that's when I notice . . . *him* again.

Over where the beach tapers off into a wooded area.

It's that boy with the red towel. He's back, and he's been watching our drills, though for how long I can't be sure. As I ride the euphoria of my victory toward the parking lot, I notice in my periphery that Red Towel Boy has picked up the towel in question and slung it over his shoulder, and now he's . . . jogging toward me with a strange confidence, like we were supposed to have plans later, like we're already familiar with each other, even though I could swear I'd never seen him before his appearance on this beach two days ago.

"Wow, congrats," he says. "That looked really, um. Hard."

"Thanks," I say politely. "Sorry, do we know each other?"

"Nope," he says with a smile. "But I was watching you out there."

"Really?" I find this response even weirder. He just admitted that he's been sitting around staring at a complete stranger, watching me swim. I point to the book in his hand—his thumb holding his page like the other day. "Looks like you came here to read."

He shrugs. "A little of both." His eyes sparkle in the sun.

I take him in more carefully. His skin is a smooth pale brown, with a few dark freckles popping through on his cheeks. His dark hair flops to the left, and he's not wearing a shirt, though I can see one tucked into the back of his shorts. He *is* wearing a white shell necklace along with a simple silver chain around his neck. His board shorts hang low on his thin but muscular hips. He's close to my age, but definitely younger. I can tell by his boyish, unadulterated smile.

"Well . . . thanks?" I say again, starting to edge past him.

"Are you hungry?" he asks, before I can fully step from the sand onto the wooden path that leads to the parking area.

"Excuse me?" I turn back around to look at him.

"I was wondering if you would be open to, um, you get it."

I stare at him. "Actually, no, I really don't!" I hate to be rude but my brain isn't comprehending what he's doing. Because what it *seems* like he's doing is trying to ask me out, but that can't be right. We have literally never met. Maybe he's just some inexperienced younger guy who thinks this is the way you flirt. . . .

"I just meant we could grab a bite to eat. You must be starving after that workout." He smiles, and I'm astounded at the confidence. He seems to have no idea how awkward he's actually being.

"Listen, that's really sweet, but I don't even know your name—"

"Benny," he says, sticking out a hand. "Benny Suarez."

"Okay, Benny, it's nice to meet you," I say, looking at his hand but refusing to shake it. "But you don't even know *my* name, and you don't know me at all."

"So you're saying your real name isn't Dolphin?"

Despite myself, I laugh. "Correct."

"So, what is it?"

I glance around, wondering if anyone is watching this interaction. Surely someone is going to walk over and tell this dude to stop hitting on me in public like this. It's not like I'm getting stranger-danger vibes at all—he seems way too innocent for that—and it's not like I don't think he's cute. He's totally adorable. But he should probably be taught some manners, and I hesitate. Would giving him my name be rewarding his forwardness?

"Look," I tell him, as kindly as possible. "You seem really nice, Benny, so I appreciate the offer. But I have a boyfriend. And I should probably get home."

If this news dampens his interest, it's only evidenced by the slightest movement in one eyebrow. Then he says, "Wait, I don't want you to get the wrong idea."

"Wrong idea?" Now I'm annoyed. *He's trying to walk it back?*

"I really want to be a lifeguard next year." He shrugs again. "I can't qualify this year—turning sixteen in a few weeks."

Ah, so he's basically Daisy's age. That checks out.

"But next year I'll make the cutoff," he goes on. "Figured since you killed it out there, maybe you could walk me through what you did to prepare? Also, this book I'm reading sucks, and I'm really bored. I have a few hours till I told Lita I'd meet up with her, and she won't care if I'm a little late."

I take a small breath and relax a bit. Maybe I was just reading into things because of Benny's flirty personality, his winning smile, and that unwavering gaze. He's just an eager kid who wants to become a lifeguard.

"Well . . ." I stall. I know I don't have to pick up Daisy—Mateo will give her a ride. And Mom certainly won't care if I stay out for a bit. She doesn't have a problem with us coming and going as we please, as long as we always text her our locations. Half the time she's so lost in a manuscript she truly won't notice whether we're there or not. As for Dave, he holes up at the Laurel library every day anyway.

It's not my custom to hang out with boys I've never met before. But there's something disarming about Benny, how easy-breezy he is, that puts me off guard. I hear myself saying, "I guess so, sure," before I've even fully registered it.

His smile grows, revealing dimples. "Great!"

"Put on a shirt first, though," I say, starting to walk ahead of him, toward my car. Then I turn to look at him over my shoulder, catching another glimpse of his sun-kissed chest and abs as he pulls the T-shirt over his head. "By the way, I'm Georgia."

It turns out Benny walked to the lake from Lita's house ("Lita" being what he calls his grandmother), the little yellow one up on Greenvalley Lane, a curving dead-end road I have sometimes gone for runs on.

He walked here because he's too young to have a driver's license.

So, naturally, I will be the one to drive.

After throwing on a pair of linen shorts over my bathing suit along with a matching top, I take Benny into town to get kale smoothies.

While we wind through the woods to get there, Benny plies me for pointers on training and how to impress Mr. Bailey, though as we talk, I realize that it's not really something you can verbalize. I'd have to see how strong a swimmer Benny is to get a realistic sense of whether I think he would qualify next time. He asks if I'll watch him swim sometime and offer feedback, and I nod noncommittally.

Then I start blathering about Rhys and how he's got this fancy financial internship and that's why he's not around. I don't know why I'm talking so much about Rhys . . . I suppose I just want to be extra sure that I've made it clear I already have a special someone in my life.

While putting in our smoothie orders (I notice Benny says, "I'll have what she's having," when they take his) he tells me this is his first time up at Laurel Lake. His abuela got a job up here and invited him to stay with her for the summer, so he thought he'd check things out.

"Are you new here too?" he asks.

I shake my head. "We used to come every summer, up until three years ago."

"Wow, you're lucky. It's beautiful here. So, what happened three years ago to stop you?" he asks, and I can feel him studying my profile.

I stare at the whirring blenders behind the counter. "Just . . ." I'm not telling this stranger about my dad's death. It's too much. "You know, life got in the way. Anyway," I say, searching for a change of subject, "if you think this is pretty, you should see what the lake looks like from above. There are some great mountain trails with lookout points. And on the ski resort they keep the gondolas open all through the summer. You can ride up to the lodge at the top and back. It's super gorgeous."

We pay separately and meet out in front of the café on the sunny sidewalk, happily slurping our smoothies.

"So can we go?"

"Go where?"

"To those gondolas! Is there time for that?" he asks.

Once again, I'm torn between thinking Benny's being too forward and realizing that he's clearly just *like* this. If he wants something, he casually asks for it, no hesitation, no sheepishness.

Even though I find it a little off-putting, I'm also kind of drawn to it. I like to think of myself as assertive, but often I hide what I really want, because being polite and going with whatever's expected seems more important. There's something liberating about Benny's whole energy.

"You know what? Why not!" I say, briefly wondering what Rhys would think of me giving the "full tour" to the new guy in town like this. He'd probably say I should be hanging out with Mateo instead. Ironically, Mateo has already been hanging out more with Daisy than me, since he's been giving her rides home from the club.

Which gives me an idea. "C'mon, get back in the car. The resort's only like ten minutes from here. Also, I want to tell you about my sister. I think you might really like her."

By the time Benny and I make it to the gondolas at the ski resort, I've already relayed a list of Daisy trivia. After all, they're pretty much the same age, and Benny does seem really sweet. He'd make a great boyfriend or at least summer fling for Daisy. Their names even sound cute together!

If I'm being honest, matchmaking him with Daisy would also make me feel a lot more comfortable about spending time together, without anyone getting the wrong idea.

And I do want to ride the gondolas. It's been *way* too long.

By the time we arrive, Benny knows Daisy's favorite '80s movies (*When Harry Met Sally . . .*, *Adventures in Babysitting*), her favorite bands (Fleetwood Mac, HAIM), and her favorite beverages (Berry LaCroix, boba).

"I hate boba," Benny says with a shudder as we get our tickets.

"Right? Me too!" I say. "I loathe slurping big chunks of pudding through a straw. It creeps me out."

He laughs. "Exactly. If I'm drinking something, I don't want to also be chewing something."

"Amen!" I laugh as we move from second in line to first in line. There's a moment of silence and I notice myself getting nervous, eager to keep the conversation going. We step forward again and get seated on the gondola. The bar comes down across our laps. "So, what's *your* favorite beverage, then?" I ask.

He thinks for a second. "Frozen Mexican hot chocolate—with cinnamon and just a little cayenne."

"Mmmm." I don't mean to sound like I'm moaning but it's been a long time since I've even had a milkshake, or really anything unhealthy and delicious.

He grins. "My lita used to make it for me as a reward for good behavior."

Our feet lift off the ground, and we begin to rise up the mountainside.

"And were you rewarded often?"

"If you're asking whether I'm naughty or nice, I would say

mostly nice," Benny says, turning to look at me. "But not a hundred percent of the time."

I clear my throat. The conversation feels like it's becoming a little more flirtatious than I'd intended. "Well, you're in luck," I tell him. "Daisy has a total sweet tooth." I look over, and he's smiling.

I turn my attention to the view, pointing out various landmarks.

We rise higher into the air, our feet dangling in the sky. It really is breathtaking up here. I'd forgotten what this feels like. Somehow being so far from the ground makes me feel . . . *free.* Like I don't have to be the one in control anymore. I can just sit back and enjoy the ride. Literally.

It's a feeling I rarely allow myself.

"There's our house!" I point through the trees. "And doesn't the lake look incredible?"

I hear Benny suck in an appreciative gasp.

"And you can see the fancy hotel across the water," I say.

Only, as I point, sadness shudders through me. I pull my arm back to my side, gripping the bar.

"Are you okay? What's wrong?" Benny asks.

"Nothing!" I'm surprised that he noticed—and I kind of wish he hadn't.

The Laurel Vista Inn is where my dad proposed to my mom. They used to tell us the story, year after year. How he'd asked the hotel restaurant to put the ring in their fondue because there's nothing that melts my mother's heart more than melted cheese, but the restaurant didn't, because they were too afraid the heat would damage the ring. So they get to the bottom of the pot and he's scraping the cheese frantically from the bottom and there's still no ring, and he starts sweating like crazy, and . . . Well, anyway, it's a great story, the way Dad used to tell it. We'd be rolling on the floor laughing. And it always ended the same way. "Luckily, she loved me enough to say yes."

They joked they had the "cheesiest" love story ever, and I guess it *was* pretty cheesy. But it was always the gold standard in my mind for what love should look like.

I try to shake away the memories, but the pain of it has lodged in my throat, and it's obvious Benny can tell.

"Hey, are you afraid of heights or something?" he asks, resting a hand on my knee.

From the spot where his hand is touching my bare thigh, tingles ripple upward. If it's been a long time since I rode this gondola, it's been just as long since a boy has touched my leg for the first time. Obviously, Rhys touches me all the time when we're together—but there's no surprise in that, no newness. I'm momentarily frozen in the sensation of it, unable to conjure words, embarrassed by how flustered I feel. All I can do is shake my head. Because no . . . I'm not afraid of heights.

What *am* I afraid of?

"Georgia," Benny says, thankfully taking over since I have lost the ability to keep up the conversation. "I need to confess something."

"Wh-What?" I stammer.

"I didn't just ask you to hang out because I want to learn how you got the lifeguarding spot. I asked you to hang out because I think you're hot."

I stare at him, speechless. It's probably the bluntest thing anyone has ever said to me . . . and I'm honestly not sure how to feel about it. Lied to? Annoyed? Embarrassed? Flattered?

"I—I told you, Benny. I have a boyfriend."

"Yeah, I know." He shrugs and slowly pulls his hand away from my thigh. "I'm not suggesting anything. I just wanted to be honest. Especially because the more we sit here, the more I realize how funny you are. And nice to talk to."

I can feel myself blushing, so I turn to look at the vista instead of him. "I wish you'd admitted this before."

"I didn't realize I would also *like* you as much as I do."

"Benny!"

"What?" he asks, smiling.

"You're just so forward. And you barely know me. I've given you more facts about Daisy than myself. She's the one you're supposed to be into!"

"In my experience, being into someone isn't really a *fact*-based experience. It simply. . . happens."

"Well, regardless, you're too young for me! And I'm taken!"

He laughs. "Okay, okay, I'm sorry I threw you off. I shouldn't have said anything. I am not very good at hiding what I'm thinking."

"Yeah, no kidding!"

"Is honesty a bad thing?"

I look at him sternly, hoping my blush has calmed down

somewhat. "Sometimes, it's better to be appropriate than honest."

He raises his hands in surrender. "Understood. But—does this mean you won't train me?"

"I never said I'd *train* you."

"You didn't yet, but I was going to ask you. Before I blurted out my actual thoughts instead."

I sigh and shake my head. We are, thankfully, reaching the summit, and we both step off the gondola together. All the magical, weightless feeling of flight has left my body and I'm back on solid earth again.

"Benny, seriously. What am I gonna do with you?"

"You don't have to do anything with me," he says. "But it would mean a lot if you would watch me swim, give me some notes at least."

"I don't know if that's such a good idea."

"Why not?" he asks, as if genuinely curious.

Isn't it obvious? "Because you clearly have a crush on me, and you're my little sister's age. And, well, I don't want to lead you on." I clear my throat. "I'm not interested in you like that."

He nods. "Okay, that's completely fair."

For a moment, I feel a huge sense of relief, along with a little disappointment.

"But since we've already established that you aren't interested in me that way, you really wouldn't be leading me on. I think that's an antiquated, sexist concept anyway. Trying to assume what a woman wants just from her behavior is no bueno. I figure it's as easy to simply ask."

I blink at him.

"So I'm saying, if you *wanted* to train me anyway, despite my humiliating honesty up there, you can."

"Oh, I *can*, if *I* want to?" I ask, almost laughing. *He's* the one who wants me to!

"Yes. Exactly. If you want to."

"Why would I want to?"

"Because it would be fun? Because people enjoy teaching the skills they excel at? Because even if you're not *interested* in me, you at least maybe find me somewhat entertaining? And because it's possible that since your boyfriend has that internship in New York City, you're almost as bored as I am and could use a distraction?"

I shake my head. "Benny Suarez. You are funny."

He shrugs with a half smile. "I've received that feedback before. So . . . is that a yes?"

"Fine," I tell him. "I'll do it."

His face lights up. "Yes! Amazing! I'm so pumped! But Georgia, you need to promise me you won't accidentally fall in love with me."

"Oh my *god*, Benny. I cannot with you." I roll my eyes so hard it feels like they'll hit my skull. "You can meet me at the lake. Tomorrow at dawn."

"Aye, aye, Captain. But what time is dawn, exactly?"

"Is six thirty too early for you?"

He pauses for a second. "No. Nope, that works. Seriously, though. I'm so grateful. I'll repay you, okay?"

I raise an eyebrow at him. "How are you going to repay me?"

He thinks for a second. "I'll have Lita make you a frozen hot chocolate."

"Wait, really?" I ask, smiling now.

He smiles back. "Only if you're on good behavior."

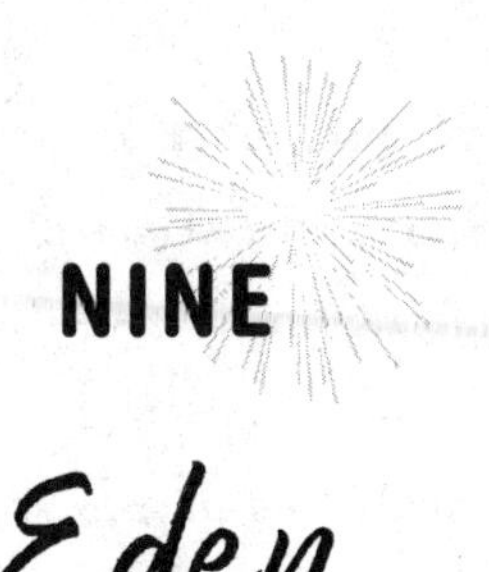

NINE

Eden

THANKFULLY, YOU DON'T NEED survival skills for basic hiking.

And thankfully, I've been able to mostly avoid my horribly smug ex-boyfriend so far this week during Boundless Horizons.

However, if I had a gratitude journal, these would be the *only* two entries. Because other than that, I've been in pure, perspiration-and-mosquito-bitten *hell*. Mother Nature is supposed to do wonders for your health and well-being, but for me, it's the total opposite. My skin is irritated and scratched up, my feet are blistered, and my nose is breaking out in unsightly zits from all the sunscreen that has sweated off my face. I feel like I've been in the woods since the time of the dinosaurs and it's only Wednesday.

Our fearless leader JJ has taught us how to use a compass (which to my surprise I'm sorta getting the hang of?) and how to collect fire-starting twigs versus longer-burning logs. (I'm dreading the day we'll have to test those qualities by actually starting a fire—in the city this would *so* be illegal.) We've even done a segment on edible versus poisonous mushrooms. (No chance I'm consuming either. And again, seems like it should be illegal. Too bad my dad's in entertainment law—I could really use a professional opinion.)

This morning, my hiking partner is Kiera. She's nice enough, but the banter is seriously lacking. I've mostly tagged along as she collected mushrooms for the past hour—she even brought a mushroom knife from home, and a magnifying glass.

"If you accidentally put anything fatally poisonous in your mouth, I'll kill you myself," I tell her, trying to be funny.

But per usual with this crowd, she simply stares at me, blinking. "That would be redundant."

I swallow my disappointment and take a sip from my water bottle. (A *small* sip. I've learned my lesson on overconsuming beverages.)

"Oh, hey, look." Kiera crouches down next to a tree. "That looks like a lion's mane! See its shaggy ball shape?"

I try not to spit out the water. *Shaggy ball shape*. Where are my friends when I need them? They'd be cracking up over this.

"Oh wow, cool, yeah, so shaggy. Like a lion's mane?" I say, winging it.

"Exactly!" she exclaims, beaming at me. I've found my way to her heart after all: acting interested in mushrooms.

But it's hard when I've been spending fourteen thousand percent of my attention making sure I don't end up alone with Leo again.

And if I'm being honest, ever since Rhys's friend Mateo put

the word *sabotage* into my brain at our backyard firepit, I haven't been able to let the idea go. It's maddening how Leo always thinks he knows best. It would be so satisfying to wipe that smug smile from his face, even for a moment. To show him that he *doesn't* know everything. To, yeah, embarrass him a little, take him off his high horse. Make him experience what it's like to be the rest of us.

After our messy breakup, we never spoke. I never got an apology. And that hurt—for a long time. I'm not saying I need revenge; I just want to feel for once like we're on even footing.

And besides, this Boundless Horizons thing is already so dull . . . so I've been working on a little plan.

The only problem is that it'll require getting close to Leo—at least long enough to execute the mission.

By some miracle, Kiera and I make it to the "rendezvous point" in decent time and we're allowed to start having lunch while we wait for the rest of the group to arrive. Leo and his partner, Jorge, are already here, along with a few other teams. I try not to watch as Leo moves a respectful distance from the group to re-douse his entire body with bug spray (he does this religiously, every hour of every day). I try not to notice what amazing legs he has—strong, taut calves, not too bulky. He's always had great legs. It's a soccer thing. But so what? If only one's calves were a measure of one's personality!

I'm snapped out of my not-staring by the rumbling of a pickup truck breaking into our little clearing. *What?!* I'm immediately shocked—I didn't know there was a way to get a car to this part of the woods! Why the hell did we have to hike our way up? I briefly hope we can get a ride back down.

But then JJ goes over to the truck and pulls out our fishing equipment, announcing that we're switching partners to practice fishing for the afternoon.

I suck in a breath. Now's as good a time as any.

Before I can change my mind, I saunter up to Leo and Jorge just as Jorge is shoving a huge bite of sandwich into his mouth.

"Hey, Leo, will you be my fishing partner?" I ask without making eye contact.

He raises an eyebrow. "Hey, Eden . . . I . . . have to say, I'm surprised you're asking me."

"I remember that story you told me once, about fishing with your uncle Ted from Florida? So I figured you already know what you're doing."

"You remember that?" he says, sounding even more surprised.

"Yeah, of course," I say with a shrug. It's just one of the many stories he regaled me with when we were dating, and I was young and naive enough to hang on his every word. "I remember everything," I add pointedly.

He steps closer, hovering nearly a head taller than me, and his gaze bores down. "I remember everything, too."

Those words send a shiver down my back. He remembers everything as in, everything he did to hurt and humiliate me? The fiasco of Becca Johnson's fifteenth birthday party?

Does he really have no regrets?

Or is he saying he remembers everything as in, all the good

times? All the quiet moments, just the two of us, laughing over our chemistry or Russian history homework, his hand finding mine underneath the library table. Hanging out alone in his apartment after school, when his parents were both at work . . . *all* the things we used to do.

As I boldly look back up into his brown eyes, all those memories flood me, too. The truth is, Leo was my first everything. My first kiss. My first . . . all the things that come after a kiss. Well, almost all the things. We didn't go *all* the way. But the point is, I trusted him wholeheartedly.

That's what made the way he ended things all the more cruel.

I clear my throat. "Okay, then, so it's settled. Do you want me to grab your, um, rod?"

"My what?" He blinks. "Oh, yes. I mean no. I'll go get all the equipment for us. Wait here."

The air feels cooler now that he's stepped away, and I shiver, momentarily wishing I'd worn something more than my gray ribbed cutoff tank top, my frayed black jean shorts, and my trusty neon platform sandals. While he goes over to the truck to load up our fishing rods and tackle boxes, I glance over at his backpack.

Now now now. After just a small moment's hesitation, I take a breath and decide to go through with it.

While Leo's back is turned, I grab a canister from my bag, jaunt over to his backpack, and swap out his beloved bug spray with my own spray can—which looks almost exactly the same, due to my extreme craftiness last night.

I manage to zip his bag and step away just as he turns around and walks back with two fishing poles and two tackle boxes.

"Come on," he says with a nod, handing me one of the poles so he can pick up his pack and strap it on. "I'll carry your tackle box," he offers.

I decide to let him carry it, even though it's annoying that he's being polite. "Where are we going?"

"According to my map, the river is northwest of this clearing," he says. "I don't know how much luck we'll have at this hour, but at least we can work on making sure you know what you're doing."

I roll my eyes, though if Leo notices, he doesn't say anything.

We trudge through the woods and I rehearse the prank in my head. When his skin reacts to the spray, I'll convince him he must've walked through poison ivy. ("I thought I noticed those clusters of three leaves!" I'll exclaim, parroting what JJ told us and pretending I have any idea what poison ivy looks like.) His legs will be covered in an uncomfortable, burning rash for at least thirty minutes, and he'll probably be yelping in pain. It'll be much funnier if this happens in front of the rest of the group.

With that in mind, when we finally spot the river sparkling through the trees, I suggest we find a spot that's not too secluded.

"I don't want to completely lose sight of the crew," I tell him. "You know I don't like feeling alone out here."

Leo cracks a smile. "It's cute how scared you are of nature."

"I'm not scared!" I retort automatically, though my brain is stuck on *cute*?

"It's okay," he says. "I feel like half of Stuyvesant kids are just like you. One time I went hiking with Mark Ling and a deer crossed our path, and you should've heard him scream. Over a *deer.*"

I laugh. "I never would have taken Mark Ling for a screamer."

"People can be deceiving," Leo says as we near the river.

"No kidding."

We climb over a couple of medium-sized boulders at the edge of the water and throw down our backpacks. I sit on the largest rock, which dips straight down into the rushing current, and Leo squats a foot away, busying himself with the tackle boxes.

"Hold out your hand," he orders, and I follow his command.

Then he swivels and drops something into my open palm—and I scream. I don't just scream, I drop the thing he put in my hand and jump up to my feet, tripping on my own wobbly sandals and nearly falling backward off the rock.

"Was that a dead *cockroach*?" I screech.

Sure, I've seen them in the basement of our building and on subway platforms plenty of times—but frankly, I've never not screamed in horror.

Leo rocks back onto his heels and laughs. "Eden, relax, relax! You're gonna hurt yourself! It's just a dead cricket. They make great bait."

I shudder, trying to collect myself. "I can't. I can't do this. No way. Why do we need to use dead crickets?!"

When you see people going fishing in movies, it always looks so peaceful, their legs dangling off the side of a dock, birds flying leisurely overhead, the sun rising up over the water. Why did no one tell me fishing involves handling *big gross dead insects*?

"Here, sit down, chill out," he says, which really pisses me off. I'm not being un-chill. I'm having a perfectly reasonable reaction to a very disgusting thing. "I'll bait your hook, and you can just—sit there."

"Fine," I say begrudgingly. On the one hand, this whole situation is embarrassing and excruciating in every way. But on the other hand, if I had any other partner from the group, they probably wouldn't bait my hook. I *am* supposed to be learning all these skills myself.

It's classic Leo to take charge, and while that can be very bossy and obnoxious, I have to admit it has its perks.

Once he's ready, we both stand up on the rock and Leo hands me my fishing pole. He shows me how to cast the line out onto the water, using his as an example. It takes me a few false starts—my line gets tangled in the hem of my shorts at one point, and I keep getting freaked out by the dead cricket dangling from the end of it, flinching when it swings near me.

"You have to kind of *flick* it," he says, reaching over to put one hand on my pole.

I yank the fishing pole away. "I *got* it. I'm trying. Just let me try it."

"All right, all right," he says, stepping back. "Let's see you give it another try."

"Ow, dammit." This time I flick too hard and the whole rod goes flying out of my hands, into the woods. I groan. Why is this hard?

And once again, Leo is in stitches.

"It's not funny."

"If you could see your face, you would agree that it is, actually, very funny," Leo gasps out.

I trudge back up the rock and wrestle my rod out of a bush, which is not fun at all but keeps Leo entertained.

Finally back on the rock, I let Leo stick another gross dead cricket on my hook since the other one got lost in the bushes. When he hands me back my pole, I stand there for a minute or two, watching the river's current glittering in the afternoon sun. Do I really have it in me to try this *again*?

"Okay, fine," I say with a sigh. "Just show me how to do it, then."

He smiles gleefully, like he's been waiting all day for this moment to show off. Setting his pole down carefully, he comes up to stand behind me, then hesitates.

"Is it okay if I do the thing where I, like—"

"Hover behind me to show me how to hold my fishing rod?" I fill in, rolling my eyes. "Yes, it's fine."

So, he puts his arms around me, gripping the pole—and my hands—in his. Even though I said it was fine, I'm still overwhelmed by the sensation of his embrace, the warmth of his chest against my back, his familiar smell of spicy sports deodorant, his . . . *Leo*-ness.

He maneuvers the rod in a professional flicking motion and the fishing line flies out straight into the water, splashing silently a good twenty feet in front of us, just as it's supposed to.

And with that, the moment is over. He lets go of the rod—and me—clearing his throat.

"Well, there you go. That should work. Just remember to wait for a tug, and be ready to reel it in if you catch something. Which I wouldn't hold your breath for at this hour, but you never know." He looks at me. "You could get lucky."

"I doubt that," I say, focusing on the river and trying to collect my thoughts.

We stand there for a while in silence, side by side. It doesn't seem like we're *fishing* so much as . . . standing. Waiting for something to happen.

"So this is it?" I ask. "This is all there is to fishing?"

He looks at me with a raised eyebrow. "Did you expect more?"

God. Why does everything between us feel like it's loaded with a double meaning?

I'm getting antsy with all this peace and stillness. I'm also getting restless about my sabotage idea, maybe even worried I'll change my mind. I glance downriver about forty feet from our spot, where I can see Jorge and his partner with their fishing lines cast into the stream. And beyond them, JJ is helping Kiera with her tackle box, which makes me feel a little better. I'm not the only one who needed help. I can spot a few more groupings, including one that's upriver from us. There are enough people in view of us that if Leo freaks out and does something embarrassing, they'll see it. Even if my triumph only lasts a few minutes, it'll be worth it.

I slap my arm hard. "The mosquitoes are bad over here by the water," I observe. "Are you getting bitten too?"

"Not really," Leo says. "But you're probably right. We should put on more bug spray."

"Mine's out," I lie.

He reaches into his bag and pulls out the canister I slipped into it when he wasn't looking. I glance away, a little nervous, a little excited. My plan is working, and it came together so easily! I don't want him to see the secret written on my face—he *could* still know me well enough to suspect something. I turn to face the water, bracing myself as I wait to hear him start spraying and screaming.

"Here, I'll do you first," he says.

"Wait, what?" I ask, swinging around to face him, but I'm too slow—he's already squatting beside me, spraying the canister at my shins.

I drop my fishing pole and start screaming uncontrollably as the pepper spray—*my* pepper spray that I disguised to look like OFF!—hits my bare legs.

To Leo's credit, he backs off immediately, confused and alarmed.

"Are you okay? Eden, what's happening?" he asks.

But all I can do is continue screaming while shaking my head. "It's— No. It's not. That's not bug spray! Oh god. It stings. It burns!"

I'm jumping around like a manic grasshopper, and before I know what's happening, Leo rushes up beside me and picks me up in his arms, baby-style.

"What! What are you doing?!" I wail.

"You need to get in the water and rinse off your legs," he says confidently.

"No!" I hate river swimming. We were just contemplating all the fish we weren't going to catch, and now I'm supposed to wade in with them?

"Yes, Eden. If you want to calm the rash, you need to remove the stimulant as rapidly as possible," he says, and while I gasp from the pain, he carries me to the edge of the river and tries to dump me into the water.

But I'm so freaked out, I grasp his T-shirt.

He teeters and falls into the river with me.

We land in about three and a half feet of freezing-cold water. How does it have the right to be this frigid in summertime?! Now I'm switching between moaning and hyperventilating less from the pain and more from the cold. Or maybe it's both. My legs *kill.* I can't *believe* I almost allowed Leo to do this to his own legs. What kind of monster am I?

"Shh," Leo's saying. "You're okay. You'll be fine. Just let the water wash your legs."

He fell away from me when we went down, and now he trudges over through the water. I can't help but notice the way his now-soaked shirt clings to his chest as he once again wraps his arms around me, this time not to show off his fishing skills but to reassure me.

Despite everything, I lean into him. I can't help it. I'm shivering.

But also, okay, there is part of me that has to admit—even after two years, and all the awful shit he put me through back when we broke up—that I still wonder what would've happened if things had gone differently. Part of me that misses the *idea* of Leo, the idea of the boyfriend who comforts you when you're hurt, and has your back when you're at your worst.

Then I remember that Leo showed me his true colors once before, and I shouldn't fall for this one modicum of charm. He's still the pompous asshole who broke my heart *and* made it seem like my own fault. And I'll never, ever, forgive him for that.

I pull away from his arms, realizing my own shirt is also completely soaked through, and my bra (not an outdoorsy sporty bra but a normal wire cup bra) is blatantly showing through my thin tank top. I wrap my own arms around myself just as JJ trudges up to us huffily.

"What exactly is going on here?" she demands. "The rules were strict and clear. We do not enter the water except when instructed, on water sport days."

I'm about to tell JJ exactly where she can put her damn rules and regulations: straight up her—

"Sorry," Leo takes over. "It was my fault. I left my fishing rod on the rock, where it tripped Eden."

JJ tsks. "Leo, I'm surprised. You should know better. We don't leave rods unattended."

"I know." He shakes his head like he's disappointed in himself. "I've relearned that lesson the hard way."

This seems to appease JJ somewhat. "Well, get yourselves out and gather your supplies. We'll be hiking back to the parking lot in ten."

She marches off and I sludge out of the water, clambering up the slippery, moss-covered rocks. I realize I'm barefoot.

"Oh no, what happened to my sandals?" I blurt out. *Please tell me they aren't floating down the river, and I'll have to walk all the way back through the woods barefoot!*

"I took them off your feet before I threw you in the water," Leo says. "You didn't notice? They're right there." He points to a spot on the boulder beside our abandoned fishing rods.

"Oh" is all I can think to say. Because no, I didn't notice him doing that. I didn't notice anything except him carrying me, and the intense, throbbing burn in my calves.

I look at my legs now as I gain my balance on the rocks. They are red and patchy and still feel like I put a curling iron straight to my skin, or a fresh sunburn, but the pain is manageable enough that I can at least walk—or hobble.

"What happened?" Leo asks as we both squeeze out of our wet shirts and gather our stuff.

"I—I don't know. So strange. I must've had a weird reaction to your bug spray. I'm gonna throw that stuff away," I tell him, and grab the canister back from where he dropped it, before he can question me further.

I zip up my backpack, regret filling every fiber of my being, then stand up and sling it onto my shoulders.

Leo comes over to me and hands me my tackle box. As he

passes it to me, he stands close, looking deeply into my eyes, as if searching for an answer to something.

Does he suspect what I was trying to do? That I'm behind it?

"Eden," he says, so quietly it's almost a whisper.

A shudder goes through me. There's something so intimate about the way he's looking at me, and standing so close . . . I can't help but once again think of his arms around me, him carrying me, him comforting me in the water, and now, his hair and chest dripping as he hovers . . .

"Yeah?" I whisper back.

"I just want you to know . . ." he says slowly, still gazing at me, almost like . . .

Well, almost as if he wants to kiss me.

I stand there, staring back up at him, waiting for whatever he's about to confess.

"I just want you to know," he repeats, a tentative smile twitching at the edge of his lips, "that you owe me big-time for covering for your ass with JJ just now."

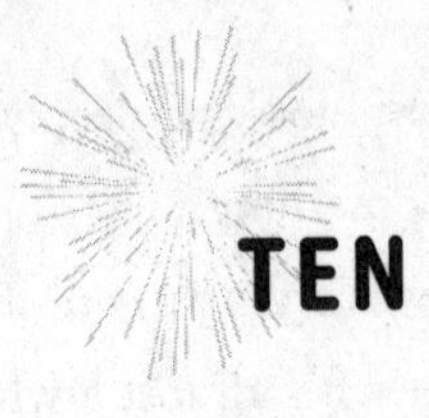

TEN

Daisy

"LET'S SWING BY THE beach," I say, kicking off my sandals and putting my bare feet up on Mateo's dusty dashboard. He doesn't seem to mind. We've just left the tennis club. He's been driving me home from work since Monday—though we've been hanging out instead of going straight home, wandering aimlessly and listening to music while I point out local landmarks. Killing time until Eden's done with her survivalist stuff, then picking her up on our way back.

I'm assuming this afternoon will be no different, but Mateo shrugs off my suggestion.

"I don't really feel like swimming." His long tan fingers tap the steering wheel to the beat of the indie rock streaming from his speakers.

"Yeah, but the beach will officially open to the public this weekend," I say, scanning his profile, trying to read him. "Once the lifeguards go on duty. Georgia told me there's only one more day of training. Which means one more day before it gets insanely crowded, and all the camp kids start taking over."

He shrugs again. "Your call."

"I just made the call! It was my idea."

"If only you had a driver's license and didn't need a chauffeur every time you want to do anything," he says.

I'm pretty sure he's teasing as usual, and not actually annoyed. Although the thought does cross my mind that he could easily find another girl—probably thirty other girls—who would be more than happy to spend their afternoons in his car. I've seen the way waitresses and cashiers and girls on the street—guys, too—eye Mateo up. It's hard to deny that he's extremely attractive, but it's more than that. There's an energy about him that makes you want to know more. Something about his soft voice that makes you want to lean in to hear what he has to say.

Honestly, I feel lucky to be the one who gets to have him all to myself, even if we're not dating. We're not even really *friends*, exactly, more like friends of friends who both need a buddy so we don't die of boredom.

Mateo is not the most emotive person in the universe; *moody* and *unreadable* are his two favorite settings, followed closely by *mysterious* and *quiet*. Except with tennis, when he's *ruthlessly competitive*. He likes to think he's a hard person to know—he's even told me that. ("Rhys is one of my few close friends. Most people think I'm an asshole, even though they've barely spoken to me," he said.) But I can tell he's just masking a lot of pain and messiness in his life that he doesn't want to deal with. Which I totally get. And I'm finding that despite his mysterious vibe, he's pretty chill, easy to be around. His sarcastic side is coming out more, and I feel like he's starting to trust me; he's been cracking more jokes, teasing me like we've known each other for years already.

Hanging out with Mateo every day after work also stops me from spiraling about Owen. I got another postcard from him yesterday. From Sweden.

Daze,

Please help me plot Grampa Dan's murder. I know the guy is already up there in age, but he's not slowing down, and I'm pretty sure only one of us is gonna make it out of Europe alive. So far, odds are in his favor. The amount of mountain hiking we've been doing is not for the faint of heart. Today we hiked all day in the pouring rain and I legit slid in a landslide of mud. It probably improved my outfit, but still. I feel like I'm in a World War II movie about soldiers on the front lines. The rain—and Gpa D—are showing no signs of letting up. But you know what they say. When it rains, it . . . sometimes rains even harder next.

Owen

I reread it five or six times, searching for double meanings, for some hint. I don't know what I expected. That he would talk about that kiss outright? Why would he put that in a postcard?

But without talking about it, how am I supposed to know what he's really thinking? Or is he even thinking about it at all? Somehow in the gap, I've completely lost the ability to understand what happened between us, and what it meant. I guess I never really understood it, but with each passing day, I'm less and less certain it was anything at all. People kiss at parties all the time. Don't they? I mean, *I* don't, but it seems like other people do.

It makes me feel foolish to have gotten so flustered and excited about it. If Owen really liked me, he easily could have said so. Instead, he's sent me two postcards that are decidedly friendly. In retrospect, it seems obvious he is friend-zoning me, trying to reestablish normalcy with all our familiar inside jokes. Make it clear that nothing's changed.

"Well, look," I say to Mateo now, pushing back my questions and insecurities around Owen. "I can't exactly help the fact that I'm not old enough to get my license."

"Yo, age faster."

I laugh. "Believe me, I would if I could." A thought flashes through my mind—would Mateo see me differently if I were his age?

I clear my throat and stare down at my stretched-out legs, which have already gotten a little bit of a tan just from these first few days of summer. "So do you want to go to the beach, or is this your not-so-subtle way of saying you don't want to hang out with me?"

"It's not that—I want to hang out."

"You do?"

He looks at me, surprise written on his face. “Of course. You’re a cool chick, Georgia’s Sister.”

“Ha. Ha.” I hate the fact that I’m blushing.

“If only I could remember your name. . . .”

I swat his arm. “Shut up.”

He laughs, then glances quickly over at me again. “Don’t play dumb. Obviously, I know your name.”

“Prove it.”

“Daisy. Daisy Daisy *Daaaaaaisy*,” he says in a singsong voice.

“Slow clap, Mateo. So are we going to the beach?”

“Wait.” He eyes me in a way I can only describe as mischievous. “I have a better idea.”

“You do?” I ask, mentally adding *mischievous* to the list of traits I know about him.

“Come on, I’ll show you.”

He takes a right turn, and soon we’ve left the wooded area surrounding the lake and are heading toward the highway.

“Where are we going?”

“Patience, young grasshopper.”

“I’ll be patient as long as you promise you’re not taking me to an abandoned field somewhere to murder me.”

He laughs. “There are probably a thousand other ways to murder you right here in Laurel.”

“Wow, so comforting.”

“Sorry, sorry, I’m just trying to find a town that’s more remote.”

“So no one will hear my screams?”

"No, silly." He smiles. "So I can teach you how to drive. We don't want a bunch of other cars or pedestrians around."

"Oh!" A flood of mixed emotions rises in my chest at once. Excitement (learning to drive sounds fun!), nervousness (will I embarrass myself in front of this cute older guy who clearly only sees me as a kid sister type, but still?), anxiety (what if I kill a squirrel, speaking of murder?).

And there's a pang of something else I can't quite pinpoint. Something between gratitude and grief. No one's ever offered to teach me to drive. It's kind of a dad-and-daughter cliché. One I'll never get to experience.

"Is that cool?" he asks, side-eyeing me through his sweep of dark hair.

I swallow the lump in my throat. "I'd love to."

We pull off the highway and take a few turns, following signs for an apple orchard. I roll down my window as we drive through fields of grass and tall weeds and apple trees, the sun beaming down. I wiggle my toes on the dashboard, and a sense of peace washes over me. This is what summers are *supposed* to feel like. Like freedom and open spaces and sunshine.

Like anything could happen next.

Mateo pulls over onto a gravelly shoulder on the side of the road. "All right, kid, switch seats." He gets out, leaving the keys in the ignition, and walks around to the passenger door.

I shove my feet back into my sandals and fumble with my seat belt.

He peers into my side of the car. "Are you getting cold feet?"

"My feet are actually the perfect temperature," I inform him, pulling my legs off the dashboard.

He reaches a hand out to me, like a gentleman helping a lady out of a carriage. I take it and let him pull me up and out of the car. He doesn't step back, though, so now I'm standing face-to-face with him. I have to look up, squinting.

"We don't have to do this if you're too scared," he says.

My heart is hammering in my chest. "I'm not too scared," I say. "I'm . . . I think I'm just the appropriate amount of scared."

"Are you sure?" he asks softly.

For some reason, this causes my heart to pound harder. I nod.

He pulls me toward him ever so slightly. "Good!" And then he lets go of my hand and gets into the passenger seat, where I was just sitting.

I take a breath of fresh air and regain my senses. *Get a grip, Daisy.* Literally, what did I think was about to happen just then?

I climb into the driver's seat, wiping the sweat from my palms onto my jean shorts. I'm still wearing my hideous, baggy work T-shirt. If I were Eden, I would have tied it into a cute midriff-baring knot, and I'd be wearing stylish strappy sandals instead of Tevas. Oh well. I am who I am!

"Okay, so what do I do? I don't even know where to put my hands!"

Mateo laughs. "Hang on, you're too far from the wheel." He leans all the way across my body, kind of like giving me a sideways hug, and I hold my breath for a second while he's draped across my lap. "The button is over here on the side," he explains, finally finding what he's looking for. He hits a lever on the side of my seat that slowly pushes me forward.

"I think I could've found that myself," I tell him.

I look over and—am I insane or is he blushing? "Oh right, sorry."

"That's okay. I'm totally used to having hot guys climb all over me," I blurt out. His blush deepens, but now I'm blushing too and wishing I hadn't just said that. Why am I such a weirdo? I clear my throat. "So, um, now what?"

He shows me where to put my hands, where to position my feet, then turns on the ignition. I feel a surge of adrenaline shoot straight to my heart.

He shows me how to take the gearshift out of park. I press my foot on the gas pedal, and we fly forward a few feet. I immediately hit the brake, and we jerk to a gravelly stop. Mateo is laughing hysterically, which is not at all helpful.

"Maybe this is a bad idea," I mutter.

"No, no, you're doing great, try again. Touch the pedal *lightly*, but leave your foot on it. And steer us off the shoulder."

As if it's that easy!

But somehow, after a few tries, I start to get the hang of it. We get back onto the two-lane road. There is not a single lick of traffic anywhere to be seen, thankfully, and I start to coast along the flat country road at around thirty miles an hour. After a few minutes, it starts to feel really good.

"Wow! I'm doing it!" I say, which comes out a little more squeal-like than I intended. We go down a little hill and I let out a terrified *whoop!*

I glance over at Mateo—is he seeing how I'm absolutely slaying this?

"Whoa, watch the road!" he says, grabbing the wheel as we start to swerve into the opposite lane. "Jesus."

"Sorry! Sorry!" I grip the wheel, humiliated now.

"It's okay, you're getting it," he says with a smile. A smile that I have to stop getting so distracted by.

We keep going. He shows me how to slow down at a couple of intersections; thankfully, there is no one passing us, and the risk of danger feels extremely low. Yet somehow, I feel like I've been injected with a powerful drug. I had no idea driving could be such a thrill, that it would feel so . . . I don't know, liberating.

I start experimenting, taking us up to forty miles an hour, and then forty-five, which is in fact the speed limit around here. As we ride up and down gently sloping hills, through sunlit fields, a feeling of euphoria washes over me. It feels like the road belongs entirely to us, and for some reason I start laughing.

"What's so funny?" Mateo asks.

I shake my head. "I don't know," I say, giddy. "This is just so *fun*!"

"You're doing great," he says encouragingly.

The breathy laughter keeps flying out of my chest, and then all of a sudden, I can't explain it, but there are tears coming down my face.

"Wait, are you laughing or crying?" he asks, bewildered.

"I don't know!" And I really don't. I don't know what's happened to me, what's come over me, but I'm starting to shake, tears rolling down my cheeks. I'm starting to feel—breathless.

"Pull over. Daisy, pull over," Mateo orders.

"How?" I ask-laugh-cry. My arms are trembling.

"Gradually lift your foot from the pedal and place it on the brake pedal but not too hard. Turn the wheel this way. . . . Yes, and then press the brake all the way—whoa!" We jerk to a stop. "Yup, just like that. Now gearshift," he says, but his words sound far away. He puts the gearshift into park for me and turns the key. The ignition settles into silence.

"Want to switch back?" he asks.

I nod, still overcome and shaky. I don't know why I'm crying.

I get out of the car slowly and walk to the front. Mateo gets out on his side and meets me at the hood of the car.

"Are you all right?" he asks quietly.

I shake my head. "No? I don't know. I'm not upset, I'm . . ."

He wraps me into a hug. "It's okay. Just breathe."

I try to—I inhale a deep, shuddering breath, but it only makes me cry a little harder, straight into his chest. "It was fun," I blubber. "I don't know why I'm crying."

"It's probably an anxiety reaction or something," he says. "Maybe you're relieved we're both still alive."

I laugh through my tears. "I wasn't that bad, was I?" I pull back so I can see his face.

He still has his arms around me. "Nah, you were fine. A little more practice and you'll nail it. I mean, you could win a race with a turtle or a bicyclist any day."

I laugh again, and he reaches down and wipes a trail of tears from my cheek with his thumb.

"You're okay," he says.

I nod. "I know. Thanks."

"Thanks for what?"

"For being so . . ." But I choke up again and shake my head.

"Don't worry, I get this reaction all the time. Hot girls crying all over me."

Once again, my tears turn to laughter . . . and somehow through it all, I feel my cheeks heating up again.

I back up out of his embrace and wipe my face on my T-shirt sleeve. "Ugh, I'm being so gross. Sorry. I guess I was just overwhelmed, and . . ." I lean my butt against the hood of the car, and Mateo takes a seat beside me. "I always thought my dad would teach me how to drive, which probably sounds stupid. Out there on the road—it felt so great. I felt so free. But it was also like letting go of this fantasy that I didn't even realize I was still holding on to, you know?"

Mateo sighs. "I'm not gonna pretend I know how that feels. But what you're saying makes perfect sense."

"I guess when I say it out loud, yeah." I let out a breath, starting to feel calmer again. "That's probably what it was. *And* relief that I didn't kill anyone, ourselves included."

He nods, quiet.

"Anyway, thank you."

"For teaching you to drive? Or attempting to, at least? I'm not sure I really taught you all that much, but no problem."

I laugh. "And for calling me a hot girl."

"When did I call you a hot girl?" he asks.

I blush. "Shut up! Just then. The *hot girls crying all over me* comment."

"Oh," he says. "I was speaking generally, you know . . ."

"Oh."

He nudges me in the ribs. "Daisy."

"What?"

"Look at me."

I look over at him.

"I'm kidding. Of course you're hot."

My whole body feels overheated and shivery at the same time. It's not just that he's calling me hot—not exactly the world's most original compliment. It's *how* he's saying it, how he's looking at me.

"Shut up." I swat at him. Because honestly, how else am I supposed to respond?

"*You* shut up," he says, swatting me back lightly.

"No, *you* shut up." I swat back again.

But this time he grabs my wrist—not tight, just enough to prevent my hand from making contact with his upper arm. "Make me."

I nudge him with my shoulder, and he drops my wrist. My hand falls onto his thigh, and then . . . I don't really know what happens, but we're turning toward each other, and his hand reaches up to my face. He tilts my chin, and I feel his intake of breath as I lean up toward him. And our lips meet.

The kiss isn't intense and urgent, like the kiss with Owen was. *That* kiss had felt like a long time coming. But *this* kiss . . . I don't know. It's . . .

Perfect?

Fluttering and hesitant, each of us a little uncertain.

He pulls away just enough to ask, "Are you . . . okay with this?"

I nod.

We kiss again, deeper this time, and his tongue gently finds the tip of mine, and his lips are so warm and soft and . . . oh wow. Mateo is a *really good kisser.*

Electricity moves up and down my spine, and I never want this to stop.

It doesn't seem like Mateo does either.

I can't believe this is happening I can't believe this is happening I can't believe this is happening.

It's the only coherent thought in my brain, which is fine, because I don't need any distractions right now.

His hand finds its way to my waist, sending tingles everywhere, and *oh, so this is how older guys kiss.*

I've kissed a few boys before; nothing fancy. Once at camp, as a dare, when I was all messed up about Dad's death. Once at a high school dance. And then Owen.

And now: this. It's a whole other level. Sexy and exciting and overwhelming. I'm afraid to show how much I like it, but Mateo pulls me closer. He stands up and leans over me, and we press together, and the kiss is slow, and . . . in a weird way it feels just as liberating and exciting as driving for the first time did. Like I'm learning as I go. Like I'm both more in control and also less in control than I've ever been in my entire life.

And then—a car whizzes by along the road—that road that I briefly thought belonged to us—honking loudly, and we pull apart, catching our breath.

I start to laugh, and Mateo does, too.

"So," he says once we've both recovered somewhat. "Still want to go to the beach?"

I look at my watch. "Oh wow, it's time to pick up Eden. Let's get her and we can all go."

I'm relieved to have a plan, otherwise I'm not sure how I would know what to do with myself next. On autopilot, I get back into the passenger seat, and Mateo takes the wheel. He puts his music back on, and we're quiet on the drive to Laurel—the tension of that kiss lingering in the air between us, taut as a stretched rubber band, while out the window, the fields fly by, speckled with gold.

ELEVEN

Georgia

WHEN I FINISH TRAINING for the day, I get out of the water and see Daisy, Eden, and Mateo waiting for me, sitting on a picnic blanket on the sand, drinking seltzers and laughing.

I squeeze out my wet ponytail and climb onto the dock. I need to do a few quick stretches, then I'll head over to the group. I'm excited to see them, but wishing Mateo wasn't here. It's been such a busy week already; aside from breakfasts and dinners I've barely had time to see Daisy and Eden, and I'm dying to talk to them alone. Specifically about Benny. He's sweet and funny and we've been meeting early every morning to work on a few drills. Though he clearly has a flirtatious personality, I think he understands we can only be friends. But I feel this urgency to introduce him to the girls—and especially to Daisy, since they're the same age. I'll just feel a little better if I can set them up. Daisy will be happy, and I can continue helping Benny without it being weird.

Even though, if I'm honest, it already is a *little* weird. Like, last night I was on the phone with Rhys before bed, babbling on about my day, and something stopped me from talking about running drills with Benny.

Luckily, Rhys started talking about Mateo, asking if I've been helping him get a better sense of Laurel. I told him Mateo seemed to be enjoying the tennis clinic and that he was driving Daisy home after work every afternoon.

"That's right, he mentioned he's been hanging out with her this week," Rhys said. "Just, you know. Don't leave him alone with her for too long."

"Rhys! What do you mean?"

"Oh, it's just Mateo. You know what he's like."

I don't pay *that* much attention to Rhys's friend group, but I thought I knew what he was hinting at. "You're saying he's a player. But he'd never go for Daisy, right? She's so young!" I exclaimed, trying not to sound totally scandalized.

"It's not that out of the question, baby. Mateo hooked up with a sophomore earlier this year. At least one, maybe two, actually. I wouldn't put it past him."

"Jeez, you make him sound like a predator!"

Rhys laughed. "Oh, come on. You can see everyone wants a piece of that guy. He's like a kid in a candy shop. He can have whoever he chooses."

Something rubbed me the wrong way about how Rhys spoke about Mateo, but I couldn't put my finger on it, so we just said our *good nights* and *I love you*s and I went to sleep. But this morning, I realized what bothered me: Mateo is Rhys's best friend. They're equally handsome, in different ways, and they're both clearly coveted by nearly everyone they meet. When Rhys was describing Mateo last night, I couldn't help but picture both of them strutting around the halls of their high school this past year, seniors at the top of their game, knowing they could have anyone they wanted. The picture made them look entitled . . . and obnoxious. If Rhys thought that anyone would be so lucky to hook up with Mateo—wouldn't that apply to Rhys, too?

Or maybe this was just my jealousy talking.

Rhys says it's cute. "I like a territorial woman," he's always telling me. But—couldn't he help reassure me by not making subtle comments like that so often?

I finish my stretches and tip my head, shaking water out of my ears, *trying* to shake off the unsettled feeling I've had in my body all day.

As I walk across the sand, I eye Mateo suspiciously, trying to get a read on whether he's trustworthy, whether to take Rhys's "warning" seriously. He's leaning back on his hands, his legs stretched out in front of him across the blanket. He's still in tennis clothes, as usual. Beside him, Daisy is bouncy and giggly in her gross oversized work T-shirt and cutoffs. Both of them are looking at Eden, who's wearing a triangle-printed romper that looks like an '80s vintage find, and a pair of thick-soled lavender flip-flops. When I make it over to the picnic blanket, Eden is in the middle of a dramatic reenactment of her fiasco from yesterday with Leo and the failed prank. Her legs have recovered, thankfully, but her ego? Not so much.

"Hey, guys!" I sit down with them on the blanket, just as

Mateo's saying, "If at first you don't succeed, try again, Eden. You've got to take the sabotage up a notch."

Daisy laughs into her LaCroix can, but I frown.

"Um, that is horrible advice, Mateo! I think Eden learned her lesson. It's probably time to do what I said from the very beginning and just have a conversation with the guy."

Eden blows her bangs out of her eyes. "There is no possibility of a *conversation* with Leo," she insists. "Since Spray-Gate, he's been more aloof than ever."

I sigh. "What would convince you to talk to him like you're two adults?"

Eden grins at me. "First of all, Georgia, we're *not* adults. And second of all, Leo never once apologized for what happened. How he treated me. He still doesn't think he did anything wrong. He thinks our breakup was my fault, and I can tell his opinion of me has never changed. He looks down on me. The only chance of clearing the air would be if he apologized profusely, and I don't see that ever happening."

"What exactly did happen?" Mateo asks.

I jump in again. "Not your business, Mateo."

"Fair enough. You're the boss," Mateo says.

"Georgia!" Daisy bursts in. "You're being rude."

"No, I'm not!"

"Sorry, Mateo. Ignore her," Daisy says.

Mateo looks back and forth between us. "Okay, no way. I'm not getting in the middle of whatever's going on here. Georgia's right, anyway, I should let you three have your girl talk or whatever."

He starts to stand up and dust sand off his shorts.

"You're leaving?" Daisy says.

"Yeah. See you tomorrow, kid." He nods to all three of us and heads out.

"Thank god he left, I really need to talk to you guys!" I tell them.

But Daisy is pouting. "You didn't have to send him away like he's in trouble or something, jeez. You treat him like he's our employee."

"I didn't! I do not! He left of his own free will!" I retort. "It's almost dinnertime anyway! And besides, why are you so worried about Mateo's feelings all of a sudden?"

"I don't know, maybe since we made out?" Daisy says defiantly.

My jaw nearly falls off my face, and dread lands like a pile of dirty laundry in my gut.

"Whoa! What?!" Eden's saying, bouncing on her knees. "Daisy, no way!"

She nods, blushing, still annoyed with me but also unable to hide a proud, beaming grin. "Literally today after work, before we came to pick you up, Eden."

Eden looks aghast. "But you let me have the front seat! I rattled on about my day the whole time we drove here, I had no idea."

"It's not like we were gonna hold up a sign," Daisy says, wrapping her arms around her knees.

"What does this *mean*?! Was it amazing?" Eden demands.

"Wrong question," I cut in. "Daisy, what were you thinking?"

Daisy glances between the two of us. "For your information, yes, it *was* amazing. And to answer your question, Georgia, I guess I was thinking why not?"

I sigh and shake my head, trying to control my reaction. "Daisy. I can't believe this. I can't believe this!"

"What can't you believe? That a guy like him would even be interested in me, when he could have anyone? I thought you'd be happy! Imagine if I start dating Mateo, and you're with Rhys. How perfect would that be?"

"Oh, that *is* nauseatingly cute," Eden says unhelpfully.

"Eden, no. Do not encourage this. Mateo is way too old for her. And Daisy, no, I'm not happy. Mateo is a nice enough guy, but you shouldn't trust him. He's a player and he's going to Cornell in the fall. He's a smart, ambitious guy and—"

"And he's out of my league, you're saying," Daisy finishes. "Wow, thanks for sharing your true opinion of me, Georgia."

"Why are you twisting what I'm saying? I'm saying you deserve *better.* A good guy your age who is sweet and fun and not quite so . . . *experienced.* Guys like Mateo, they expect things."

"Like what?" Daisy asks, glaring at me.

"Like *sex,*" I hiss at her. I'm extremely aware that I'm the most experienced of the three of us. Obviously—I've been with Rhys for nearly three years now. Eden's had her share of hookups but nothing serious, and she never got that far with Leo before they broke up. I know she lost her virginity at some point last year, but she basically swore off going all the way since then. As for Daisy? Not even close.

Eden starts laughing. I glare at her. She is actively *not* helping right now.

Daisy rolls her eyes. "Georgia, you sound like a Victorian book of manners."

"No way. Edwardian, maybe."

"What?"

"Never mind. Just please, Daisy, I want you to be careful with your heart. That's all."

"Kinda sounds like you want her to be careful with her cooch," Eden says.

"Well, that too! They're related!" I shout, exasperated.

Daisy and Eden look at each other, and then at me . . . and then we all start laughing.

"The sacred cooch-heart connection," Eden gasps out through her laughter.

"Stop calling it that!" Daisy squeals, swatting at Eden.

Still laughing at myself, I try to calm down. "Look, sorry, I'm just being a protective big sister, okay? And also, I'm annoyed because I have someone else I wanted to set you up with. He's this really cute kid your age named B—"

"Georgia, it's okay." Daisy puts her hand on my arm to stop me. "You don't have to set me up with anyone. I think I like Mateo."

Now it's Eden's turn to squeal. "You do?! That *is* pretty fast. What about Guacamole Boy?"

"Guacamole Boy?" I ask. "Who's that?"

Daisy glares at Eden, and I feel a flash of annoyance that they have some secret code I don't know about. "No one. Just a friend.

I know it's fast and I'm just figuring out what I think about him. But I promise I'm not getting too carried away, okay? Could you please trust me for once?"

"I do trust you," I tell her. "Just . . ." Clearly, now is not the right time to force-feed Benny on her. It needs to feel more natural. "Wait, I have an idea," I start, thinking fast. "Let's have a party this weekend. I'll bring the guy I want you to meet. We can . . . see how it goes."

"Ooh, a party! Yes!" Eden says, clapping her hands. "*Now* you're starting to make sense!"

"Fine, but Mateo has to come, too," Daisy says.

"Fine, of course!" I tell her. "Rhys will want him there anyway." I turn to face Eden. "And Eden, you're inviting Leo."

"What? No way."

"Yes way."

"Is it Georgia's-the-Boss Day? Because you're really leaning in," Eden says.

"I'm going to force that guy to apologize to you if it's the last thing I do," I tell her. "He needs to do the right thing. And if he doesn't, I promise I'll kick him out. Deal?"

"Well, what if he says no?"

"He won't, trust me. He'll come. And if he doesn't, he's a dick."

"He *is* a dick, though," Eden grumbles . . . but doesn't refuse, so I can tell she doesn't hate my plan as much as she insists.

I know the girl better than she'd like to admit. I know how heartbroken she was over Leo. And I also remember how in love with him she was. I know it'll be healing to have this conversation.

She needs it. Her parents kind of left her in my charge this summer—I mean, in Mom's charge, but basically in mine—because they felt like she needed a reset. It's more than just country air Eden needs. She needs to get over her past.

Pleased with my new plan, I start packing up our stuff, eager to get home and shower and help Mom with dinner. I'm starving after a full day of training—and I need to keep moving before the girls try to change my mind.

Friday morning, I wake early—even for me—feeling reinvigorated. After I drove home from the beach with the girls, we had a cozy night. It started raining softly, so we had tacos inside while Dave told us a story about how he'd gotten reprimanded at the Laurel library—for the great sin of humming to himself while working on his paper. I found this whole anecdote wildly embarrassing, but Mom seemed to think it was the absolute most adorable tale a man could tell. Later we put on a movie no one really liked; we mostly just talked and laughed and fell into bed exhausted. I had a quick sleepy call with Rhys and told him about the party idea. He loved it, which made me happy. Daisy would meet Benny, and Mateo would get the hint, and Leo would apologize to Eden, and Rhys and I would hold hands, be a unit again, and it would all be perfect. I fell asleep sure of that.

Last night's rain left a lingering humidity; the sun's only partly out as I slip out of the house at six fifteen in my first bathing suit of the day—a white bikini and matching visor, along with a pair of navy striped shorts. With all the fans whirring and air conditioner units buzzing, no one hears my car as I pull out of the driveway.

I'm not sneaking out, exactly. I've just been coming and going in the early mornings before anyone else is awake because that's the best time to meet with Benny. Before it gets too hot, and before I'm too busy with training. The beach opens to the public Saturday, and then I'll be on duty most days, though our shifts will trade off a bit, with two of us working at any given time. Anyway, I like this hour. The lake is quiet, and we aren't disturbing anyone. I've been getting home by seven forty-five, in time to trade my wet bathing suit for a clean one-piece and come down for breakfast with everyone else a little after eight. It's requiring a serious amount of bathing suit switches, but otherwise the system works fine, and no one's the wiser. Not that I care if anyone knows. It's just easier this way, like I said. I know how cranky this family gets when they don't have enough sleep.

I love pulling into the empty beach parking lot. My first glimpse of the still water, with no one else around. It's serene, meditative.

This morning, Benny's here first. He greets me with a huge smile and a wave before I'm even out of the car. I have to say, it's a great way to start the day. At home I'm rarely greeted with smiles of enthusiasm—usually it's Mom tearing the house apart looking for something she lost, or Daisy grumbling about homework she forgot to do or, if it's a weekend, pissed that someone woke her up.

"Hi, Benny." I get out of the car and slam the door shut with my hip, tightening my ponytail. I keep it high on my head and mostly avoid getting my hair wet during these sessions. Makes the transition into outfit number two easier.

"Hey, Georgia," he says, walking over. He's already wet, lake water dripping down his bare chest, his necklaces glinting in the early light. "Got a few laps in already to warm up."

"Nice," I say, impressed. "Okay, let's get to that sidestroke, then."

We grab the rescue tube from the shack and walk down the dock, and I sit on the edge with my stopwatch while he hops into the water.

"Okay, left side now. You need to be agile."

"If I rescue someone, won't I just use my stronger side?"

"You could get a cramp," I tell him. "Or an injury. Better to be prepared for anything."

He switches to his left side, powering through the water. It's very pleasant, sitting here with my feet dangling in the water, watching his body ripple through the lake, strong and certain. He's been taking my feedback, and I'm satisfied to see real improvement after only a few days.

"Form is more important than speed on this stroke," I remind him when he makes his way back to me. "Remember, you're using sidestroke because you've got a person in your other arm. Speed is for getting to them, steadiness and endurance for the return."

"It would be easier if I could practice *with* a person," he says, squinting up at me from the water.

"What, like me?"

He shrugs. "No, I was thinking Mr. Bailey, when he gets here."

I sigh. "I'll get in, but please don't get my hair too wet."

"Why not? That's crazy. Your hair is wet all day."

I splash my feet a little. "Not before breakfast, it isn't."

"Georgia. Are you keeping these practice sessions a secret?"

"No! Why would I do that?"

"I don't know, you tell me."

"I'm not!"

"So who knows?"

I pause. "Me . . . and you. But that doesn't make it a secret. Plenty of things happen that no one else knows about, and they aren't secrets. Like that," I say, pointing to a hawk flying high over the distant shore. "If no one sees the hawk, does that mean its flight pattern is being kept a secret?"

"Wow," he says with a laugh. "So philosophical."

"Oh, come on," I say, standing up. I toss him the rescue tube, then shimmy my shorts down my hips and kick them off, aware that Benny is staring at me. It is one of my best bikinis, after all, and I can't exactly wear it for work, so I figured I might as well wear it for this. I splash off the dock and into the water beside him. "Stop being annoying and start saving my life."

I breaststroke out about forty yards or so into the deeper part of the lake, keeping my head above water, and turn back, treading water. I wave my arms in a fake signal of panic, and then, still treading water, I set my stopwatch.

Benny's fast, but I'm still a little out of breath by the time he gets to me. It drives home just how easy it would be for a lesser swimmer to drown this far out. Alertness and speed are everything in this job.

When he gets to me, he approaches from behind like he's been taught, grabbing my hand and speedily turning me so I'm facing up, while hefting me backward onto the rescue tube. I feel it squeak below my shoulder blades.

"Lower," I instruct him.

"Hey, who's saving who," he grunts, repositioning it down below my lower back.

"I guess we'll see, won't we? And it's *whom*. Who's saving *whom*."

He laughs, out of breath. "Don't crack jokes, or you really will be the one saving me."

"Grammar's not a joke to me," I tease.

"Stop!" he laughs again, spitting out lake water.

I feel his arm tighten strongly around me as he begins to pull me back in toward the dock.

My ponytail is definitely getting wet, but I have to admit, I feel . . . safe. Secure. Like he knows what he's doing.

And that makes me feel proud too, because in such a short time, while I'm still going through training myself, I've taught him these skills.

I relax, going limp, as someone exhausted from nearly drowning might do, and allow him to pull me all the way in, feeling the cool water stream along my body.

Benny's fully out of breath by the time we reach the side of the dock in waist-deep water.

He lets go of me, his hand grazing accidentally along my

stomach. I'm not sure he noticed—he definitely didn't do it on purpose—but I inhale reflexively, unused to being touched by anyone who isn't Rhys. I recall his hand on my leg on the gondola and blink the memory away.

"Not bad," I tell him, standing up.

"Thanks," he pants.

"But your endurance definitely needs work. We should do some running drills for that." He groans, and I laugh. "Not right now. I've got to get home."

He smiles. "Same time tomorrow?"

"Oh—I don't know if I can do weekends," I explain. "I'm starting work for real tomorrow."

"Ah," he says. "Monday at dawn, then?"

"Absolutely."

"Georgia, would you be open to meeting up later today? I . . . have something I want to show you."

"I—" I'm tempted to ask him what it is, but then remember it's Friday. "I'm sorry, Benny. My boyfriend is coming up later today. We'll probably want to spend every free second we have together."

He nods. "Would your boyfriend have a problem with you training me? Is that why you're keeping it a secret?"

"No! He's not possessive at all. Rhys is the most confident guy I know. And I told you, this isn't a secret."

"Okay . . ."

"What?"

He shrugs. "I mean, if I were him, I wouldn't love it."

"That's kind of sexist," I inform him. "But good to know."

"I'm just saying, you're a very special human, Georgia, and if I were your boyfriend I'd be constantly sweating losing you."

"Well, Rhys isn't 'sweating' anything, so don't worry. He knows he won't lose me."

"Okay. I guess that's good. I mean, if it's good for you, then it's good."

I'm finding this conversation annoying, but then remember something. "Hey! We're throwing a little party at my place on Saturday. You should come to that! And you can finally meet Daisy." I add a wink, regretting it instantly.

He laughs. "Has anyone ever told you your wink looks more like a flinch?"

"Ha. Yeah, I could feel that."

He laughs again. "Party sounds great. What's the address?"

"I'll text it to you," I say.

He smiles. "I actually don't have a phone."

"Oh!" I tell him the address, and he nods.

"I'll remember that. Thanks for inviting me."

I smile. "Of course!" I say, feeling charitable. Because while I don't think I've done anything to lead him on, I know that I'm one of his only friends at the lake so far, and he's probably just bored and lonely and can't think of anyone else to hang out with on a Friday night.

But tonight is for me and Rhys.

"Bye, Benny," I say with a wave. "Keep up the good work."

* * *

It isn't until I'm taking my lunch break in the shade of the beach shack that I get the text from Rhys.

Rhys:

So, so sorry to do this baby but I can't come up to the lake this weekend.

My heart plummets like a broken elevator. Bubbles appear on my screen, and then:

Rhys:

It's my first weekend here, and all the other interns are doing this network party. Gotta show face. Hope you understand.

Can't wait to see you and kiss you soon.

Next weekend, for 4th of July.

Sorry again.

My hand hovers shakily over the screen but I'm too shocked to write back. He didn't even call, only texted. I can't explain why it stings this much. After all, it's not like we haven't weathered canceled plans before. And he's probably texting from work—he probably can't make a personal call but wanted to tell me right away. He's trying to do the respectful thing. That's Rhys. He's always trying to do the right thing, and I know that. But it still feels like an insult, a rejection. His fun internship in the city is more important than spending time with me.

Without meaning to, I remember what Benny said that morning, about Rhys not being afraid of losing me. This tiny voice in my head adds: *because he takes you for granted.*

I try to swallow that thought away.

Does he even remember I'm throwing a party this weekend? That he's supposed to come to?

I hover my fingers over the screen again, trying to figure out what to say back. A wild impulse takes over, and I almost want to text Benny instead, to tell him I'm free tonight after all, but remember I don't have a way to reach him. A hotness tingles my fingers, a feeling of anger and defiance.

But then I scroll back to Rhys's text. And write: **Oh no. I'm so sad. I miss you and can't wait to see you next weekend instead. I'll be thinking about you all weekend. Love you.**

Because that is the mature thing to do.

Because that is the *right* thing to do.

TWELVE

Eden

TRULY, THANK GOD AND modern technology for indoor plumbing, because I feel like I'm going to explode suspense-induced diarrhea. Okay, well, it might be Diet Coke–induced, I'm not sure. But the rumbling in my stomach is fierce, and it's all because of Georgia and this stupid party.

I mean, it's *not* a stupid party, it's actually a very pretty, well-decorated backyard soiree with swaying fairy lights and flickering reflections of the lake through the trees. But everything feels off. Georgia's been in a *mood* ever since Rhys said he was staying in the city. I'm happy Georgia has someone she's so into, I guess, but the guy really rules her emotions. And if you ask me, it is a little selfish of him.

But no one asked me.

Aunt Elena and Dave are having their own grown-up party on the porch, drinking chilled red wine with a handful of adults I recognize vaguely from around Laurel. The sound of their laughing voices trails out into the yard and then fades into the sounds of a killer playlist on the speaker, thanks to yours truly. We've used the strings of lights to section off the part of the yard that runs through the trees to the edge of the lake. We have the firepit going, dusk is fading into night, and the stars are breaking through the clouds.

We actually have a pretty good crowd out here already, given we've only been in town a week. But Leo, I can't help but notice, hasn't arrived.

One of the first people to show up was a boy named Benny. He's apparently the hottie Georgia wants Daisy to meet . . . but Daisy has pretty much had blinders on ever since Mateo got here, along with a lanky blond guy named Sam from his tennis clinic. They've been hoarding the cornhole set. So, Georgia commandeered Benny to help her finish hanging the lights and get the firepit started.

Daisy also invited a guy named Tre from the club's snack kiosk, and Tre brought his impressively pierced partner, Jaclyn. The two of them are my favorites so far. Tre sauntered up and the first thing out of his mouth was a compliment to my playlist, so that obviously won me over.

Georgia invited the other lifeguards (or "LGs") from the beach, an assortment of extremely fit guys and girls who all arrived together and, for reasons I can't quite discern, all refer to Georgia as "Finn." I finally ask one of them, a kid named Zac, why the nickname. "Finn as in Phinny as in dolphin! Because of how she squees when she comes in first on a race," he says, as if it's the most obvious thing in the world, then jogs off to fist-bump someone. These LGs are a bit rowdy, celebrating the first day of the beach being open to the public. The party has barely gotten into full swing when they start daring each other to do dumb shit like climb a tree or steal a bottle of wine from the porch. Leave it to the lifeguards to be the least responsible people here.

At least that's better than the eight or so total randos *I* invited. Because yes, I invited the entire Boundless Horizons group. What choice did I have? There was no way I was going to only invite Leo—the last thing I need is him thinking I actually *want* him to come tonight. The best way I could think to get him to show up was to activate his competitive side, or his pride. He clearly fancies himself a leader of the group, which meant that if I invited everyone, he'd feel like he had to be here. And I figure it's nice for me to try to make some actual friends while I'm up here. Kiera and Jorge, who is usually Leo's partner in crime at BH, are already off wandering the woods at the edge of the yard. I have no doubt she's got him helping her forage for edible mushrooms.

I start to relax. Leo clearly isn't coming, which means I can just enjoy myself and be normal. Even the adults are letting loose—at one point Dave drags Aunt Elena out onto the lawn and I see them dancing together before they retreat to the porch to refill their glasses. I dance with Tre and Jaclyn and a couple of the BHers and another tennis clinic guy I didn't even know had shown up. Georgia and Benny join us, but then Georgia pulls me away.

"Where are we going?" I ask as she drags me by the elbow.

"I need a selfie of me, you, and Daisy. Let's go get her," Georgia says, a determined look on her face. She pulls me over to the cornhole board, where Daisy is still hanging out with Mateo and his friend.

"Who's gonna be our fourth?" the friend protests as Georgia grabs Daisy with her free arm.

"I'll play!" says an LG named Francesca, though everyone's calling her "HP." ("You know, HP for printer for prints for princess because she's a total princess about not getting sand on the lifeguard tower," someone explained not very helpfully.)

Georgia marches me and Daisy over to a vacant corner of the yard and pulls out her phone.

"Get our outfits," I instruct, forcing Georgia to hold the camera up high. We do look cute. I'm wearing a pair of lilac barrel jeans and a lacy white tie-front tank top that shows my belly button and would also show cleavage if I had any. Georgia's wearing an impractical but very flirty white linen minidress with puffy sleeves that shows off her sun-kissed shoulders, freckled collarbones, and tan legs. Even Daisy has pulled it together—she's for once not wearing her ugly tennis club T-shirt and cutoffs, trading them in for a denim skirt I loaned her and a mint-green vintage '90s camisole that makes the hint of strawberry red in her hair really pop.

After we take the photos, Daisy starts to walk away.

"Wait," Georgia says. "Hang on." Daisy pauses. "Will you guys help me replenish the snacks?"

"Of course!" I say, and we follow her into the house.

As soon as the screen door shuts behind us, Georgia turns. "Do you guys feel like this party is a success so far?"

Daisy shrugs. "Yeah! A lot more people came than I expected this early in the summer. I'm guessing they had nothing else to do." She heads into the kitchen to grab a fresh bag of chips.

I follow her and start loading up on the sodas for the cooler.

Georgia nods to herself. "The timing was good. This is the week people arrive at the lake and have no other plans except to prepare for July fourth next weekend." But her face looks distant.

"Georgia, is everything okay? Are *you* happy with the party?"

Georgia blinks and nods. "I guess so. I mean, it's not exactly what I'd envisioned. . . ."

"Because Rhys isn't here," I fill in.

She sighs. "It's totally fine. I get why he has to network. It's not that, really."

"Then what?"

Georgia looks between me and Daisy. "Are you seeing how Mom and Dave are all over each other?"

I glance at Daisy. "On the porch? I hadn't noticed. Can't say I've been paying much attention to Old People Corner."

Daisy laughs. "Georgia, they're drunk on red wine. Who cares?"

"But it's kind of embarrassing, don't you think?"

"I don't think so," I tell her. "If I had a nickel for every time my parents got drunk in public, I'd be the planet's richest person under twenty."

"It's not the wine; I don't care about that," Georgia says, tearing open a package of napkins and, for no apparent reason, counting them. "It's just, doesn't she have any decency? Everyone up here knows about what happened."

Daisy looks astonished. "You mean about Dad?"

Georgia puts down the napkins. "What else would I be talking about? Of course I mean Dad."

"G, he died *three years* ago. She's allowed to move on."

"Of course she is! But there's a line."

"A line?"

"You can date, that's fine. But I never liked the idea of her parading him around up here. This place was, like, Dad's sacred happy place."

I see the pain written on Georgia's face and realize this really has nothing to do with Dave, or Elena, or wine, or Rhys not being here.

There are some things bigger than all that.

I wrap an arm around Georgia. "I wouldn't take this too seriously. Just let them have fun tonight." I pause. "And you know what? Let *yourself* have fun."

"I *am* having fun," she insists. But she looks like she's going to cry.

Daisy and I look at each other again. "Okay . . ." Daisy says, "well, in that case, can we go back to this fun party we're throwing?"

"Daze!" I say. Sometimes the girl is so caught up in her own world it's ridiculous. Or maybe it's a little sister thing.

"What?"

"Group hug first," I command, wrapping my arms fully around Georgia and waving Daisy over. She joins the hug, and I breathe in the smell of all three of us together, a mix of floral and peachy perfumes and body sprays and leftover sunscreen. For a moment, it's just like it's always been, the three Holliday girls all together, a unit. Sweet and cozy and indestructible.

I hear Georgia sniffle a little. Then she gently pushes us both away. "All right, all right, you guys are messing up my hair." She laughs. "But I love you both."

I fix her smudged mascara with my thumb, and we grab all the stuff we came in here for.

By the time we're outside again, someone has spilled a stolen bottle of wine all over Francesca; Sam and Mateo are arguing over a game of beer pong (with lemonade, not beer) because those two seriously can't *not* compete. A couple of the LGs are filming a YouTube video, and Jorge and Kiera are legit making out in the woods against a tree. It's starting to feel like mayhem out here, and that's when I hear my name.

"Eden."

I turn.

It's Leo.

Oh lord. I really need to lay off the Diet Coke, because instantly, the artificial sugar and caffeine elixir spikes in my veins and I can literally feel it manifest into anxiety in my gut.

It's not just Leo, it's Leo *looking really good*. (And oh, how his ego would bask in the knowledge of that thought passing through my head.)

He saunters over to me, hands hidden in the pockets of his hideous cargo shorts, which show off his not-at-all-hideous calf muscles . . . and nauseating Velcro Dockers sandals that threaten to ruin everything. At least he's paired the outfit with a white linen button-down that looks extremely posh-summer-party in all the right ways, complementing his white-teeth smile. His dark, floppy curls look a little tighter than usual, and I wonder if he used hair product. Leo Goldbaum, putting in the effort?

This should be a new form of mythical creature, like the centaur, except instead of half man, half horse, it's catalog model on top, stupid clueless high school dude on the bottom.

"Sorry I'm late," he says. "Took longer to get out of the house than I'd planned."

The Leo I know is Mr. Punctual, so I can sense there's something else behind this casual comment, I just don't know what it is. Maybe he was torn about whether to come at all. By now, I'd assumed he was a no-show. What made him change his mind?

I raise an eyebrow. "Agonizing over which shoes to wear, I assume."

He laughs. "Sure, something like that."

"I was joking. I'd be happy to sacrifice those to the firepit."

He shakes his head, still smiling. "I hadn't planned to give up any of my clothes, but I guess we'll see how the night goes."

I clear my throat. Now what? "There's a bunch of drinks in the cooler." I wave my arm helplessly in that direction.

He nods, and as soon as he starts walking over to the cooler, I dart over to Georgia, who's laughing at some story Benny's telling her. Am I hallucinating or are Georgia's off-the-shoulder sleeves hanging even *more* off the shoulder?

"*He's here*," I hiss.

"What? Who is?" Georgia pulls her attention away from Benny.

"*Leo!*"

"Okay, relax." Georgia looks at me innocently.

"*What do I do? You're the one who made me invite him!*" I remind her.

"So what?" she asks with a shrug. She looks over at Benny and laughs. He plays with his necklace. I look between the two of them. What the actual hell is going on here?

"How's your plan to introduce Benny and Daisy going, by the way?" I don't mean it to sound so catty. It's Leo's fault. His presence clearly brings out the worst in me.

Georgia turns to face me fully. "We're not making a lot of progress, honestly. Benny's been great, but we have a problem with Daisy. She's way too . . . *distracted*," she says, nodding over to Mateo. I look over and see Daisy's holding on to Mateo's arm, balancing on one leg while doing the ankle grab dance move.

"She's got some interesting mating rituals, that's for sure."

Georgia gives me a pained look. "Don't say *mating*, Eden, gross."

"Okay, Miss Manners, can we get back to me? I can't talk to Leo. It's too awkward. I really wish you hadn't convinced me to do this."

"Like I really twisted your arm?" Her eyebrow goes up.

Benny steps closer and asks, "Who's Leo?"

I point him out—he's holding a sweaty can of seltzer and

mingling with other Boundless Horizons people, looking completely comfortable, almost as if *he's* the party host. It's very annoying.

"Wow," Georgia says. "He's even cuter than I remembered."

I roll my eyes. "He's aged well. Unfortunately."

"So, what's wrong with him being here?" Benny asks.

Georgia stands up straighter. "Leo is Eden's ex, and I told her to invite him tonight because he owes her a major apology and Eden has some personal healing to do." She glances at my face, and then adds, "What? It's true!"

I turn to face Benny. "If you haven't noticed already, Benny, you're about to discover that my dear cousin here is a Stage Four Meddler."

Benny laughs, his necklaces glittering under the fairy lights. "Sounds to me like she just cares about the people she loves?"

"See?" Georgia says smugly, arms crossed, looking pleased as punch and throwing Benny the most generous smile I've seen on her in days.

"Georgia! *Help*."

"Okay, okay, don't worry, I'm on it."

She is not, in fact, *on it*. At least, not in the way I expect. Georgia does not get up and take Leo aside to, I don't know, give him a stern lecture? Not sure what I expected, but it certainly wasn't this.

"Party games!" Georgia is shouting, clapping her hands together and calling everyone over to the firepit area.

To her credit, she's very good at bossing people around; soon everyone is sitting in a relatively coherent circle formation.

Tre suggests Never Have I Ever, but Zac, one of the LGs, boos that idea and says we should play Truth or Dare instead. Everyone rallies around that suggestion quickly.

"I'll go first," Zac volunteers, and, to no one's surprise, he picks dare.

Georgia thinks for a second. "I dare you to climb up that tree with a beanbag and toss it into the cornhole set. If you make a score, pick someone to kiss. If you miss, you have to . . . wrap yourself in toilet paper like a mummy."

Jaclyn nods their head, impressed. "That's one hell of a layered dare."

"I accept," Zac says formally, then climbs the tree and proceeds to totally miss the target. While he's mummifying himself with toilet paper, the game goes on.

Zac dares another LG named Mike to skinny-dip in the lake (he does).

Mike dares Francesca to sing her favorite song (she does, but only part of it).

Francesca dares Sam to burn his T-shirt in the firepit (Georgia vetoes this).

Sam dares Daisy to hold a handstand for as long as she can (forty-two impressive seconds).

Daisy dares Mateo to chug a seltzer in less than a minute without burping. He ends up spraying seltzer all over himself. Daisy giggles like he's a stand-up comedian.

Mateo then turns . . . to me.

I usually love dares, but I'm less into the outdoor variety, so I say, "Truth." And instantly regret it, sensing this could go badly.

Mateo tilts his head, thinking. "Well, since I don't know you that well, all I can really ask is how that sabotage plan is going."

I can feel my face burning under everyone's curious stares. "I—I— There is no sabotage plan," I stutter, realizing Mateo has no idea that Leo is even *here*. I try to indicate with my eyes that he should *shut the heck up*, but he either doesn't get it, or ignores me.

"So you're saying you *didn't* switch out bug spray with pepper spray in order to ruin your ex's day?" he asks with a smile.

I chance a look over at Leo now. He's frozen in place, realization gradually registering in his eyes, his whole face morphing from relaxed to shocked. I'm going to throw up.

"Pepper spray is an important method of self-defense," I squeak. Before anyone can protest to my lame response, I swivel around and desperately point at Benny.

"Benny," I say loudly. "Your turn." I feel like I'm burning up, like Leo can see right through me. I don't dare to catch his eye.

"Dare," Benny says with a shrug.

I think for a second. *This* should be fun. "Pick someone here that you like and kiss them." Time to put the obvious flirtation between him and Georgia on full display. I'm practically daring him to call Georgia's bluff about setting him up with Daisy.

But Benny blushes. "Actually, can I switch to truth?"

"Fine, just tell us who you think is the most attractive person at the party."

He thinks for a second. He definitely glances over at Georgia, and as much as I'm still dying of mortification from my turn, I'm *also* dying to hear his answer. "Elena Holliday," he responds calmly. When several of us scoff, he says, "What? She is a very elegant woman." He gestures at Daisy and Georgia. "And she clearly passed down good genes."

People laugh and roll their eyes, someone piping up about Benny being into older women. It was clearly a dodge. But I guess I can't say I blame him.

Benny picks Georgia to go next, and she selects truth as well. He looks her right in the eyes, across the roaring fire. "What's something about your boyfriend that you can't stand?"

I hiss out a breath. *Ooh*, that's a good one.

Georgia pauses for a second, blushing, unable to come up with an answer. "That's not a fair question."

"Just answer it, Georgia." I nudge her.

She glares at me. "Okay, fine. I can't stand the way Rhys chews gum. It is the most annoying sound in the world. Next! I pick . . ." She scans the circle as if contemplating. "You. Leo."

My stomach flips. *Here we go.*

"I'll take a dare," he says. His face is unreadable, but I can see behind his eyes there's a flash of something—pride? Anger?

"No, pick truth," Georgia says.

Leo shakes his head. "I get to choose. I choose dare."

Georgia sighs. "Fine. Kiss the person you have the best connection with here."

There's a beat of complete silence. Then Leo stands up. "You know what? I don't think I have a connection with anyone here. I should probably head out."

A bunch of people start booing, and Leo dusts off his cargo shorts and turns to walk away.

Georgia nudges me as I watch him leave.

"What?" I ask, panicked.

"Go after him! Talk to him!" she hisses.

"No!" I hiss back.

"Do it!" she says.

I can't sit here and act calm, anyway, so I get up and run after Leo.

By the time I catch up, he's getting into his car.

"Hey." I scramble for the right words. "Look, I can explain," I begin, having absolutely no idea how to explain anything.

But he shakes his head. "I don't need you to."

"You don't?"

"No," he says, "because I can see that absolutely nothing's changed about you. Disappointing, but not exactly surprising." He turns on his engine.

I feel an old, indignant anger roaring to life in my chest. It feels like Becca Johnson's fifteenth birthday party—and the rumors that stemmed from it—just happened yesterday. I can still remember Leo's scorn. The cruel way he broke up with me. Storming off without even letting me explain anything. Kind of exactly like he's doing now.

"Oh, *I'm* the one who hasn't changed?" I snort. "Right. That's really rich, coming from you."

"What's that supposed to mean?"

"You're still a righteous, judgmental asshole. I *don't* owe you an explanation. You deserve far worse than a stupid prank."

"Whatever, Eden. See you around." He shakes his head again, closes the driver's-side door, and pulls out of the driveway.

And I just stand there, stunned, watching him go.

THIRTEEN

Daisy

I WAKE THE MORNING after the party to the faint sound of a *click* below my window. Scrambling out of bed, I see Georgia in a matching pale blue Alo sports top and bike shorts, blond hair in a ponytail, slipping out of the house and getting into her car. I know she thinks she's being stealthy, but she underestimates me.

We may seem like we're oblivious, but trust me, little sisters always know.

If she were just going out for morning runs, she wouldn't be so cautious about waking us up. And she wouldn't be coming home with wet hair.

I get back into bed and throw the covers over my eyes for another hour or so. It's Sunday, after all.

When I finally emerge, Mom and Dave's bedroom door is still closed—I bet they're sleeping off hangovers. I trudge down the stairs and find Eden slumped on the couch in her pajamas, eating a bowl of cereal, staring into space. Eden and I both have nothing to do today; no Boundless Horizons for her, no tennis club restaurant shift for me.

"Are you okay?" I ask her.

"Huh?" She looks up. "Oh, I'm fine. Some party last night."

"I thought it was pretty fun." I plop down next to her. "But what happened to you after Leo left? You just disappeared! I knocked on your bedroom door later, but you didn't answer. I figured you must've gone to bed."

Eden blows her bangs out of her face. "I had a lot on my mind."

"Care to share?"

Eden shakes her head. "There's nothing to say. Leo did me dirty back then, and he hasn't changed at all. And he acts like everything is always *my* fault. Like I'm the immature one who hasn't changed."

"Boys are stupid. Who cares what Leo thinks?"

"True," she sighs, but I can tell she does care.

"I guess Georgia's plan to help you get closure backfired," I observe.

Eden snorts. "Like many of her plans. She wanted to set you up with that guy Benny, then spent all night talking to him herself."

I shrug. "She probably just wanted someone to flirt with since Rhys couldn't be there."

Eden turns to look at me. "Do you think something's going on between her and Rhys?"

"Like what?"

"Like . . . trouble in paradise?"

That never occurred to me. "Those two are so solid," I say.

"They've made it work for almost three years."

"I know, but now high school's over."

"But they're going to college together," I point out. "And they literally have their future kids' names picked out already. I think they're a forever thing, I really do."

"And what's going on with you and Mateo?" Eden asks.

I start to blush. "I mean, I don't want to get carried away. It's just a good time," I say carefully. "But like, how cute would it be if we were a couple? Georgia and Rhys, me and Mateo."

Eden laughs. "Okay, Jane Austen, let's not go ahead and plan a double wedding just yet."

"Shut up! I'm not!" But she's kind of right. I don't *want* to get carried away, but I have to admit . . . it's maybe a bit too late for that.

"So are you guys like officially *together*, or is it more of a situationship thing?"

I sigh. "I don't know. Labels are so confusing. It's only been *three days* since we kissed. But also, it's been three *amazing* days. And last night we realized we met at least once before, when I came to that football game with Georgia and we hung out with Rhys and him and their whole crew. That was over a year ago, so we've technically known each other for more than a year."

Eden laughs. "I've never heard a better example of girl math."

I nudge her shoulder with my own. "Fine, but still, there's a connection."

She wags her eyebrows. "I can see that. But also, Georgia's right. You should be careful."

"Why, because he's older?" I ask. "I can't believe you're taking Georgia's side."

"Not just that," Eden counters, setting down her cereal bowl. "Have you thought this through? It could be really awkward. What if you guys start a relationship and then he breaks your heart, and then you have to be Georgia's maid of honor in her wedding to Rhys and there's Mateo, the guy who broke your heart, standing there as his best man. Have you thought about the consequences?"

"That sounds like the plot of a *fantastic* rom-com," I tell her. "Maybe you've been reading too many scripts." Her dad's an entertainment lawyer and he sometimes gets early access to watermarked Hollywood scripts; he's been known to let Eden peek at them from time to time.

My phone pings and I look down at the text bubble.

Mateo:

Beach day?

"Speak of the devil," I tell Eden, typing back at the same time. "Mateo wants to go to the beach. Want to come?"

She rolls her eyes. "No, I'm good."

I look at her. She does not seem *good*. More like depressed. "Are you sure? Everything's always more fun when you're there!" Which is true; usually Eden is the life of the party. But secretly, all I really want is more alone time with Mateo.

A series of scenes from the past couple of days flash before my eyes: Mateo pulling me aside at the tennis club on Friday and us making out against the wall behind the entrance to the locker rooms. After work, driving back to one of the apple orchards we'd passed on Thursday, and wandering around the rows and rows of trees, talking about nothing—music and college and tennis and just random stuff I can't even remember. It got a little chilly and he handed me his oversized sweatshirt, which smelled like him, and I never wanted to take it off. We went back to the car, and he opened the rear passenger door. I got in and he got in after me and we kissed lying down on the back seat like in an old movie. I really didn't know people actually did that. It was kind of uncomfortable with all the seat belt sockets poking into my back, but I was too caught up in how good a kisser he is to care. Then, yesterday at the party, we hung out the entire night, basically as if we were already a couple.

"Daisy?" Eden says, waving a hand in my face.

"Sorry," I breathe, blushing again.

"Go upstairs and change. Trust me, I'm fine. I need a day of couch rotting anyway," she says, grabbing the TV remote.

"Doth my ears hear the phrase couch rotting?" Dave says from the stairs, where he and Mom are finally emerging in their sweatpants. Dave's glasses look crooked on his face—the classic adult *I drank too much last night* look.

"Our favorite!" Mom says. "But you're gonna have to share, Eden," she warns, pushing her butt onto the sofa and tucking Eden's feet up onto her lap.

"I'll run out and get the Sunday paper," Dave says. "Anyone want anything? Fritter, Daisy?"

I'm impressed he already knows my breakfast order. "Not today, actually. I'm heading out. Thanks, though!" I turn back to Eden. "Call me if you change your mind," I tell her, then run giddily up the stairs, skipping every other one.

I'm standing in the driveway in my black two-piece bathing suit and overalls shorts, a tote bag on my shoulder with a rolled-up towel and book I'm definitely not going to read.

"Get in, kid," Mateo says through his open car window. We've been driving for a few minutes when he asks, "So should we go to the beach or do you wanna do something else?"

I shrug. "It's a great day for swimming; the beach will probably be crowded. Georgia will be there."

We both know what that means. Georgia doesn't exactly *approve* of us hanging out. I push down the insecurity and hurt that I don't have her support. I really thought she'd be excited for me to be with one of Rhys's friends.

"Well, is there somewhere more private we could go?" he asks.

"Actually, yes!" I sit up taller. "There's a great little swimming hole we used to go to when we were kids. It's shallow, and in the summers the current is pretty mellow. You have to hop across these rocks and then there are parts that are deeper. It's known about, but not *that* known. And it's still early enough in the summer; maybe it won't be crowded."

"That sounds amazing," Mateo says. "How do we get there?"

"Um, I actually have no idea," I admit, pulling out my phone and scrolling around Maps, hoping to find it.

"Let's grab some snacks while you figure that out," he suggests.

My stomach rumbles in response. I forgot to have breakfast. "Yes. Snacks."

We drive into downtown Laurel and wander the aisles of the Green Frog, the posh little corner grocer, picking up fancy flavored chips like dill pickle and ketchup, bottles of locally made root beer, and a big bag of candied popcorn.

At the checkout, Mateo grabs a baseball hat that says "The Green Frog" and plops it onto my head. "This looks cute on you."

The cashier lady looks at us. "Are you buying the hat?"

Mateo nods. "Sure. My treat."

Our first gift! That must mean something. I grin, carrying our paper bag of snacks out of the store feeling lighter than I've felt in a long time.

We end up having to drive around for an extra forty minutes, getting lost on back roads, but just as I'm about to admit defeat, we spot a couple of cars parked on the side of the road, at the edge of the woods. And I see a little path that looks vaguely familiar.

"That's it! At least, I *think* that's it." I bounce up and down in my seat.

When we get out of the car I know I'm right: Dad used to take us here. The memories flood in, threatening to overwhelm me. I remember coming here when I was young enough to wear pink inflatable floaty wings. But I blink the memories away, trying to stay in the lightness I was feeling before.

We carry the snacks and our towels down the narrow path through the trees, birds chirping in the branches overhead, toward the splashing sound of the river. There's a couple of women in beach chairs on the shore, watching their two little kids playing at one end of the river, but otherwise the place is totally empty.

We take off our flip-flops and I lead Matteo barefoot across the stones to the other side of the river, where we set down our stuff on a big flat rock that's hidden from view. I sit at the edge of the rock with my feet in the icy water, leaning back on my arms. Mateo sits down a couple of feet behind me. The sun filters down through the canopy, and the air smells like the woods, like the river, like childhood. It's magical.

"Wow, this place is incredible," Mateo murmurs.

"My dad always took us here because he could fish while Georgia and I splashed around in the shallow pools, even before we could swim."

"He sounds like such a good dad," Mateo says.

"Yeah. We were lucky."

"My dad probably thinks of himself as this great father," Mateo muses. "He was always working, but he'd show up at tennis tournaments and soccer games on the weekends. Putting in face time with the other parents. But it was all a show, you know?"

I turn to look at him. "Not really, no."

"Like . . ." Mateo pauses, searching for the words. "He was auditioning for the role of the Good Dad in public. But at home, he was just an asshole. He was cold and disinterested. And honestly, when the scandal hit, I wasn't even that surprised. I was more. . . freaked out about what it would mean for me and my brothers and my mom."

"What *did* it mean for you guys?" I ask.

Mateo hasn't really opened up to me like this before, about what happened with his dad.

"Well, my older brother dropped out of school. He went to LA to become an actor. So far, he's only booked a couple of commercials. But he's got the face for it. He'll probably succeed. He's the handsome one in the family."

I laugh. "You have an older brother who's the 'handsome one'? I have trouble believing that."

Mateo just sighs. "I used to be so jealous of him. But we're very different."

"How did your mom handle things?"

"Swore off men completely, but I don't think she liked men much before anyway. We were okay. My mom's family back in Italy helped us out a lot. Financially, I mean. We didn't have to move. But trust me, there were plenty of times where I wished we had. Everyone knew, ya know? That part was so brutal. So embarrassing. And I was just *angry*, all the fucking time."

"Are you still?" I ask. "Angry, I mean."

He sighs. "Yeah? I guess I am. But I try not to think about that dipshit any more than I have to."

We're quiet for a moment and then I say, "Thanks for telling me about it."

"It's easy to tell you things, Daisy. You're a cool girl, you know that?"

I smile and watch him smile back, dimples appearing in his cheeks. "I am? Like how?"

He shrugs. "Your energy. It relaxes me. You're very yourself. Very confident. It's not a common thing to find."

"It's not?"

"Not in my experience," he says.

"Which is, from what I understand, vast."

He laughs that off.

"Seriously, though, Mateo. You've dated a lot of girls."

"Who cares?" he says with a shrug. "It means nothing."

"I'm not insecure about it. I mean, not exactly. It's just, I probably seem really inexperienced." Thankfully, my new hat is shading my face, hopefully hiding how embarrassing it was to say that out loud.

"Come here," he says.

I scooch backward on the rock so that I'm beside him. He tilts back my hat and kisses me. It's smooth and slow, and I feel my entire body tingling like it does every time we kiss, every time he touches me.

"I like you the way you are," he whispers.

"Okay," I whisper back, deciding to trust him. Because why shouldn't I?

We kiss some more, and he runs his hand through the open side of my overalls, against my bare skin. I arch my back, nervous and excited at the same time. There's part of me that wants to take off my overalls and lie down on this rock in only my bathing suit with Mateo, but I'm also afraid . . .

Afraid of what it would lead to. Not that we would *do it*, out here in the open. But when I'm with Mateo I start to lose all sense of what's realistic, of what might happen next. That's what's so intoxicating and also so confusing about this.

"Mateo," I whisper, pulling back.

He groans softly. "What?"

"I'm just . . . I'm worried."

He furrows his brow. "About what?"

I say nothing, trying to find the right words.

He leans back on his hands. "Tell me. What are you worrying about? You don't need to worry with me."

"I don't?"

He shakes his head. "Of course not."

"Okay, well . . . I don't think I'm ready. To, ya know."

It takes a second to register, and then he laughs, and shrugs. "Oh, like, *that*. Yeah, I wasn't expecting that. Like at all. I promise."

"Really?"

"Yes, really."

I practically throw myself at him then, and we fall back onto the rock, with his arms around me. "Thank you for getting it."

"It's all good, Daisy. You're younger than me. I'm not stupid. I just like . . . spending time with you. It doesn't have to lead to anything more."

I feel so relieved. He's not disappointed that I'm inexperienced. That I'm not ready for, like . . . *sex*. Which he's probably done multiple times. With multiple people. Which I can't think too much about right now.

I nuzzle my face into his T-shirt and breathe in the smell of it.

"Seriously, Daisy. You've made this summer so much better for me. I wasn't in a great place. And I know it's only been a week, but I'm really, really glad I met you."

"You mean, *re*-met me," I remind him.

"Oh, right. Yeah."

"I'm really glad too," I say.

He lifts my chin, and we kiss again. And I start to understand what people mean when they say they *melt* into each other. I can't help but feel like there's some strange twist of fate to all this. Some reason why Owen friend-zoned me right at the start of the summer, and why Mateo and I met again here, and even why Rhys has barely been around, leaving Mateo in need of someone to spend his free time with.

And even though it seems crazy to me, and I know I'm not ready *yet*, I can really see a world in the not-too-distant future where I *am* ready for more . . .

For . . . all the things.

With him.

FOURTEEN

Georgia

I ADJUST MY VISOR and look out at the sparkling lake from high up on the lifeguard tower. It's six p.m. on Sunday, so the beach is finally calming down, families packing up their towels and chairs and sand toys, teens tossing their magazines and earbuds into their bags. I sigh, finally able to relax. It's not that I mind it being busy. We're not allowed to read or scroll our phones up here, for obvious reasons, which means a quiet beach can be peaceful but a little boring. A crowded day gives me a lot to pay attention to, and the time goes faster.

Eden came by earlier and hung out reading on a blanket for a while. I was glad to see her, even though we couldn't really talk. I still feel bad about how last night went. I had no idea Leo would react like that. It was a weird night all around. I was proud of how the yard came together and how many people showed up, but I felt my attention being pulled in a million directions, and responsible for making sure Benny was having a good time, conscious that he didn't really know anyone else there. Not that I minded; I've been having a blast hanging out with him, and it was refreshing to see him in real clothes instead of swim trunks. But also, I can't stop thinking about when he asked if I was keeping our practice sessions a secret. I hadn't thought I was, but seeing him mixed in with my family and our other friends felt like the intersection of multiple worlds. In a way, I'm glad Rhys wasn't there after all. The collision would have been too much.

I climb down from the tower, blow the whistle to signal to the remaining swimmers that we're closed, then head over to the dock to unroll the string of buoys we use to block off the swimming area during off-hours. Then I go to grab my stuff from the shack, masking a yawn. My whole body is exhausted. Yesterday was my first full day of work, and I had a full shift today as well. Not to mention the party last night. I'm looking forward to flopping face down into bed tonight.

I got a double load this first weekend because next weekend is the Fourth of July festival, and while some of the other lifeguards don't mind working on a holiday, I really want to be there. The fireworks and the whole day of festivities leading up to them are iconic here in Laurel. It's a magical time, one of my favorite events of the year, and I've missed it.

And, obviously, Rhys will be here. But that feels far away. I still have a whole long week to wait.

Speak of the devil—when I unsilence my phone, a string of texts from Rhys pops up:

Rhys:

Baby, how was your party? Did you miss me?

I met so many great contacts last night!

I feel like I'm finally on the right path.

Just tried you. Where are you? Why aren't you answering the phone?

Baby, are you mad at me?

Just kidding.

You can try me later but I might be out with a few of the other interns.

I try to think of what to say, but my mind is drawing a blank. The truth is, I'm too tired to listen to a long recap of a finance networking event full of people whose names I surely won't remember anyway.

"Busy?" a voice interrupts.

Startled, I drop my phone back into my bag and turn around. It's Benny, walking toward me across the sand. A sight I've become very used to this past week—I just saw him this morning.

"Hey!" I say, surprised. "What are you doing here now?"

He smiles. "I was so focused on my backstroke this morning, I didn't thank you for inviting me to the party last night. I had a great time."

"You came all the way back to the beach to say thanks? You know, this is where phones really come in handy."

He shrugs. "It's a short bike ride from Lita's. And it's still so nice out. Unless you don't want me here?"

"No, it's not that," I say quickly. "I was just cleaning up and closing out. It's swim-at-your-own-risk o'clock."

"I enjoy swimming at my own risk."

I smile and shake my head. "Why does that not surprise me."

We walk back out across the sand to the edge of the lake, letting its gentle laps kiss our bare toes.

"Have you actually been in the water today?"

I shrug. "Only once, and it was a false alarm. Looked like a little kid was stuck underneath the dock, but it was just a life jacket someone shoved under there."

"Let's swim, then," Benny suggests. "We have the whole lake to ourselves."

"We always have the whole lake to ourselves," I remind him. It's literally why we've been getting up so early to meet here.

He laughs. "True. But usually, you're sitting on the dock barking orders at me, or you're only in the water to demo something. I don't think I've ever seen you swim not for exercise or training purposes, but just, like, for *fun*."

I shrug. "What can I say? I spend most of my leisure time doing things for other people. I like to stay busy."

He shakes his head. "Do you even *like* swimming?"

"Of course I like it!"

"But do you *love* it?" he asks.

I shrug. "Benny, I enjoy swimming just as much as the next person. Why are you asking this?"

"I'm trying to get to know you, Georgia. Not the things you

like as much as the next person, but the things you're passionate about. Is swimming one of them?"

I shake my head. "I don't know. Maybe?"

"Maybe?"

"I feel like you're making this a big deal. I mean, are *you* passionate about swimming?"

He nods, squinting out at the water. "Yes."

I stare at his profile. I hadn't noticed how long his eyelashes are. "Why?"

He shrugs. "I like how it feels to be submerged. I like the sensation of water against my skin. I like testing the limits of my endurance. And I like just . . . floating. When else do you get to defy gravity, you know? Come on." He wraps his hand around mine, and the sudden intimacy sends a jolt of confusion through me as he starts to pull me deeper into the water. He drops my hand, as if realizing maybe it wasn't appropriate, and turns back to face me. "Are you coming?"

"Hang on." I walk up onto the shore and toss my bag on the dry sand. My keys and phone spill out, and I almost go back to fix it but then figure, hell, I'll deal with them later. When I turn around again Benny's already plunging elegantly into the water.

I pull out my ponytail and shake out my hair, then run in after him.

We're both well out into the lake when Benny dives, coming up spitting water at me.

"Gross!" I splash at him, and he tries to tackle me, but I swim away.

I will admit, it feels almost alien swimming and splashing around with no real purpose or goal. I can't remember the last time I *played* in the water. Probably not since I was kid, when Dad would take me and Daisy to the swimming hole in the woods.

"I love that," Benny says, pointing up to the sky. "When you can see the moon even though it's still light out."

I float onto my back and look up. The moon is a white stamp etched onto the violet-blue-pink of the sky. I can hear the sound of the lake whispering in my ears as I float, arms outstretched. Benny's right. When *do* we get to feel this weightless, this held?

Time seems to slow; I look over, and Benny's floating on his back too. We stay like that for I don't know how long. Long enough that something shifts in me. I feel myself doing that thing I always say I hate; I feel myself *relax*. And it's the strangest, most freeing sensation, like a knot undoing itself from deep within me. I'm soft at the edges—not physically, but in some other way. Soft at the edges of who I am. Some faint voice starts stirring within me, rising into my mind.

What if you didn't have to hold everything you're holding?

What if you didn't have to succeed, or try, or prove, or get ahead?

What if you didn't have to be so strong, after everything that's happened?

What if all you had to do was just be?

What would you let yourself love?

The sky suddenly seems so wide it could swallow me, and there's a momentary flutter of panic in my chest—the panic of not knowing how to answer all these questions. Except then the answer *does* come, and it's so simple, I don't really understand it, but I don't have to. The answer to what I would let myself love beats back to me with the rhythm of my pulse:

This. This. This.

I swear I could have fallen asleep like that—just lying there right beneath the surface of the lake, my hair splaying out around me like a mermaid's, feeling the water tickle my rib cage and sway me like a floating leaf—if Benny hadn't touched my shoulder, breaking the trance.

I've floated into chest-deep water, and Benny's standing there pushing his wet hair out of his face.

"You looked so peaceful, I was afraid you were going to nod off and drown," he admits.

I smile and stand up in the water, facing him, my hair wet and stuck to my shoulders. "Luckily there's someone here who could've rescued me."

He smiles. "Glad I didn't have to, though."

"Obviously."

"*Obviously*."

We laugh.

"Hey, Georgia?" he says. He's squinting a little, though by now the sun has begun to dip below the horizon line. Water droplets glimmer on his shoulders.

"Yeah?"

"This," he says slowly. "This thing. Whatever it is. This was never really about setting me up with your sister, was it?"

I swallow a lump in my throat.

"You don't have to answer that," he says. "But I know."

I look at him. "What do you know?"

Through the water, his hand finds my waist. He looks into my eyes searchingly, and I don't pull away. I feel like I'm under some sort of spell; maybe the lake water didn't just go into my ears but all the way through my brain, rinsing it out until all the things that used to fill it have been washed away . . . including all the reasons.

All the very good reasons why this is wrong. They've floated away.

That's the only explanation for why I can't take my eyes off his, except to notice him lick his lips quickly. His inhale has a tremble to it, as if from the cold.

It's the only possible way I can explain what happens next.

I'm not even thinking of kissing him. I'm not thinking *at all.* My body has taken over for me—or the lake has, floating our bodies together until we're pressed up against each other, and his lips find the corner of my mouth, kissing me there, and then more fully, his tongue lightly parting my lips. I shiver, kissing him back, standing up on my toes, wrapping my arms around him. He lifts my legs and I wrap them around his waist, losing myself completely in the kiss.

It feels like we could kiss forever—but eventually Benny falls backward into the water, and I come down with him, splashing. He laughs and we pull away, rising back up to the surface, and I'm snapped out of the moment with sharp awareness.

"*Oh god*," I breathe.

"Georgia," he says, but I shake my head.

"This was a mistake. I'm so sorry. I—" I feel like I'm going to choke, or start sobbing, or I don't know what. I just know I need to get out of this enchanted water before I let myself do anything crazier than what I've already done. "I have to go," I tell him, splashing out of the water so hard my thighs burn with the effort.

I bend down, dripping wet, and hurriedly gather my stupid sandy phone and keys and flip-flops, while my hair, sticky with lake water, flops into my face and drips all over everything. *Dammit, dammit, dammit.* I shake the keys free from the sand and without turning to look behind me, I race straight to my car. I don't even bother to dry off. I fly into the driver's seat, turn on the ignition, and pull out of the parking lot, only catching one fleeting glimpse of Benny as I do.

He's standing alone in the middle of the beach, one hand pushing his hair back, watching as I drive away.

FIFTEEN

Eden

I AVOID THINKING ABOUT Becca Johnson's fifteenth birthday party as much as I can possibly help it. Whenever my mind does go back to that time, there's just this raw, resentful anger. It was over two years ago, and yet the memory lurks, not exactly an open gushing wound but not quite a healed scar either. It was one of those events that, like it or not, changes the way you see the world forever after.

The party started out like any other: Becca's parents weren't home. They own a spacious converted loft with three bedrooms and a roof terrace on a very cool block in the West Village. She's one of the richest kids at our school—we have a pretty big mix of economic backgrounds, with at least half the school being families who live in tiny rentals in remote parts of the outer boroughs. But Becca's parents are loaded, and her loft is a great party space, so this wasn't the first time she'd had a ton of people over. She'd always tell her parents it was a slumber party with her three best friends, then invite everyone. I don't know how she got away with it—she must have been paying off the doorman or something.

There was flowing alcohol, as there always was at her place; I'm not super into drinking and I hate the taste of beer, but Becca's best friend, Gina, was making her famous Mountain Dew cocktails (literally it's just Mountain Dew and vodka) and I swear, you cannot taste the alcohol. Blame peer pressure, or my addiction to sugary sodas, but I had two huge plastic cups of it. Leo hadn't come to the party; there was a big game the next day. So I guess I felt a little awkward and wanted to fit in.

Looking back, I don't know how much of that night was a setup from the start. Did Becca and her friends get me drunk on purpose? I don't know that I can totally blame them for that, but I do know that several people in her group of friends kept cornering me, trying to convince me that Leo wanted to dump me, that I wasn't good enough for him, and that everyone knew I was only dating him to try to make myself more popular. At some point, we were dancing in Becca's living room, and Becca told me her older brother, Eddie, thought I was cute. I didn't even really know which guy was Eddie until he started dancing close, putting his hands all over me. The next thing I knew, he was trying to kiss me. I pushed him off and fled to Becca's parents' room, where I ended up puking up Mountain Dew and vodka in their en suite bathroom.

I came out of the bedroom after washing off my face and gargling with the Johnsons' winter-fresh mouthwash, to find several of Becca's friends, who all high-fived me. I didn't know what the high fives were about, so I just went along with it, feeling kind of embarrassed and a little dizzy. It gets a bit hazy then, but I remember Becca racing up to me and throwing her arms around me in a hug and whispering something like "Don't worry, I don't mind that you hooked up with my brother. I think it's so funny!" I just shook my head. I should've said something, but I wasn't thinking clearly. I figured she was referring to the sloppy kiss attempt when we were dancing, and instead of correcting her, I called an Uber and went home.

I thought that was it—a kind of gross, awkward, barfy night that could've gone better. I didn't realize that it was only the beginning.

I knew something was wrong the next day when I opened my phone and saw I'd gotten a bunch more followers. At first I thought maybe the party had boosted my popularity or something—until I realized I was getting tagged in unflattering, blurry photos from Becca's, and people were commenting about how I was this wild party girl, throwing myself at rich boys who were out of my league. As I scrolled, I realized people weren't just talking about my sloppy kiss dodge on the dance floor or how drunk I had accidentally gotten. They were saying that when I'd gone into Becca's parents' bedroom, I'd gone in there *with* Eddie. And that we'd hooked up.

I was in shock—and the shock continued in school that Monday, where people were looking at me differently, shunning me, whispering about me. I didn't think "slut-shaming" was even a thing anymore; I thought we left that all behind in the '80s and '90s when our parents were teens, but apparently not, because I don't know what else to call it. I didn't realize people could be so gleeful about taking own someone who they hardly even knew. Soon, it was comments about my family, my brother, my dad. There was actually some relief in the fact that the negs were so random—clearly none of it was based in fact. People were just looking for a reason to pile on. About a month later, all the heat turned on someone else—a nerdy kid in the Young Republicans Club who everyone said was ableist because of some video he'd made about a ramp—and they forgot about me. But it took a long time for me to be comfortable enough to make new, real friends.

And in the meantime, I had to deal with the fallout with Leo. That was the most surprising part—the way he so readily assumed everything people were saying about Becca's party was true. "I saw the photos," he kept saying, like that was proof of anything.

I tried to tell him I was just dancing—in a big group of people—but he rolled his eyes and made some comment about how we all know I like attention. It was *mean*. And cruel. That's the only way I can describe it. He just turned so cold; it was like the Leo I'd known, and had been head over heels for, had flipped a switch.

We sat in the library, and I refused to cry as he coolly said, "I think we both knew where this was headed anyway."

I nodded, because what was I supposed to say? I was just trying to keep it together and not look like a blubbering loser where other kids from school could see me. So I held it all in and agreed with him. "You're right. We both knew this wasn't going to last."

"Okay, well. I guess I'll just . . . see you around, then," he said.

I watched him stand up and leave the library, thankful that

the shock was so intense I couldn't cry even if I wanted to. I mean, I did cry—at home, later—but for the rest of that day I was, mercifully, emotionally paralyzed.

And that was it. He never apologized, never came around asking to hear the whole story. Never said he felt bad for how people were treating me or expressed regret for not standing up for me. Nothing. He just *moved on* as if we were never together.

After a few months, we were spending time in such separate circles that I could go through most of my days barely seeing him. And when we did happen to pass each other in the halls at school, we'd both look the other way.

Obviously, it's something I've spent a significant amount of time processing, wondering why me, why did this happen? In retrospect, I think Becca must've had a crush on Leo; she was much cooler than me and had no reason to be jealous, but she obviously didn't mind sabotaging me to get what she wanted. Plus, she and Gina and a few of their other friends never really liked me, though I never knew why. They were a totally separate crowd from the friends I've been hanging out with since then—Ray, Alex, Suzanne, Jackson, Isla are all friends I made after that night, but until then, I was a little bit of a floater. I guess I was so caught up in all things Leo, I wasn't spending a lot of time cultivating a core friend group. Maybe that was my real mistake—being so starry-eyed over a guy that I lost touch with what was going on socially around me.

Do I regret dating Leo? I don't know. I do regret the way I lost myself. I regret trusting him. I regret thinking I knew what love was. I regret not realizing how cruel people can be.

But I also miss the time when I was innocent and trusting. When everything seemed simpler. Because I know now I'll never get that back.

Other than a brief trip to the beach to see Georgia and get some vitamin D, I barely left the house Sunday after the party, and that's probably a good thing. Leo bolting during the game of Truth or Dare triggered memories of the Becca Johnson debacle, and I just needed some time to wallow and stay curled in a ball.

But now it's Monday and I have no choice. There's still a whole other week left of Boundless Horizons.

The morning drive is quiet. It's a gray day, heavy with the threat of rain, though so far none has arrived. Georgia came home yesterday exhausted from work and skipped dinner, saying she was going right to bed. But from the looks of things, she didn't sleep well.

"So, when you caught up with Rhys, was he tragically disappointed he missed the party this weekend?" I ask.

I'm only trying to make conversation, but she nearly gives herself whiplash swiveling to face me. "What do you mean?"

"Whoa, eyes on the road, Georgia," I say, thrown off by her reaction. "I just know how bummed you were that he couldn't come!"

Georgia looks at the misty gray street ahead. "I don't really want to talk about Rhys."

"Are you guys fighting or something?"

Georgia sighs. "No, no, of course not. We don't fight."

I scoff. "You *never* fight? That seems unhealthy."

She's quiet for a minute. "Speaking of apologies, I should apologize to *you*."

"For what?"

She sighs again. "For thinking I could get Leo to make amends. I overestimated my persuasive abilities, clearly."

"No, you just underestimated what a complete jerk Leo is. I tried to tell ya."

Georgia glances over at me. "But you were so in love with him two years ago. Explain to me how you can be so into someone and then so *not*."

I shrug, a squirmy, sad feeling gathering in my gut. "Simple. They show you their true colors."

"Hmm," Georgia says, turning her focus back to the road. She pulls off at the coordinates and leaves me in the parking lot. "Good luck today," she says.

"You too," I say automatically. For some reason I feel like she needs luck too.

As she drives off, the day's humidity wraps itself around me instantaneously. This is gonna be a hellish day for mosquitoes. But now I can't even think about bug spray without feeling guilty and embarrassed.

When we gather around JJ for our morning huddle, I try to analyze Leo's face without catching his eye. Is he still pissed? Does he regret how he acted on Saturday? I don't know why these questions are even bothering to occupy space in my brain; I meant it when I told Georgia I've seen his true colors. Leo isn't one to apologize. And he probably has no idea that I spent all of yesterday distraught and low-key depressed, reliving our breakup. He was probably up bright and early taking a morning jog, then blissfully going about his day like the party never happened.

But then I remember the shocked look that flashed across his face during the Truth or Dare game. It was a look of disbelief, and something else. Could it have been hurt?

I need to stop reading into things. But it's kind of too late. I've spent so much energy trying to guess what Leo is thinking while also avoiding eye contact that I end up completely missing JJ's lecture. The huddle breaks up, and I have no idea what we're supposed to do.

I turn to Kiera. "Hey, wanna be partners again?"

She looks at me like I've grown mushrooms for ears. "I'm partnering with Jorge," she says. "Weren't you listening?"

"I, uh—"

"I know, it's super gendered, forcing all the girls to pair with guys. Hello? Not everyone is binary-conforming."

I nod, like that was my concern too. "Totally."

As I watch everyone pair off, my heart starts to sink. Leo is looking right at me. When our eyes meet, he nods.

Much as I don't want to, I go over to him. I can be angry, but I don't want to feel guilty, so I may as well rip off the Band-Aid. "Look, about the bug spray—it was immature. I shouldn't have—"

"I'm sorry, Eden," he says, cutting me off.

"I— You— *What?*"

"I know you'd rather die than be partners, but you're stuck with me."

I can't read his expression at all. "But . . . you basically hate me. Why don't you just partner with someone else?"

His eyes seem brighter on this sunless day, sparkling almost. "I don't hate you. *You* hate *me*."

I stare at him.

I mean, yeah, he's not wrong. I do kind of hate him. I hate him for the hurt he caused me. He *earned* that hate. So what am I supposed to say?

He shakes his head. "I just feel stupid."

"*You* feel stupid? You're not the one who ended up with pepper spray all over their legs."

He laughs dryly. "I feel stupid for thinking we could be friends. But I thought about it, and I decided I'm not ready to stop trying."

The statement sits there in the heaviness of the air, and I yearn for a breeze, for anything to interrupt this tension, this stillness. *Friends?!*

His eyes scan my face, but I still don't know how to answer him. He sighs. "I guess sometimes there's just too much history, huh."

I nod slowly, still processing the idea that he wanted to be friends. . . . When two years ago, that day in the library, he acted like he didn't want to be in the same room with me, or even the same *school*. Now I just feel . . . confused. And a little sad. If he really can't see how badly he betrayed me, if he can't apologize for it, then what kind of friendship could we ever build? You can't be friends with someone who runs that hot and cold. You can't be friends with someone you don't trust.

By now, all the other partners have started marching toward the woods. I look to Leo. "What are we even doing?"

"You mean me and you?" He shoves his hands into his pockets.

"No, I mean, *us*, as in, Boundless Horizons." I gesture at the disappearing groups. "I wasn't really listening to JJ's speech this morning. I guess I was . . . distracted."

Leo shakes his head, in an *Oh, Eden* kind of way, that's both familiar and condescending. And annoying. But I feel a little rush of relief, too because *here's* the Leo I know. I almost feel more comfortable when I can tell I'm irritating him. At least then I know where we both stand.

"I'll give you a hint," he says as we start walking in the same direction everyone else went—directly into a swamp of trees. "It starts with a *K*."

My mind spins. "Kickboxing?"

"What? No."

"Um . . . karaoke? Koala observation? KFC?"

He shakes his head again and laughs. "*Kayaking*, jeez. Didn't realize that was going to be so challenging."

"Hey, I think karaoke with koalas—and a quick KFC run first—sounds like a dreamy way to spend the day. They should really have let me plan this."

"Maybe next year. Though I should warn you . . . I don't think koalas eat chicken."

We continue trekking through the woods, with Leo leading

the way. "That's fine, I'll get extra cherry pie poppers for the koalas."

"You always did have a sweet tooth," he says.

I remember everything, he said last week.

Not everything, clearly, I want to say to him now, but I keep my mouth shut. "We can't all be health freaks," I say instead. "Some of us have to live our lives."

"And you've always marched to the beat of your own drum," he says. "That hasn't changed either."

I straighten my shoulders as I walk. "I'll take that as a compliment."

"Good, you should," he says. "I love that about you."

I swallow hard at a spike of pain in my chest. The word *love* makes me feel ill with confusion. Like a long, fine acupuncture needle going straight through to the tenderest muscle.

How dare he use that word with me, after everything.

We're the last people to arrive at the boathouse, which means we get the shitty oars, and a kayak that is almost definitely going to sink to the bottom of the lake from the looks of it. We shove it into the shallows, and he holds it "steady" (not possible) while I climb in first, crawling awkwardly to the front.

He gets in after me, and we wobble a bit. I gasp, trying to act not freaked out.

Then things smooth out as he shoves us away from the shore and begins paddling, sprinkling my back with droplets from his oar.

I frankly hope we *do* sink to the bottom of the lake so I don't have to sit here at the front of the kayak, feeling Leo's eyes boring into my back. At first, he tries to give me instructions on how to "optimize" the angle of my paddle to "maximize impact," but eventually he gives up. I'm sure he's sitting there silently judging me now.

I guess it's better than me being at the back, having to stare at *him* all day. His rippling back muscles as he maneuvers the oar, cutting cleanly through the water with expert precision.

Eventually, the peacefulness of the lake stretching out before me starts to bring a sense of calm. Birds I don't know the names of swoop and dive and soar above us. Because it's gray, and a Monday, there aren't any noisy motorboats or water-skiers. I start to see something beautiful in the shades of misty gray: the blue-tinged surface of the lake, the charcoal of the shoreline, the deep forest gray-green of the trees, and above, the pale white-gray of the sky, clouds dancing in slow motion across it. Everything seems blurred and wet, like a watercolor.

Maybe the past is like that, too—misty and interpretive, shape-shifting to the eye of the beholder. I start to wonder if Leo and I just have two totally different ways of seeing it.

For the first time, I'm curious to know his version.

Not that I'll ever ask. He doesn't need to know how much weight it all still holds for me. The crap I went through is mine to process, not his. It's mine to hold on to or let go of or heal from when I'm ready, at my own pace. There's nothing I need from him anymore.

I'm at peace with it, I tell myself. *Everything happens for a reason.*

I feel a new kind of sadness filling my chest. The sadness of accepting that sometimes bad things just happen. I know it's not the same as what my cousins went through when Uncle Mitch died. What our whole family went through.

But there's a little piece of that same feeling inside me right now—a little piece of grief.

And I finally realize what it is I'm grieving when it comes to Leo.

I'm grieving the Eden of before.

The Eden who didn't know any better.

The morning floats by slowly, like the clouds, and then in a blink, it's over.

It starts to rain during lunch, and JJ tells us we can go home early today. A gift I wasn't expecting. Normally, she warns, we need to be prepared for any kind of inclement weather. But her weather app is reporting a storm, and we don't have to deal with it today.

Oh, so she gets to use apps out here? Still, I'm happy. I'll take a storm right now. I've needed a storm, I think.

But then, right as we're all packing up our gear again, JJ adds, "And folks, whoever you're partnered with today, you'll be with all week—plus for the final overnight camping trip on Friday."

What?!

I dare not make eye contact with Leo. I just hurriedly stuff my things into my backpack and pull out the deeply impractical poncho I got from Zara, which looked effortlessly chic and casual on the online model but makes me look like a walking kite. I throw it on and start trudging in the direction of the parking lot.

"Eden, wait up!" Leo jogs up and says, infuriatingly, "You're going the wrong way again."

I huff out a breath and turn around without saying anything.

"Look," he says. "We're going to be partnered all week, so let's just try to get along. Please? Truce?"

I stop walking and stare at him. The rain is soaking through his dark hair—I'm actually shocked he doesn't have some sort of perfect rain attire for that. Water drips down his face, like tears, and he's breathing heavily. Maybe from jogging to catch up with me.

Truce. Can I give him that? I think of the peace and acceptance I found on the lake this morning.

"Fine," I say, sticking out a hand. "Truce."

He takes my hand in his, slowly, gently. I feel a flood of warmth at his touch, at the tenderness with which he's holding my hand, like it's a delicate thing he could break. Like he doesn't want to let go.

"Truce," he says quietly, and shakes my hand.

Then he lets it go.

We start walking again.

"Do you need a ride home?" he offers.

I think about calling Georgia. She's probably off work, given the weather. But then I'd have to stand there in the rain waiting for her to come.

"Okay," I say. It's just a ride. It's not a big deal. He owes me that much.

He owes me so much more.

We get into his car, and I pull the poncho hood back off my head. Rain comes down loudly on the windshield and roof. I shiver.

"Are you warm enough?" he asks.

"I'm fine," I say, though I still feel shivery, fluttery, like my muscles can't relax.

We drive back to my house in silence.

"Eden," he says as we pull up in the driveway. He turns off the engine and faces me.

I turn to face him, too. With the engine off, the sound of the pouring rain consumes everything. The air in the car suddenly feels electric.

"Thanks for the ride," I say haltingly, before he can finish his sentence.

And then I grip the door handle and fling the door open, throwing myself out into the storm. I run across the soggy lawn with my head down. I don't look back to see if he's watching me, or if he's already left. The rain is too heavy, and anyway, I don't want to know.

SIXTEEN

Daisy

I'm in a total DAZE, Daze. We left Austria. We're in Germany now—we took an overnight train and it was like sleeping on an active construction site (horrible). I got this postcard at a museum in Berlin. It's kind of a cool city, actually. I guess all I really knew about Berlin before was the wall. We saw it, by the way. It's . . . a wall. But you'd like it. What remains of it. It's covered in art. Anyway, I'm rambling. We should travel together sometime. It would be way better than this. I can just imagine the trouble we would get into. Or okay, the trouble I would get us into, and you would somehow get us back out. Hope your summer is maximally chill and that you're sleeping in super late every morning and wasting as much time as humanly possible, because that's what summers are for. Wanna waste some time with me when I'm back? Shit, gotta go. We are catching another train, this time to . . . somewhere. I forget. Can you handle the suspense?

Owen

I laugh, thinking of the trouble we *would* get into together if we were traveling abroad, and tuck Owen's postcard away, trying to go back to my shift. The restaurant is totally *dead* today—the dreaded midweek slump—and Mateo hasn't come by at all yet. Tre and I have been taking turns with the playlist, and I've already refilled all the salts, peppers, and ketchups. Now I'm just bored out of my mind.

"What were you reading?" Tre asks, coming up to me where I'm standing at the cash register on the counter.

"Oh, nothing, just a postcard from a friend."

"Was it funny? Can I read it?" he asks, putting out his hand.

I hesitate. "I mean, sure, why not." I pull the postcard back out and hand it to him.

He reads it and then looks down at me with the funniest expression. "I can see why you like him."

"What? I—I don't *like* him. I mean—" I falter. I still don't really know how I feel about Owen and that kiss. But in only a little over a week, it feels like my whole life has changed, and there's no going back. "We're just friends!"

"Does *he* know that?"

"He's the one who is friend-zoning *me*," I explain. "Or was. But it's mutual. We've been friends for years."

"Well, he's definitely in love with you," Tre says, handing the postcard back.

I stare at it, baffled. "What do you mean? Why do you say that?"

Tre shakes his head. "First off, no straight guy sends a girl postcards if he's not in love with her. It's just not scientifically possible."

I roll my eyes. "You don't know Owen. This is *very* Owen. He's a postcard guy."

"Oh, so he's sending postcards to everyone?" Tre asks.

I pause. "Well, no. I don't think so. But that's because I'm one of his closest friends. . . ."

"Uh-huh. Right. One of his closest friends who he's in love with."

I laugh. "Whatever. You don't know anything! You've never met him."

"I've only finished argument one. Then there's argument two, which is the content of said postcard."

"There's nothing romantic in here whatsoever, Tre."

Tre shakes his head. "He talks about art. He talks about the future. He talks about a future *with you*."

"He's talking about a vacation."

"Is he?"

"Yes! Like a college vacation you take with friends."

"Uh-huh," Tre says.

"Stop saying *uh-huh* like that!"

He laughs. "I'm sorry, girl, but I call complete BS with all of this. He's in love with you and he wants to 'waste time with you.' Be still my heart. If that's not romantic, I don't know what is!"

I reach out and push him in the direction of the kitchen. "Please go tend to the French fries, this conversation is over."

He swats me away. "You're not the boss of me!" But he heads toward the kitchen doors. "You're the boss of Owen!"

"No, I'm no—" But the kitchen door swings shut before I can have the last word.

Tre's teasing leaves me feeling off-kilter through the lunch shift, pondering what he's said. I don't want to think about Owen liking me. I don't want to think about *me* liking *Owen*, either. If I let all these thoughts take over, it could ruin our friendship completely. It could make things pointlessly awkward. I'm already worried about it being awkward when we go back to school. I think—I can guess from his postcards—that he's just as eager to act like nothing has changed, and I'm all about that, too. I've wanted things to go back to normal this whole time.

At least, I think that's what I wanted. Because, obviously, it's hard to evaluate what I really wanted *before* . . .

Before there was a Mateo.

I mean, the kiss with Owen was *extremely* good. And exciting. And fun. And the next morning, if you'd asked me, I probably would have happily agreed to do it again.

But Mateo is like this dark tide that's overtaken my life. I hate to say that I feel "swept away," but I kind of do. There's so much

I don't know about him, so much mystery that feels impossible to fully unravel. And I know it's not just made up in my head. Unlike Owen, Mateo has made it very clear he likes me back *in that way*, that he finds me attractive, he wants to spend time with me. And he's opened up about stuff that he normally keeps hidden from everyone. He's shown me glimpses of his true self in ways that even Owen, who I've known for years, hasn't done.

And the fact that he's best friends with the guy my sister will probably marry someday? I've never been one of those people who believes in "fate" and all that, but if I were, there'd be no arguing that there's something fateful and romantic about me and Mateo.

And yeah, maybe it's more than that. It feels good to have the attention of an older guy who could choose anyone but is choosing to hang out with *me*. I'm so used to being the little sister, left behind when Georgia's out living her cool, boyfriend-filled life. I like being the chosen one—to be chosen at all. Is that so bad?

I'm still having this inner war with myself—I can't even focus on book seventeen of the romantasy series, where Ronaldo the vampire and Sahara the demigoddess have become each other's sworn enemies after Ronaldo's unspeakable betrayal—when my shift finally comes to an end.

As usual, I wander out to the tennis courts to watch Mateo wrap up his clinic practice for the day. It absolutely poured yesterday afternoon, but today the weather is brisk and the rain's gone, though it's still misty and gray.

As I watch Mateo play—the ripple of his muscles under his shirt, the huffs of breath that hint at the effort he barely shows, the concentration on his face—I fantasize about the last few days. We didn't mind the rain on Monday. We just drove around and talked about everyone who came to the party, and laughed, and played music, and then when the storm really started to get strong, we pulled over and made out in the car until my leg literally fell asleep from the weird position I was sitting in, half straddling the gearshift, half on top of Mateo.

It was like a scene from *The Notebook* or something. Less raunchy but still somehow steamier even than some of the scenes I've read between Ronaldo and Sahara (and those get pretty dang steamy. Though sometimes the descriptions of anatomy are completely gross).

Yesterday, Mateo showed me a few tennis strokes and we volleyed for a bit, then went for a swim and got ice cream. We tasted each other's ice cream cones. It felt like we were in a movie montage where the couple in the rom-com fall in love. Which I know sounds crazy, but in nearly two weeks of spending this many hours together . . . crazier things have happened.

After Mateo's finished playing, he packs up his bag and holds my hand as we walk to his car. I could be sick with happiness. I've literally *never* walked around holding a guy's hand except once in third grade with Jordy Falmouth, and everyone made fun of us, and we never played together again.

Once we're in the car, Mateo looks at me, his dark hair framing his face. "So where to today, Miss Daisy? Your chauffer is at the ready."

"It's kind of kinky, thinking of you as my chauffer."

"Whatever you're into," he says with a laugh.

I'm into YOU, I want to say, but don't. Because I don't want to seem like a completely lovesick puppy. It's too soon for that. *Rein it in, Daisy.*

"Seriously, though, are you getting sick of driving me around?" Nervousness cuts through my voice as it occurs to me that he could be getting bored with me.

He taps his fingers on the wheel and shrugs. "I'm down for whatever."

This is not super reassuring. I'd really prefer something more like *I'd drive you anywhere, I just like being with you.*

"There are some hiking trails," I say, trying to think of ways to entertain him, show off more of Laurel. "A few lead to pretty great lookout points. I know we went to one of them when Rhys was here, but there are better ones you can only get to by walking."

He shrugs again. "Sure, that sounds cool."

I wish I wasn't so paranoid about him, paying attention to every little sign that he could be losing interest. I remind myself this is always how Mateo acts. Chill and a little above it all, easygoing but sometimes distant. I remind myself it takes a lot to get a person like him to open up, and he's already done that with me, and I can't expect him to be open every second that we're together. I *like* hanging out with him when he's brooding; it's sexy. I remind myself I liked hanging out with him before we started making out.

Still . . . even now that I know he likes me, I feel like I have to worry about making sure he *still* likes me. Ugh. I've never felt like this before, and I can't believe how stressful it is.

I direct him to one of the trailheads, and we get out of the car. "It's kind of chilly. Do you have a sweatshirt I can borrow again?" I ask hopefully.

He searches around in the back seat. "I didn't bring one today. Sorry," he says.

I try to hide my disappointment. All I want is to be wearing his sweatshirt again, to be wrapped in his smell. Which is so random, since I'm literally *with* him.

"So, Daisy, what's new in Daisy-land?" he asks as we begin walking the trail.

"You already know everything," I tell him. We've been spending a lot of time together. It's not like he's missed much.

"Then what's new in Eden and Georgia land?" he asks, grabbing a stick and using it to needlessly whack at weeds and underbrush on the sides of the path.

I shrug. "Well, Eden had a really hard time with Leo showing up at the party Saturday. We already talked about that."

"Yeah, that was my bad. I made him storm off. I didn't even know the guy was there!"

"I know. But it's not your fault at all. He was being weird. That's on him."

Mateo shrugs. "Think I should say sorry to Eden anyway? I really thought it was just a funny inside joke, the whole sabotage thing."

"You don't have to do that," I tell him. "It's nice of you, though."

"Eh, I don't know if it's that nice of me. I think you give me too much credit sometimes, Daisy."

"Do I?" I don't know why this statement bothers me, but it kind of does. Like he's suggesting I'm wrong about him.

He laughs. "Nah, you don't. Changed my mind. I'm just as great as you say."

I laugh, too. "You are! Anyway, Eden's struggling, but honestly, it's Georgia I'm more worried about. She's been so off lately."

"Ever since the party?"

"Actually, maybe even before then."

Mateo sighs. "I guess she probably has a lot to process."

"A lot to process?"

"Well, Rhys must've told her the truth. Maybe they broke up because of it."

I stop walking. "Wait, what?"

Mateo stops too. "I mean, I'm not sure if they broke up, I'm just saying I would understand if that's what she wanted. I think it was probably inevitable anyway."

"*What?* What's inevitable? You lost me. What did Rhys tell her about?"

Mateo puts his hands up. "Sorry, sorry, maybe I misspoke. I don't know what they talked about, I just know that he was going to tell her about Lindsay. I don't know when, though."

"About *Lindsay*?! Lindsay who?" My face feels like it's going to burn right off, and I'm starting to hyperventilate. "Who the hell is Lindsay, Mateo?"

Mateo looks suddenly guilty. "Oh shit. You don't know any of this. *Shit shit shit.*"

"Now you have to tell me," I demand shakily. Even though part of me really, truly does not want to hear what he's going to say next.

Mateo shakes his head. "It's none of our business—mine or yours. Rhys and Georgia were gonna take a break once college started anyway. Let's just say it's probably coming a bit sooner than that now."

"Take a break? No, they weren't! They have a whole *life plan*," I say, aghast.

"That's not what I heard."

"From who?"

"From Rhys!" Mateo says with a shrug. "He's always said to me that he wants to be able to play the field in college. It's only natural. We're all pretty young to be thinking about settling down."

I stare at him. We've both stopped walking, and though we're standing still, it feels like the earth is spinning too fast beneath us. All I can do is blink. Am I going to throw up? Am I hallucinating this whole conversation?

Mateo sighs again and puts an arm around me. "Daisy. Don't look so shocked."

I swallow a hard lump forming in my throat. "I can't. I *am* so shocked."

"They'll figure it out together, okay? I'm sure they will. They're both mature."

"But you never said who Lindsay is?"

Mateo squeezes me closer. "Come on, let's go look at that view. Are we close to it?"

I pull away. "Rhys is cheating on my sister, isn't he, Mateo? You understand why you need to tell me this, right? It's my *sister.* It's her heart on the line. I can't just do nothing with this information. You have to tell me everything."

Mateo runs his hand through his hair. "She's just one of the other interns in the program. I don't know that any actual cheating has *happened.* But he has expressed . . . interest. That's all I can say. That's truly all I *know.* But this isn't even about her, really. Lindsay is just the symptom."

The symptom?! My heart feels like it's being twisted and wrung out like one of the towels in the tennis club locker room after it falls into a gross puddle outside the showers. My head suddenly kills—a pressure headache from the cold humidity and the overwhelm of this information. What do I do? What do I *do*?

"Do you still want to keep hiking? I didn't mean to murder the vibe completely," Mateo says.

"No. No, I need to get home. Right now."

"Okay, sure, no worries." He sighs. "I feel really bad about this, Daisy. I feel like such a dick. First, I fucked things up for Eden, and now this."

As we start to walk back to the car, my mind is reeling, but this gets through somehow: Mateo *did* kind of mess things up for Eden at the party. He says he didn't mean to—just like he didn't mean to blurt out anything about Rhys possibly cheating and wanting to dump my sister just now.

He brings these things up so casually. Like he doesn't care what the consequences are, doesn't see how anyone could be hurt. They're just punch lines. It's so . . . insensitive. Does he even know he's doing this?

I'm suddenly very, very angry at Mateo. I know it's not really his fault—it's Rhys's—and you're not supposed to kill the messenger. But seriously, how does he not get how horrible this is? I choke back a rising sob in my chest. *Poor Georgia.* She has to know.

She has to know *now.*

We get back to the car, and before I can open the door, Mateo stops me. "You're not going to say anything, are you? I really think you should let Rhys tell her when he's ready, if he hasn't already."

"Are you kidding?" I nearly scream. "No way am I just sitting on this information."

Mateo frowns. He gets into the driver's seat and slams the door. "I understand you're upset. But you do realize this is going to put me in a really bad position. If Rhys hasn't spoken to Georgia yet, he'll kill me for saying something."

I swing toward him. "You really think *that's* my biggest concern? Rhys is a selfish, narcissistic *asshole.*" As I spit this out, I feel the truth of it—since long before this news. Rhys has strung my sister along for years, made her feel like she's the center of the universe when they're together, then out of sight, out of mind when they're apart. He's always praised her "independence," but

I bet he just wanted to protect his own opportunities to flirt with other girls and live his life.

All while my sister was planning their life *together.*

I'm so angry I don't know if I'm going to punch something or puke or burst into tears.

Mateo turns on the engine. "I'm sorry, Daisy. I thought you knew. I thought they'd already talked. Maybe they have? Maybe that's why Georgia's been acting strange?"

I shake my head. "No way. If they'd had *this* talk, I would know. Trust me."

We drive in silence for a few minutes, and I hear Mateo take a breath, like he's trying to figure out how to say something. I'm so tense, braced for whatever comes next, that I almost don't want him to open his mouth.

But eventually, he does. "Look, I hope this doesn't make you hate me. Or Rhys, for that matter. For what it's worth, I really don't think he's done anything wrong."

"You *don't*?!"

"It's not that he doesn't care deeply for Georgia. I'm his best friend, and I know he does. But it's really not . . . *unreasonable* to, like, want to figure life out after high school. It's not a time to be in a relationship."

My chest feels like it's caving in. *Not a time to be in a relationship.*

I feel so stupid. So very, very, *very* stupid.

I look at him out of the periphery of my vision, afraid if I turn to face him fully, all the emotion will break out of me like rain from heavy clouds. "Call me naive, but I guess I didn't realize there was a right or wrong time for a relationship, if you actually care about each other."

Mateo just sighs.

I stare at the road ahead of us, watching the broken middle line dissolve over and over again as we drive onward, leaving all my pathetic little hopes and fantasies in the past. "I guess your theory applies to us, too."

"Daisy." Mateo's voice sounds broken. And I can't help myself. I turn to look at his face, desperate to see regret written there, or reassurance, or *some*thing. Instead, I see him working his jaw like I've seen him do in the middle of a tough tennis match. "I hope I didn't give you the wrong idea about us. I really do like you. These past few days together have been such a blast."

These past few days.

"You're sexy and refreshing and a barrel of laughs," he says, only making it worse.

A barrel of laughs. Is that supposed to be a compliment?

"But we both agree it's just a casual thing. A summer thing. Right?"

I try to nod as if I'm completely cool with what he's saying, but I can't. The lump in my throat is so big that I know if I move my head at all, it's going to come spewing out in the form of an embarrassing sob. I try to choke it back, but it hurts too much.

He puts a hand on my leg, keeping the other on the steering wheel. "I just want to make sure we're on the same page."

The same page. The same page?!

We are barely on the same *planet* right now.

Again, it's too painful to speak. I try to breathe and regain control. I don't know if I'm more hurt or humiliated. I blink back approaching tears.

"Daisy," he says, more softly. "Oh, Daisy. Come on. It's been fun, but what did you think this was? A real relationship? I mean, we're not even sleeping together. I don't feel like I need to apologize for anything."

I stare at the road, though my ears are ringing loudly now. I'm helpless, gripping the door handle for dear life. There's no way I can speak without revealing the truth of how I'm really feeling.

And that isn't for him to know. He doesn't get to see my true feelings.

We pull up in front of the lake house silently. I gather my stuff and open my door, summoning all my willpower. Then I get out of the car and finally turn to face him.

"Thanks for the ride," I say. "I think I can find my own way home after today."

I slam the door.

Inside, I march straight upstairs, swiping wetness from the corners of my eyes, to knock on Georgia's bedroom door. There's no answer, so I peer in—empty. I remember I didn't see her car outside, so she's not home yet. Though the truth of what I've learned is burning up inside me, I also realize I don't know how I'm going to break it to her. I need to process. I need to prepare. I need to find the words.

I can't bear to think of how hurt she's going to be. I can't bear to have to sit there and see it.

Besides, I can barely keep myself together anyway.

So, I walk past her room and head to my own, throwing myself down on the bed, and let it all come pouring out.

When I've cried for close to an hour into my pillow—replaying every single excruciating moment with Mateo, the good and the bad, hating him, wanting him back, wishing I hadn't basically ended it, but also proud of myself for doing just that—I roll over and stare at the ceiling, wiping my eyes.

And then I do the next most natural thing to do. I go to the desk and pull out a sheet of paper.

Dear Owen, I'm more ready for that European vacation than you can possibly imagine. Things up here at the lake haven't gone like I thought. You'll probably think this is absolutely dumb and embarrassing—because it is—but I feel like I need to tell you everything. I trust you to burn this after reading it. I trust you to not tease me ruthlessly for the rest of time. I trust you—well, that's really it. I trust you. And I hope that what happened at Holly's graduation party won't ruin that. Because there's a lot that's happened since. . . .

SEVENTEEN

Georgia

OVER THE NEXT FOUR days, the gray skies slowly give way to perfect, blissfully breezy, sunny weather that couldn't fit my mood less.

Four days, sitting up on the tower chair, staring out at the heads and arms of hundreds of people, responsible for their safety. Responsible for their *lives*.

I can't even take care of my own.

It's been four days since I made the biggest mistake of my life, but it could've been four minutes ago. It's all I think about. That stupid kiss plays over and over and over in my mind. The shivery, helpless surge of something—lust? insanity?—that rushed through me, taking over. Benny's lips, soft and wet from the lake water pressing against mine, making my body do crazy things. Falling on top of him, as if falling out of the clouds, falling out of a dream, crashing hard back into reality.

I've tried to analyze it from every angle: that strange moment where I slipped completely outside of myself and became this Other Georgia. One who, for a few blissful seconds, didn't care about any of the things she normally holds so dear: propriety, loyalty, maturity.

On Monday, I obviously didn't wake up early to train Benny. When I got to the beach for my shift, though, he was here, wanting to talk. I told him that what happened was a mistake. And besides, I needed to work. He asked if he should come back later, at the end of my shift, and part of me wanted to say yes. So we could process what happened between us. So I could make it *clear* how much I regret it.

But I also knew that seeing him alone again was a bad idea. "Just give me space, Benny," I said. "I can't be around you right now."

He nodded, looking sad. "I understand. I'm disappointed, but I understand."

He looked so forlorn that I rushed to add, "Obviously this is a public beach. You can come here and swim or practice as much as you want. But we can't interact. I have a job to do."

"I understand," he said again, looking down.

"I have to figure out how to fix this horrible mistake." I stopped short of blaming him—I only blame myself. But he needed to know how serious this is to me.

He looked up into my eyes, searching my face, maybe wondering if I really meant it. Whatever he saw there, I guess it convinced him.

I've seen him around the beach since then, practicing his sidestroke and doing push-ups in the sand. But I've averted my eyes, and he's stayed away.

He's behaving very well—he's listened to my request and respected it.

I know there's not much more I can ask.

And yet, the tension inside me is so intense I feel like I could snap in half. The kind of anxiety I've been experiencing since that kiss would give Doechii a run for her money. Regret doesn't even *begin* to describe it.

The craziest part is that the guilt isn't even completely about Rhys. Yes, the idea of him finding out, the idea of me having to tell him what I've done, consumes me with sticky, nauseating shame. But there's something even worse roiling deep in my gut.

And it took me until today to realize what it is: I feel like I didn't just betray Rhys.

I betrayed *myself.*

I am someone who people admire and come to for advice. They trust me because I'm responsible; I know the right thing to do in any situation. I take care of others. I work hard. I care about making good impressions and moving through the world in a respectable manner. And I know Rhys does, too, which is why we're so good together. We have the same values. We want the same kind of life.

When my dad died, and Mom and Daisy fell apart, I was a rock. I held it in, held us all together, even helped Mom with groceries and bills, organized her schedule. I pitched in with funeral planning too, picking out Dad's favorite songs, sorting through family photos for the slideshow. I can't tell you how many times Mom has said she wouldn't have survived without me, without that strength I showed. I know it's true, and I'm proud of that. It's important to me. It's who I am.

And while I was being a rock for everyone else, Rhys was mine.

Now I've taken that rock and I've sunk it right down into the middle of the lake, and there's nothing—nothing anchoring me anymore.

How can I say I'm a good person now? How can I look anyone in the eye, ever again?

All week, Daisy's been trying to talk to me—presumably about whatever's going on with her and Mateo. Mom keeps asking if we can find a moment, just the two of us, to catch up. Eden's been in her own world, maybe still upset with me about the party. But I can't bring myself to face any of them. I've been nearly silent at dinner, forcing myself to consume enough food to not draw attention. I'm sure they can sense something's wrong, though I've tried so hard to hide it, to paste on the smile they're used to. I can't let them know; I can't let them *down.* It would be too unbearable to see the shame and disappointment written on their faces.

The sun is too bright. I adjust my visor, subtly wiping tears from the corners of my eyes while I try to keep my focus on the water.

The seconds tick by as the hot sun pours down on my shoulders, and I feel like I'm sitting in a torture chamber. Every morning has felt like this.

During my break, I barely touch my lunch, then jump into the water to cool off. But the burning sensation isn't just coming from the sun, it's coming from within.

Somewhere around four, Benny shows up.

True to form, he ignores me completely.

I watch as he strips off his T-shirt and walks confidently into the water. It's been super crowded; after all, it's perfect beach weather after several gray days. And the Fourth of July festivities start tomorrow, going into the weekend. It's a busy time in Laurel.

I can almost lose sight of Benny among everyone else in the water, but like a game of Where's Waldo, I keep spotting hints of him. The arm stroke that's unmistakably his. The flash of his red-and-blue swim trunks. The specific way he shifts his weight to one side when waiting in line at the snack shack for a Popsicle.

It would be so much easier if he would just not come here at all. I have to concentrate so hard to avoid him, it ends up being the thing I'm most focused on all day. Benny, Benny, Benny. Everywhere I turn my gaze.

I should be glad. He's keeping his distance, playing by the rules.

But instead I feel overheated and frustrated and, frankly, furious. He gets to just splash around and chill out and enjoy the summer like he hasn't been involved in ruining someone's life.

Okay, maybe that's extreme. He didn't ruin my life. But he's half the reason my good conscience has been ripped to shreds; half the reason I haven't been sleeping, the bedsheets hot and stiff against my burning, tingling skin.

He's the whole reason that when I *do* drift off to sleep for brief stretches, I dream of things I shouldn't dream of, and wake feeling guiltier and sicker than before.

I train my gaze back to the water. I shouldn't be watching the snack shack.

Somehow the remaining minutes of the day tick by, and it's finally time to pack up. But I can tell that someone's approaching, and turn around.

Benny. It's like I have a sixth sense for him now, like I can tell where he is not by looking but via some supernatural awareness in my fingertips, behind my ears, the backs of my knees.

He smiles, handing me a mango Popsicle.

"What is this?" I ask, mystified. Why is he smiling? How can he possibly be joyful when I'm completely wrung out?

He shrugs. "A peace offering. I saw you glancing over at the snack shack." I blush, but I'm not sure if he registers this. "Figured you were hungry."

He's not wrong. I take the ice pop—no sense letting it melt in his hands.

"Thank you," I say, unwrapping it and feeling an instant burst of relief at the sweet coldness against my tongue. Maybe this was all I needed to take the edge off my misery—something to cool me down and a few calories.

He stands there watching me. "I'm glad you like it."

"Benny," I say. "Please. Don't do this."

"Do what?"

"Look at me like that. Be nice to me. You're supposed to be giving me space."

"Is that really what you want?" he asks.

"Of course it is. It's what I need," I tell him, hating the shakiness in my voice. He's only a year and a half younger, but he's somehow so clueless.

"Georgia," he sighs, shaking his head.

"What?"

"Nothing."

"It's not nothing. What is the sigh for?"

"I think you're lying," he says, looking me right in the eyes.

Indignance rises in my chest. "I'm *lying*? That's interesting."

"Is it?"

I realize he's never lied to me. In fact, it's the opposite; Benny has always been painfully blunt. That's part of what got us here in the first place.

"I haven't lied to anyone," I tell him. "I certainly haven't lied to *you*. So what are you suggesting? That I lied to Rhys? That I should tell my boyfriend about our—" I stop myself from saying the word *kiss* out loud. Because there are still a bunch of people clearing out of the beach who might hear. And also, because the word *kiss* makes it seem so much smaller and more trivial than what it actually was.

He has the grace to blush.

I go on. "For your information, I *do* plan to talk to Rhys about this, when I see him in person. I don't take this—I don't take any of it—lightly."

"Oh, I am very aware of that," he says, his eyes tracing every twitch in my lips.

"So who am I lying to, then?" I demand, crossing my arms.

He shakes his head, trying to hide a half smile. "Yourself."

"I am not lying to myself. *You're* lying to *your*self. Clearly you think what happened between us wasn't that big of a deal, but for me it very much was."

"It was a big deal to me, too," he says, the smile disappearing. "But Georgia, you're lying to both of us if you say you didn't like it. *Love* it, even. Come on. I just need you to admit this."

I feel heat overtaking my brain; the mango Popsicle is suddenly mushy and about to dissolve all over me. "I will do no such thing."

"So, it isn't true?"

I throw my hands up, my frustration erupting. "So *what* if it felt good in the moment, Benny? That is beside the point completely."

"I don't think it is. I think it's the *whole* point. Why don't you let yourself be happy, Georgia?"

The heat gathering in my chest is starting to feel like something other than anger. Why is he asking me this? "I do. I *am* happy. I am very happy. Or I was, until you came into the picture."

He lets out another sigh. "You are stuck in some idea of what your life is supposed to be like. But there's obviously so much more to you, beneath the surface. It's no secret that I like you, and I want you to admit that you feel this too. But even if you never admit it to me, I just . . . I hate how locked up you are. It's not fair. For someone as special and beautiful as you to be living in this, like, this . . . I don't know . . . this *box* you've put yourself into."

I am dumbfounded. I just don't know how to respond to this. I don't recall ever being so . . . *seen.* It's something other than attraction—or attention, even. It's like being completely exposed.

I hate it.

"I'm not in a box, Benny. This is who I *am.* And now if you'll excuse me, I need to go home."

I chuck the melting remains of the Popsicle in the trash can and climb into my car, where the sticky-sweet mango scent still lingers on my fingers.

The whole drive home, I can see the sun flashing between the trees, bright and beautiful, but it's shining on a faraway land, not on me. The walls of my life are closing in.

This box you've put yourself into.

Is he right? But who is he to tell me how to live my life? After all, I rationalize, my favorite place to shop is the Container Store. My favorite thing to do is draw little boxes on my to-do list and then check them off, one by one. Maybe I *have* put myself into a box, or a series of them. Maybe I *like* boxes. They are contained. They are organized, safe, predictable. Boxes are the building blocks of society!

And yet . . . that image of being inside a box—like Barbie in the movie—makes me itchy with uncertainty. What am I missing out on? What would I let myself love if I could . . . let myself love?

I don't realize that tears are streaming down my face until the road ahead goes blurry and I have to pull over.

I pat my face dry with my beach towel, leaving sandy crumbs stuck to the sunscreen. *Get it together, Georgia.*

Before I turn the engine back on, my phone pings.

Speaking of sixth senses. It's Rhys. **I have a surprise for you! Can't wait to see you soon.**

I swallow hard, but all I can taste in my throat is the suffocating flavor of mango.

I burst through the door as soon as I get home—between the sweat and the sand and the sunscreen and the mango Popsicle and the tears, I'm desperate for a shower. But instead of the usual bustle of the house—Mom in the kitchen transitioning from writing to cooking, Dave home from the library and lighting the grill, Daisy and Eden prattling on about their days—it's quiet. And everyone is sitting in the living room.

They look up when I walk in. Mom, Dave, Eden, Daisy, and . . . that's when I realize.

Rhys.

"Surprise!" he says.

"I— What? You're here early? How?" I try not to show how flustered I feel, but I'm afraid it's obvious from the way my hands are fluttering around like birds released from a cage.

He gets up to wrap me in a hug, but I pull away. "Sorry, don't hug me—I'm completely gross."

He laughs. "Okay, why don't you shower?"

"Wait," Mom says. "Before you do, take a seat, both of you."

Irrational fear jolts through me like I've been hit by lightning. *Do they know?* Why is everyone sitting here, so quietly and seriously? Is this an intervention? Are they going to force me to publicly admit to cheating on Rhys?

The panic starts ringing in my ears as I take a seat on the couch next to Rhys.

Mom clears her throat and takes Dave's hand. The gesture alarms me even more. Like she needs strength to confront me. I glance at Eden and Daisy, trying to read their expressions. Are they on my side? But I can't tell what they're thinking—they're focused on Mom too.

"Dave and I wanted to share something with all of you. Rhys, too, of course, since you're here. And we're so happy that you are," she adds, which drives a knife through me.

"What? What is it?" I blurt out, desperate for them to just spit it out. If I have to have the walls crumble down around me, I may as well get it over with. The suspense is worse.

"Just say it, Mom," Daisy prods.

I look to Daisy—was this her idea? She clearly already knows, or guesses, what this is about. . . .

"Okay, okay!" Mom says, suddenly breaking out into a huge grin. She looks at Dave and then around the room at us. "We're engaged."

There's a beat of silence. Then Daisy and Eden start squealing and jumping up and down.

Rhys reaches over and squeezes my hand. Then he gets up to give my mom a congratulatory hug.

I feel like gravity has socked me in the stomach, sinking me into the couch.

This can't be happening.

This can't be happening.

This can't be happening.

It's like they're all operating in a different version of reality; laughing and crying and hugging and asking questions and congratulating Mom and Dave, while I'm watching from the outside through a foggy window. I'm in some nightmare and can't connect to the other side. The ringing in my ears is so loud I can't even think.

Somehow, I manage to shove myself out of the couch cushions and stand, wobbly. Instead of approaching the rest of them, though, I walk in a daze right out the front door. I stagger toward the edge of the lawn to the trees, then down the steps that lead to the little path to the water.

Dad, I think. *Dad, you won't believe this.*

I feel the strangest urge. I want to protect him—Dad—from finding out what Mom has done.

I know he's there at the edge of the water, with his fishing pole, watching the sunset. Oblivious to this cruel twist of fate. Oblivious to the fact that everyone—everyone besides me—has decided it's okay to abandon him, leave him behind.

When I reach the water's edge, I see with cold shock that the shore is empty. Some part of me really believed, for a second there, that I would see Dad. That he'd hear me approaching and turn around, taking off his baseball cap. His figure silhouetted in fading gold-red sunlight.

But no one is there.

* * *

"Georgia."

It's Rhys's voice. He's followed me.

"Hey, baby, what's going on?"

"It's too much," I gasp. "It's too soon."

He puts his arms around me from behind, and we stand like that, facing the water, and I can't bear to turn and face him. I feel like I'm going to split into a million shards.

"Don't you want your mom to be happy?"

I let out a sniffle, thinking of my conversation with Benny. "Maybe I don't know what that even means."

"Oh, come on, don't be silly."

"I'm not," I say.

"If it's what's best for her, I'm sure it's what's best for everyone. Be rational, baby."

I pull away. "I'm sick of being rational! What good has being rational done for me? It only got me—*here*!" I'm shaking, angry now.

"What's so bad about here?" There's complete confusion written on Rhys's face.

Truthfully, it feels kind of vindicating, like, *yeah, take a good look at the real Georgia, the person I am now. Not so proper after all. Not so easy to soothe into compliance.*

"Everything," I say. "Just—everything. This was never how the summer was supposed to go. I was right—we shouldn't have even come up here. It was too soon, too close. We weren't ready. And now—you're never around. You're living your glamorous life in the city, and I'm out here dealing with everybody falling apart, including myself."

He shakes his head. "I don't understand."

"No!" I almost laugh. "No, you don't understand." I shake my head in disbelief. "I honestly don't know if you've ever really understood me, Rhys. I think you just love this *idea* of Georgia Holliday. Accomplished, smart, pretty, athletic, and fits easily under one arm. Am I right? I'm right, aren't I?"

"Baby, where is this coming from? Did—did Mateo tell you something?"

"Tell me what?"

"Nothing. I'm just trying to understand why you're so upset with *me*. What have I done?"

I shake my head again. I don't know how to explain. "It's not something you've done."

He looks relieved. "But—then what's wrong?"

I stare at his perplexed, handsome face, and the frustration is so strong in me I want to push him, shove him, make him *wake up* and see what I'm going through. Make him understand. But all I can say, all that comes to me, is the same word that came to me when I was floating on the lake last Sunday with Benny.

"*This*."

"This, as in . . . *us*?" His eyes search my face. "Georgia," Rhys says slowly, "are we breaking up right now?"

I stare at him, feeling like I've been slapped. That wasn't what I was saying *at all*. I was trying to say that he doesn't get me, doesn't see me, doesn't understand that everything until now was a lie. . . .

I was trying to tell him what I've done. That I ruined us.

But as we look at each other in shared shock, I begin to realize that maybe he's right. Maybe breaking up is exactly what I'm doing.

Even though I never in a million years planned to.

Never thought it was what I wanted.

What would you let yourself love?

A sob rises in my throat. "I'm sorry, Rhys. I don't love you anymore." I realize it's true the moment the words come out.

"Baby," he says quietly, but that word, *baby*, grates against my ears. I can't stand here and be soothed and mollified, told it's all going to be okay, when it's not. But then he shocks me even further. "I think maybe this was coming for a long time."

"It—it was?"

He looks into my eyes. "I'm so sorry," he says.

"No," I say. "No, I am. More than you can ever know." My voice is gravelly in my throat. "Goodbye, Rhys."

And then I walk past him, away from the sparkling water and the memories and the past.

Away from the person I used to be.

The yellow house on Greenvalley Lane isn't hard to find.

I feel unhinged as I knock on the door, and even more wild and embarrassed when an older woman answers. She's shorter than me, with lined skin and a kind smile. She's wearing black leggings and pale pink Crocs.

"You must be Abuelita," I say, realizing I don't know her actual name, only what Benny calls his grandma.

She looks a little surprised—understandably—taking in my disheveled appearance and tear-streaked face. "¡Benito! ¡Vete aquí!" she says loudly over her shoulder. "Alguien vino a verte."

She steps aside, and Benny appears. He's wearing jeans and a white T-shirt, which shouldn't take me aback but it does—I'm used to only seeing him in swim trunks on the beach. Here, he's a whole person, with a whole life I know so little about.

Shyness suddenly overtakes me and I don't know what to say.

But Benny breaks into a big smile. "Oh good! You're not mad at me. I thought after our conversation today . . ."

I shake my head, trying to find the right words. "Not mad" is the best I can do.

"Do you want a frozen hot chocolate? You look like you could use one."

I shake my head again. "That's not why I'm here."

He glances over his shoulder. "Should we go somewhere else where we can talk?"

I nod.

He steps behind the door for a second and comes back with a pair of flip-flops on. "Voy a salir, Lita," he shouts, and leads me back down the front steps to the road. "Where's your car?" he asks me.

"I walked here."

He looks at me in surprise. "Wow, okay."

"Can we go to the beach?"

"It's kind of a long walk."

"But how do you get there every day?" I ask.

He points to the side of the house, where a bike is resting. "We might both fit on there. Wanna give it a try?"

I shrug. "Okay."

He drags out the bike and sits on the seat, then instructs me to climb up onto the handlebars. It takes a few tries of me falling on top of him, and despite the misery that's been boiling inside me, I burst out laughing.

I finally get my butt positioned in the middle of the bars. "Can you even see around me?" I shout, but he starts pedaling, and I start screaming as we sail downhill, the evening air rushing past my face, drying the last of my tears.

The beach is empty and the sun has almost set. We leave the bike by the sand and walk down the wood-boarded path toward the water. "Dock?" he asks.

I nod, and he takes my hand.

To my surprise, I let him.

We walk to the end of the dock and kick off our sandals, sitting with our feet dangling in the water.

"Did you want to talk?" Benny asks quietly.

"You were right," I blurt out at last. It's such a massive release to say it aloud. "You were right about everything. I feel so stupid."

"You're not stupid," he says. "What happened?"

"We broke up," I say, my voice breaking. "Me and Rhys."

"Because of me?" His voice is low; we're both looking out at the water and not at each other.

"No. Because of *me*," I say. "I don't know what I want, but I know you're right that I want something more. I want something different. I want space to figure out what that is."

"I'm happy for you, then," he says, putting his hand back on top of mine.

"Also, my mom is getting engaged to her boyfriend."

"Wow."

"Yeah."

"That's a lot."

I sigh with relief. It's such a simple acknowledgment of the truth. "I knew you'd get it."

He turns to face me. "So . . . can I ask you . . . what this means for me?"

I meet his gaze. "I don't know. I don't know what anything means right now."

"Maybe we don't have to know."

I swallow, a ball of nerves gathering in my throat. "Maybe we don't have to know," I repeat. It feels so freeing—and so scary—to say that.

He reaches up to my face, brushing stray hair from my eyes. Then he smiles, letting out a small laugh.

"What? What's so funny?" I ask, surprised that a laugh escapes me, too.

"Who would've thought, when I first saw you, that we'd end up here. I just feel like the luckiest person alive," he says. "To be sitting here with you."

"Me too," I say.

And then I kiss him.

The kiss is long and slow and magical, like sinking into the water. He leans back on one arm and soon we're lying on the dock, in each other's arms. Eventually, I pull away for breath and we look into each other's eyes, and then kiss some more—with even more intention.

Like this could be our only chance.

And who knows.

Maybe it is.

EIGHTEEN

Eden

I BLOW MY BANGS out of my face and stare again at the compass. "I thought she said west-northwest." I look around us—it's just thick woods in every direction. No path in sight. "But what's the difference between that and northwest-north?"

"There *is* no northwest-north," Leo says with a laugh.

"Fine, Directional Genius, then *you* lead us," I say, handing the compass back to him.

"It's about damn time," he sings to the rhythm of the Lizzo song.

I roll my eyes. "I thought you said there was no karaoke in Boundless Horizons."

"Maybe you're rubbing off on me."

I look at him, his big dimples. Despite how hot he got since middle school, one thing hasn't changed. "You are such a dork."

He does a really embarrassing shimmy. "You love it."

"Please *never* do that move again."

He shimmies again. "I can't be stopped."

I can't help it, I laugh. "Lost in the woods with a bad dancer. This is how it ends."

"Don't be morbid," Leo says. "Now that I'm in charge, we will definitely survive."

"Unless I die of residual embarrassment."

"I'd resuscitate you. Sorry. You're stuck with me," he says.

"You know CPR?" I feel warmth creeping underneath my skin as I unwillingly picture Leo giving me mouth-to-mouth. *Relax, brain. Sheesh.*

He shrugs. "No, but I've given the Heimlich before, so."

I laugh again. "I'll keep that in mind in case I choke on an acorn out here."

But my laughter fades as I look around us. Leo is confidently marching through the woods in a slightly uphill direction, but I still can't make out any familiar path. There are no painted rocks, no signs, and no voices in the distance.

Somehow, we've made it to the Friday camping trip. Since we decided to have a truce at the start of the week, Leo and I have been getting along okay. I'm surprised to find that despite all the unresolved confusion and drama of our past, there actually *are* the seeds of a real friendship here. I've stopped focusing so much on resenting his past behavior, which means that I'm beginning to see the ways we've both matured since then.

Not that there's anything mature about his silly dance moves.

But he's not trying so hard to prove his superiority or mansplain basic things to me; we may joke about it, but he's actually been patient—when I got tangled in the tent cords during our practice setup; when I got tangled in the harness during the rock-climbing excursion; when I got tangled in a bunch of weeds during the site-clearing session. As it turns out, I have a real gift for getting tangled in things.

And his teasing comments no longer sound condescending and irritable—now it all just seems familiar, comfortable. Like the teasing between, well, *friends*.

Which is, I guess, what we're becoming.

Maybe that's all we were ever meant to be.

"Leo, can I see the map again?" I call out, jogging to catch up with him.

Before we all departed this morning, each group got an individualized map, supposedly leading us to different camping sites. We'll be completely on our own to do all the site clearing and set up our tents, cooking stoves, sleeping bags, bear canisters, et cetera. None of the campsites are visible to each other—so that we're really alone in the woods—but JJ says we're all in earshot of her whistle. Which gave me some relief at first.

But now we've been hiking with our *extremely* heavy gear packs for hours, and there hasn't been a single sound of another hiker or whistle or any indication whatsoever of human life. It's starting to feel eerie.

Leo hands me the map without slowing down, and I stare at

it, turning it around as if maybe from a different angle it'll make more sense. "The thing is," I say, huffing to keep up. "The map makes it look like we'll be camping really close to the spot where the river and lake meet up. But . . ." I huff some more. "But that would mean we should be hiking *downhill* from here, not up, right?"

Leo shakes his head. "Nah, this is the way. We have to get over the ridge and then the river's on the other side. Even if we've overshot the trail a little bit, once we can hear and see the river, we just have to turn right and follow it the rest of the way."

He says this with such calm confidence. I should just relax and let him lead; this is what he's good at, after all.

But another hour goes by, and then another, and I'm starting to get really tired. "Leo, can we stop for a snack?"

He looks up at the sky. "We're supposed to make it to the site before dusk."

"We must be getting close by now, right? I don't see the river anywhere."

He stops walking and looks around. "I know, it's strange. We should have hit it by now."

"Really? When should we have gotten to the river? Is it possible we overshot it somehow?"

He wrinkles his forehead, staring at the map. "Like at least an hour ago."

"An *hour ago*?! Leo, we've been potentially marching off course for over an hour and you didn't say anything?!"

He scrunches his brow. "I mean, I didn't think we were going off course, exactly. I kept figuring it was just a little off from the map."

Instantly, my calm and trust vanish. "You figured, huh. But you didn't tell me that. We could have discussed it. I *told* you uphill felt wrong. What if we've been going in the completely wrong direction this whole time? Do you even know where we are?"

JJ said all the camping sites are within the same three-mile radius. But given how long we've been hiking, it's possible we're not even remotely within range. And we weren't allowed to bring phones with us, which means we have no way of letting the group know we've gone off course.

Suddenly the insects sound so much louder. The leaves that had been swaying in a slight breeze are now swishing angrily, the wind picking up speed. And when I glimpse the sky between the thick branches overhead, it looks distinctly less blue by the minute.

I try to keep the growing worry from pounding through my chest, but it's right there at the ready. I do *not* like this. I do not like being lost and alone in the woods.

Lost and alone in the woods with Leo.

"We need to start retracing our steps immediately," I insist, though even as I say it, I realize with dismay that it's nearly impossible to tell which way we came from. "You're the Boy Scout; you should know what to do," I tell him, attempting to sound more confident than I feel.

"The first thing to do is not panic," Leo says. "There's nothing to be afraid of. It's just nature, remember?"

"Nature, which is full of bears, insects, and poisonous plants."

"When have we encountered any signs of bears in these entire two weeks, Eden?"

I shrug. "We know they come out after dusk."

"This would have been true whether we had found the campsite or not," he points out, but I'm latched on to his phrasing. *Whether we had found* . . .

"Are you saying you don't think we're going to *ever* find the site?" I can hear my voice rising an octave.

He glances up at the sky. I'm not wrong—it *is* getting darker. Only subtly, but still. After two weeks of these hikes, with no phone to tell the time, I recognize the telltale signs of afternoon waning into evening. And that is most definitely happening right now.

"Eden, relax. We're gonna be fine. Either we'll get to the campsite on the map, or we'll make our own. No big deal. We have everything we need. Just trust me, okay?"

I snort. "Sure. *That's* always worked out for me."

"What do you mean?"

"Nothing."

"No, it's not nothing. I thought we were friends. You can be real with me," Leo insists, his head quirked slightly to the side.

"Real with you? Fine—I've trusted you in the past and that backfired," I snap.

His eyebrows go up. "How so?"

"Well . . ." I clear my throat and take a breath. "To put it bluntly, I trusted you completely when we were together. I was all in on you, even if I shouldn't have been, and you totally turned on me. So, like, forgive me if it isn't second nature to put my entire life in your hands just because you say so. Okay, Leo? That real enough for you?"

He shakes his head. "I turned on you? Sure, whatever, Eden."

He hitches his gear pack higher on his shoulders and starts walking downhill, in a direction I would say was southeast but I really have no idea.

I race to catch up again. "Yes, Leo. You turned on me. How can you deny that? You broke up with me when I was at my complete lowest. And you never once apologized. You never showed any regret. You never even looked back. You just walked off into the sunset, while I had to pick up the pieces of my life."

He stops and stares at me. "You're going to blame me for how I reacted? You're gonna tell me that *I'm* the one who can't be trusted? Eden, that is actually making my brain hurt. You're the one who can't be trusted. Don't get things twisted."

He keeps walking, but this time I don't run to catch up. I'm too rooted to the ground. "Wow. *Wow.*" I truly can't believe it.

And then it hits me.

"To this day, you still think I did it," I say, almost more to myself than to him. Because I really can't believe it. Can't believe that after all this time, Leo really thinks I hooked up with Becca Johnson's older brother. That I cheated on him. That I was this drunk party girl who not only went behind his back but enjoyed it, and thought I could get away with it.

I stare at his backpack as he marches farther ahead through

the trees. He has a whole picture of me that isn't even close to the truth.

I would race after him and defend myself, but you know what? I defended myself enough two years ago. I'm sick of having to defend the truth, instead of just being believed.

And I'm even more sick of the power of this one stupid rumor. Because at the end of the day, even if I *did* get drunk on purpose and hook up with Becca's gross older brother, why should anyone care this much? Shouldn't a girl be able to make a few awkward mistakes in her life? It wouldn't make me a bad person, even if I *had* done it. People do far wilder things every day. People break each other's hearts every day—carelessly.

I would know.

I've done it. On purpose.

I've hurt other guys since breaking up with Leo. Let them think we were going somewhere, then ghosted them. I've watched as realization sank in that I didn't care as much as they hoped. I have even—I can admit this—savored the little high of knowing I can hurt someone first, before they hurt me.

I'm not saying I'm proud of any of this.

I'm just saying I'm human, and even if I did mess up—back then or now—I deserve to be forgiven.

Leo has shown me his true colors again and again, and I went ahead and decided to give him another chance, even as a friend. I should've known better.

I guess the joke's on me.

* * *

We've been hiking together but separately—me trailing about twenty feet behind, both of us silently seething—for about forty-five minutes when the first fat droplets of rain begin to fall.

All this time, I've been so concerned about not making camp before dusk that I forgot to worry about the weather! The forecast had said partly sunny conditions would last until tomorrow, but that's the Catskills for you. It rains when it feels like raining.

Leo stops and squints up into the canopy, putting out a hand.

Though I have no desire to be close to him, I approach slowly anyway. "What do we do now?" I keep my voice flat, dry, trying to stay focused on getting through this nightmare. We're lost in the woods, in the *rain*. In a fight. The only way this could get worse is if we were also in a bear's stomach.

He sighs. "We clear a site as best we can, and we start setting up camp."

"Now? *Here?*"

He turns to me. "Got a better plan?"

"Not unless you have a time machine." I would go back to before I even agreed to my parents that I'd do this program.

Who knows, maybe I'd just go all the way on back to before Becca's birthday two years ago.

"Shoot. Left my time machine at home with my watch and phone."

"Ha."

"Come on, then. Help me clear the site."

We remove twigs, rocks, and underbrush, trying to get enough flat ground space with no impeding branches in the air that could tear the side of the tent. We work in silence as the rain picks up. I pull my Zara poncho out and put it on, squishing around as I work. All I can hear is the sound of the rain pattering against the slick, not-as-waterproof-as-advertised material of the poncho and the sound of our heavy breathing. We manage to get the tarp spread out, but the tent gives us trouble. A gust of wind throws me and the tent over sideways into a muddy area. I hit my hip against a tree root and it really hurts, but I don't let the pain show. I just grind myself up to a kneeling position and pull the tent up with me. Mud drips off my knees. I feel it gathering inside my shoes.

And, obviously, my bladder chooses this brilliant moment to remember all the soda I had while we were hiking. I tried to limit my intake but the more stressed I got, the more I absentmindedly kept sipping. The theme of today: Eden doesn't learn her lessons. She makes the same mistakes again and again.

"I have to pee," I mutter.

"What?" he shouts, looking stressed. The wind flapping the tent around and the rain falling harder now on our heads, and the tent, and the trees, makes it hard to hear.

"Pee! I have to pee!"

"Put on your headlamp," he says, brow furrowed. But at first, I hear something that sounds like *deadlands*.

"Huh? What?"

"HEADLAMP!" he shouts, pointing to his forehead.

"Okay, jeez." He is being such a complete jerk, I can't even believe I was starting to think we could be friends.

I put on the stupidly embarrassing headlamp and march into

the trees, searching around for a secluded spot to squat. Frankly, *all* the spots are secluded.

When I finish peeing, my entire butt is drenched from rain. At least I didn't get attacked by a bear with my pants down. I'd much rather get attacked by a bear while fully clothed.

There's a moment where I freeze, unable to see Leo or the campsite.

Oh no, have I gone too far?

But then I notice a flicker of light. Leo put on his headlamp, too.

By the time I trudge back to the site, the tent is set up.

"Get inside," he says.

"What?"

"GET INSIDE WHERE IT'S DRY!" he barks out. "ISH."

"Okay, okay." I unzip the tent, but before I step in, he grabs me.

"Wait. Take off your boots first. They're muddy. Let's go in barefoot so we don't make it as muddy in there as it is out here."

He has a point, even though taking my muddy boots off while standing *in* the mud in the rain is not easy to do. I try to lean onto the tent but it veers precariously toward the ground, so I grab on to Leo instead. I feel his bicep flex beneath his rain jacket as I wrap my hand around his upper arm. *My lord.* Does he really need to choose this moment to be vain about his muscles? Come on. Stop showing off.

I kick off the shoes and step in wet socks onto the inner ledge of the tent.

"Here!" he says, holding out a hand. I hand over my dripping, gross boots. He swiftly opens his gear pack and pulls out a plastic bag, wrapping my boots in it. "Go inside, I'm fine!" he shouts. So I go in and wait for him to figure out how to get his boots off on his own.

Inside the tent is . . . small.

Like, very, very small.

After a minute or two, Leo slumps down wetly onto the tarp beside me.

"Ow, your lamp is shining straight into my eyes," I say.

"So is yours."

We both turn them off, and then it's almost too dark. I shiver. My whole body is soaked through. I don't know how I'm ever going to get comfortable.

"You look like a drenched puppy," he says.

"Uh, thanks?"

"I have an idea." He digs around in his gear pack and pulls out a dry T-shirt. "Do you want to borrow this? You could change underneath it. I've seen my sisters do that."

I really don't want to say yes, but I also don't want to sit in these wet clothes, and the alternative would be changing in front of him with no cover at all. And it isn't *that* dark in here. So, I accept the offer.

I take off my poncho and pile my wet stuff all in one corner. Once I slip on his loose T-shirt, it's easy to pull my wet tank top off by the straps. The pants are a bit trickier; the T-shirt comes halfway down my thighs, but I can't fully stand upright in the tent, so I have to shimmy and slide around to get changed.

Meanwhile, I can't help but notice that Leo has just whipped his wet shirt off and . . . left it off. Guys have it so easy! I avert my eyes. I don't need to be taking in his chiseled chest right now. Is that a tiny patch of hair sprouting down below his belly button, toward the line of his pants? No, no it's not, because I'm not looking.

Finally I manage to slip on a dry pair of shorts. "Can I just leave this T-shirt on for now?" I ask. I don't have the energy to maneuver a new shirt on underneath.

"Sure," he says.

I sit, enveloped in the scent of his T-shirt, while he sits just a few inches away from me in the tent, not wearing one at all.

"Now what?" I ask.

"Well, we can't really start a fire in this weather, but most of the food we brought doesn't need to be cooked," he reminds me, pulling out cut veggies, trail mix, and . . . a can of beans and a can opener.

As if.

"These don't need to be cooked either," I say, reaching into my pack for the extra snacks I packed: a bag of SunChips, a bunch of Rice Krispies treats, and a jumbo package of peanut M&M's. "Sorry for being a genius."

He looks at my stash with some mix of gratitude and hunger, and lets out a very sexual-sounding groan. "Never apologize for your genius."

I mentally file that groan away under *things to not pay too much attention to right now.* He used to make that sound sometimes, when we were alone together. Making out. In his room at his parents' apartment, or sometimes in the study room at the back of the library when no one was around . . .

I smile to myself inadvertently, remembering the time the librarian caught us.

"What? What's so funny?" he asks.

"Nothing."

We eat in silence, our hands occasionally brushing against each other's as we dive into the junk food I brought.

"Can we, uh, talk about our argument back there?" Leo says after a bit.

I finish crunching my SunChips, thankful to be inside the tent, safe from the rain, and consuming salt and sugar. I don't see any value in continuing to reopen old wounds again and again with him, so I say, "I'd rather not. My ass is still damp and I'm not in the mood."

He laughs. "Fine. So what should we talk about?"

"How much I'm enjoying the peace and quiet?"

He laughs again. "Eden, we're not going to make it a whole night together without talking. You do realize that, right?"

A whole night together. Obviously, I was prepared for the fact that we were going to be camping together tonight. If I'm honest, I've been thinking about it all week, preparing myself to be chill. To be *friendly* since we were supposed to be *friends* and all.

I was thinking about spending the night together (camping) when we were rappelling down the side of a rock face and my butt landed on his face.

I was thinking about spending the night together (camping) when I heard Daisy crying into her pillow two nights ago and she refused to answer the door after I knocked.

I was thinking about spending the night together (camping) when Aunt Elena told us she was getting engaged and Georgia basically lost her mind and fled the house. Elena and Dave were holding hands and telling us all about the details of their planned nuptials—they want to get married on the lake next summer—and Georgia stormed out the front door.

Everyone watched her leave, and Dave said, "Does anyone know what's going on with her?"

Rhys got off the couch and followed her. But as soon as he left, Daisy turned to the rest of us and said, "Rhys is cheating on her. They're breaking up. That's why she's upset."

Everyone started talking at once, in shock.

I was shocked too, even if I'm secretly a little glad that she's finally getting out of that relationship. I could see how much it was limiting her, even if she couldn't.

But despite the flood of big news crowding my brain—Aunt Elena was getting remarried! Georgia was probably breaking up with Rhys! Everything would be different from now on!—the loudest thought of all was:

Tomorrow I'll be spending the entire night with Leo, alone, just the two of us. (Camping.)

So yeah, I've thought about it.

But that's a lot different from actually doing it.

I shiver again.

"We could unroll our sleeping bags," Leo suggests. "It'll warm you up."

"It's so early, though. There's no way I'll fall asleep."

"You always were a night owl."

"Yup. You remember everything about me. I get it."

He's quiet for a minute. Then he starts unrolling his sleeping bag, not looking at me. "Anyway, the sooner we fall asleep, the sooner we can wake up in the morning and get out of here. Which is what you want, right?"

Of course that's what I want. To get out of here as soon as humanly possible. To make this "whole night together" end quickly. So I don't know why his comment—or his sudden return to coldness—stings so much. My emotions are completely scrambled around Leo, and there's nothing I can do about that.

We push our sleeping bags to the opposite sides of the tent, but we're only about eight inches apart. I lie still, feeling my body slowly warm up, listening to the rain falling on the sides of the tent. But the idea of trying to fall asleep right now is mathematically improbable. Torture. My mind is racing, my heart is racing, I'm wide awake.

Plus, there's definitely a twig underneath my back, below the tarp.

"Are you sleeping?" Leo whispers beneath the sound of the rain.

"Nope," I say.

"Are you absolutely miserable over there?"

I swallow. "Yup."

I hear Leo sigh. "I've never seen anyone suffer this much in nature."

"What can I say, I'm an anomaly."

"That's true, you are an anomaly. But can you admit there's something at least sort of beautiful, lying here listening to the rain fall? It's sort of . . . relaxing, no?"

Relaxing? I wish. I'm desperately thirsty from all the salty chips, but won't let myself drink from my canteen. The last thing I need is having to pee in the middle of the night.

"Tell me again why you signed up for Boundless Horizons?" Leo asks.

Now it's my turn to sigh. "I didn't. My parents did."

"But why? They thought it would be good for you?"

"I guess. They think that if I'm learning survival skills in the woods I won't be partying all summer in the city? I don't know. Their logic is beyond me. It's just their chosen punishment."

"For what?"

I sigh and blink my eyes. "I guess they're disappointed in me."

"Really?" he whispers. "Why would they be disappointed in you?"

I shake my head. "I don't know. I have zero life skills besides flirting and fashion?"

He laughs softly. "Those skills are valid."

"Leo, I don't need you to be nice to me. It's obvious that you have a very negative view of me as a person, so let's not force this whole friendship thing."

"I don't have a negative view of you."

"You said earlier that I'm untrustworthy."

"Well, you *did* try to prank me with a pepper spray bottle," he points out.

I shift around in my sleeping bag to face him, but I can't make out his expression in the dark. "Is that what you meant? Or were you talking about sophomore year, too?"

He's quiet. "Sometimes I swear you misunderstand me on purpose. Like you're always looking for reasons to hate me, or think less of me. I always felt that way, even when we were together. Everything I did was suspicious to you."

"What?" I ask, truly shocked.

"You were so mad about your brother not making varsity, and you really blamed me for that. Which wasn't fair. I'm not the coach. I had no real say over his decision. And anyway, your brother was talented, but he didn't want the spot. He wasn't a serious player."

"That wasn't your judgment to make, though," I tell him.

"It was just my *opinion*, Eden, and it turned out I was right. He dropped out to focus on music. My opinion didn't come out of nowhere."

"But at the time he really wanted it. And you were dating me. And he's my brother. So you should have been loyal, instead of gossiping about him behind our backs."

He shakes his head—I hear his hair rustle against the sleeping bag. "I wasn't gossiping. The other guys were. A lot of guys on that team were jerks, you know. A couple of them had already bullied Jesse. I didn't think he'd be happy on the team anyway."

I prop myself on an elbow—which causes my head to hit the side of the tent. I blow my bangs out of my face. "Hang on. Jesse was bullied?"

"You didn't know?" Leo asks. "I guess that's good. Maybe I managed to protect him from the worst of it."

I lie back down, reeling. "Okay, so let's say you didn't do anything wrong with Jesse. There's still the much, much worse way you behaved after Becca Johnson's birthday party."

"The way I behaved? What did *I* do?" Leo asks. Now he's the one propping up on an elbow.

I prop myself up again too. Now we're in a face-off. "You dumped me. When I was so alone and scared. If what you say is true, and you cared so much about my little brother not getting bullied by older kids, then what in the hell did you think was happening to me?"

"You were bullied?" he asks, and his sincerity hits me like a punch to the gut.

"How could you not have known that? I got attacked online for months. For something that didn't even happen."

He shakes his head. "I'm really sorry, Eden. I truly didn't know that."

"How? You were my boyfriend! How did you not know that was happening? It was possibly the worst thing that had *ever* happened to me!" I feel hot all over, just reliving the tiniest sliver of that humiliation and pain.

"I was at an away game. I came back and you were avoiding me. Yes, I knew there were rumors about you being into someone else. I didn't know about the online stuff. As you may remember, I had all those restrictions on my phone, and I didn't even have an Instagram account. I still don't."

"But you had to be pretty oblivious to not realize something was wrong."

"I *did* realize something was wrong. I just thought that what was wrong was *us*. You were always angry at me, always withdrawing and blaming me for things. And then the party happened, and it seemed like the last straw."

"Because you believed everyone. You thought I cheated on you, and your pride couldn't take it."

He sighs, searching my face. "I didn't think you cheated on me. But honestly, I did think that you wanted to. That you could be into someone else? That someone else could be into you? Of course I believed that."

"Seriously? You looked down on me then, just like you do now." I try to choke back the tears, but the truth feels so raw and vulnerable as I hear myself say it out loud.

"Eden. Is that really what you think?"

"Why else would you believe the worst about me?"

"I *didn't*. I believed that you were out of my league. You were so effortlessly beautiful and funny and weird and unique. You still are. I was a nerdy Boy Scout. Soccer was the only cool thing I did, and it was my whole life, and you don't even like sports. I was always waiting for you to move on. So yeah, maybe I was a bit susceptible to believing those rumors. And I truly am sorry for that. If I had known you were hurting that badly, I would have done things differently. At least, I like to think that I would."

His words are so comforting and surprising, I just don't know what to make of them. "But how could you have not *seen* how much I was hurting?" My voice is low, trembling.

He sighs. "I feel awful. But I didn't know. And Eden? You didn't tell me."

I let this sink in, but it's too much. I lie back down, blinking away tears. The rain is pattering more lightly now. "You walked away so fast, that day in the library. So cold. Like you'd become a totally different person."

Leo is lying down again, too. "I'm sorry, Eden," he says. "I was caught up in my own hurt. I thought, okay, the time has come, she's totally over me. Let me just make this as clean as possible. I didn't want you to see how upset I really was."

"You were upset?" I roll over to look at him.

"I was completely devastated. I tried to hide it. That's why I had to avoid you so intensely, for so long. I couldn't trust myself to be normal around you. It was hard for a while."

"But then you moved on. You dated other people."

"So did you," he points out.

"But that's different," I say.

"How?"

I sigh, searching for the words. "Because I moved on, but I didn't. Some part of me never recovered. I guess that's why I did the stupid pepper spray thing. I would've gone further with my sabotage plans, too, if that hadn't backfired so badly. Even after two whole years, I still wasn't completely over it after all."

He laughs softly.

"Are you *laughing* right now? What's so funny about all this?" I ask, wiping a tear from the corner of my eye.

"It's just, you know—same."

"Same?"

"Seeing you on orientation day for Boundless . . . I thought I was over you too, but it quickly became clear that I wasn't. That I'm . . ." He clears his throat. "That I'm still not."

"You mean you hadn't gotten over what happened between us? Our breakup?"

"No, Eden. I mean I haven't gotten over you, period. You still have the same exact effect on me that you always had."

"Which is what? That I make you crazy?"

He laughs again. "Yeah. In the best way."

"Why are you saying all this now?"

"Because unlike the immature kid I was two years ago when I hid my feelings from you, after the party last weekend, when I realized how hurt I was . . . something clicked. I realized I didn't want to keep avoiding the painful stuff. I wanted to be different. I wanted to see if we could get past the past."

"Get past the past," I repeat. "I don't know if that's possible, Leo. It's part of us now."

He stares at the top of the tent, and sighs.

"But," I say, turning toward him again.

He rolls toward me. "But?" Even in the darkness, I can see the hopeful smile on his face.

"I guess there is such a thing as forgiveness."

"Is there?"

"Yes, Leo. There is. And I forgive you."

"Really?"

"Yes, really," I say. And I mean it. I had no idea what his side of the story was. And he's right: *I never asked.* I was just as judgmental as he was. We both made assumptions. We were both wrong. It doesn't make it okay. But it makes me see how much I'd like things to change.

"Pinky swear?" he says, pulling one arm out of his sleeping bag and reaching it toward me.

"Pinky swear," I say, catching his pinky. But before I can pull my hand away, he takes it and holds it, lacing his fingers through mine.

We lie like that for a while, scooching our sleeping bags even closer to each other, neither of us willing to let go of the other's hand. Eventually we're close enough that I can easily nuzzle my head into his shoulder.

The smell of the rain, minerally and fresh, and the smell of Leo, citrus and smoke and *him*—it may be the most delicious, comforting blend of scents I've ever experienced. And despite the part of me that knows if I tilted my face upward the tiniest bit, we'd be kissing, I stay where I am, just breathing in this moment. Listening to the rain fall. Feeling Leo's chest rise and fall underneath the sleeping bag.

And before I know it, I'm asleep.

NINETEEN

Daisy

WHEN I HEAR THE soft click of the front door below my window Saturday morning, I'm ready. I glance at my clock—6:12—and leap out of bed in my pajamas, then tiptoe down the stairs toward the front door, determined to follow Georgia and confront her.

Eden was gone yesterday for her camping trip and won't be back until later this morning, just in time for the Fourth of July festival. But I haven't had a chance to really talk to Georgia since Rhys showed up on Thursday. I need to tell her I'm sorry. For blurting out their business to the rest of the family. But also for not telling her what I knew sooner.

I'm assuming she's going to get into her car and drive off—and I plan to stop her. I want to know where she's been going. I hope I'm not too late.

But as I step outside, I watch Georgia walk right past her car, and past the driveway completely.

I follow her.

She's walking toward the trees at the edge of our yard, the wooden steps to the path.

I find her sitting at the little rocky outcropping of our own private snippet of lakeshore. The other spot where she and I used to splash around while Dad fished. Sometimes Mom would come out here, too, and perch on a rock with a book in one hand.

"Hey."

She looks up, and I take in her face. She's one of the prettiest people I know, but I haven't really studied her face in a long time. Her nose is a little pink from too much sun and starting to peel. There are pale lavender shadows under her eyes from not sleeping. She still looks beautiful—but also changed somehow.

"What are you doing awake this early?" she asks.

"Stalking you," I admit.

She snorts.

"What are *you* doing up so early? You don't have to work today. You could sleep in."

She picks up a stick and starts playing with it, scraping it around on the rock beside her. "We both know I don't sleep in."

"That's true. But you've been sneaking out in the mornings."

"Yeah? And what else do you know?" she says, suddenly very consumed with her stick.

Guilt roils in my guts. "Mateo hinted to me that something might be going on between you and Rhys. Or that Rhys might be thinking about cheating. Or about breaking up with you. Or . . . or both. I'm sorry, Georgia. I should have said something right away. I tried to, actually. But you were already being so distant. You're never around."

"It's okay, Daisy."

"It is?"

"You're right. I really haven't been around much. I've been . . . preoccupied."

"Is everything okay? Is there anything I can do?" I ask, sitting down beside her, filled with relief that she doesn't seem angry with me.

"No, everything is not okay," she says, with a kind of forlorn heaviness I haven't heard in her in a long time. "But," she adds, "it *will* be. Eventually."

"Are you not okay because of you and Rhys? Because maybe you two should talk again. Maybe you can still work things out. Maybe—"

She shakes her head. "No. Rhys and I are not getting back together. It's not about that, not really. It's about me."

"What about you?" I ask, suddenly worried. "You're not, like, dying of some terrible disease, right?"

She laughs and shakes her head. "No, no, not at all. I'm just . . . You know what's nuts?"

"What?"

"I think I might be processing Dad's death for the first time."

This is not what I was expecting her to say. "For the first time? It's been three years."

"Being up here at the lake . . . I don't know. It's unleashed something. I think I was holding it all together. For you. For Mom." Her voice breaks a little.

I wrap an arm around her. "You don't always have to be strong for us. We're strong too, you know."

She laughs and sniffles at the same time. "I just can't believe Mom is ready to move on."

I sigh, looking out at the water. "For what it's worth, I don't think of it as her moving on. I think you can carry grief and love at the same time. Don't you?"

She turns to look at me. "Since when did you get so wise?"

I shrug. "I guess I've been busy this summer too."

She laughs. "You really have. Are you and Mateo . . . ?"

I shake my head. "Not anymore."

She nods. "I never thought that was a good idea. I tried to warn you."

"If you say *I told you so*, I'm going to shove you in the lake," I tell her.

She puts up her hands in surrender. "Sorry, sorry."

"Just let me make my own mistakes, okay, Georgia? And you can focus on your own."

She cracks a smile. "Oh, I have."

I wait for her to say more, but she doesn't. After a minute of silence, I squeeze her again in a side hug. "When you're ready, you should probably talk to Mom. She's upset about you storming off Thursday night. She's worried you really hate Dave, that you think he's some devilish aquatic expert." Georgia sniffle-laughs a little at this. "But seriously. I don't think she'd even go through with marrying him without your approval."

Georgia shakes her head. "She doesn't need my approval. I'm not the parent."

"Could've fooled us," I say, standing up and brushing off my pajama shorts.

"Where are you going?" She turns and squints up at me, and for a moment, I see this rare glimpse of vulnerability. This loneliness in her voice, and I have the craziest thought that maybe, just maybe, Georgia needs me. And it makes my heart swell.

"Back to bed, of course. It's way too early for us regular humans to be awake."

She laughs. "Okay. Sweet dreams."

"You coming back in?"

"Nah. I'm gonna sit out here a little longer."

"All right." I walk up the path toward the house, but turn to look over my shoulder one last time. With her back to me, facing the water, Georgia looks a little bit like Mom.

When the doorbell rings a few hours later, I have to forcefully pull myself out of the thickness of dreams. At first, I think it must be Eden, returning from her camping trip. But then I realize she wouldn't bother with the doorbell. I sit up, rubbing my eyes, and hear someone downstairs opening the door. Then I hear a low male voice.

It must be Rhys. Coming over to talk to Georgia. Maybe he thinks there's still a chance to make amends. I yawn and stretch and flop backward onto my pillow again, prepared to drift off for one more hour before I start the day. The festival doesn't really get going until around noon, then it goes all day with celebrations in the town center that last into the evening, ending with music and fireworks over the lake. Lots of people go out in their boats to watch the fireworks from the water, but since we don't have a boat, we usually just go to the public beach, which is always crowded with picnic blankets.

I'm lying there thinking about what sweet snacks I want to buy, what carnival games I want to play, when there's a knock on my bedroom door.

"Daisy?" Mom calls. "Are you awake? Someone's here for you."

I sit up again with a sudden pang of dread. I thought I heard Rhys's voice downstairs, but what if it's Mateo? Coming over here to—what—try to make up with me? Would he care enough to do that? What would I say? I contemplate pretending to be sick and hiding under the covers. I've managed to avoid him at the club, but if I had my wish, he'd just leave Laurel Lake for the rest of the summer. Rhys is barely ever here, and without me to entertain him, won't he be bored? Or will he just glom on to some other girl—some cool, carefree older girl who doesn't get emotionally attached after less than two weeks of making out?

Ugh. I'm spiraling.

Which is why it's even harder to comprehend what's happening when Mom cracks open my door and pokes her head in, saying, "Oh good, you *are* awake." Then she pushes the door open the rest of the way, and reveals . . .

"Owen?!" I blink, wondering if I'm still in a dream.

His hands are shoved in his pockets, but he pulls one out to brush his long hair out of his eyes. "I know I left kind of early, but I thought you'd be dressed and eating Pop-Tarts by now."

I leap out of bed and give him a huge hug. He hugs me back, and I'm suddenly aware that I'm just wearing a thin sleep shirt over my pj shorts. Not that I should care—it's just Owen. Right?

I pull back. "What are you doing here? Aren't you in Europe?"

He looks down at his body. "Apparently I'm not."

I laugh.

"I got back last night."

"Wait, you got back last night to Rhode Island? And now you're here?"

He shrugs. "Nothing to do at home without you there."

"Seriously?" I scan his face. This seems untrue—Owen always has things to do. Projects he invents for himself. The guy could keep himself occupied in a bunker in a zombie apocalypse, probably designing and testing zombie-trapping devices.

He shrugs. "Also, I got your postcards. And letters. And it kind of seemed like you were having a shit time. So, I figured I'd come cheer you up."

I have to admit, seeing him *is* cheering me up—it's an instant boost to my mood.

Though alongside the excitement that he's here, there's this nervous flutter in my chest, and I can't stop thinking: *We kissed. We kissed. We kissed.*

Now what?

I clear my throat. "But how did you get here?"

"I drove."

I go to the window and see Owen's dad's car in the driveway.

"Your dad let you borrow his car?" I ask, incredulous.

Owen twists his mouth. "Not exactly."

I run over to Owen and swat him in the chest. "You took your dad's car without asking?! On your first day back?!"

He laughs. "Stop! Don't hit me! I did nothing to you!"

"Your parents are going to be so worried! This is *so* typical of you." Normally I would be worried he's going to get in trouble—his parents try to be understanding with him, but they have their limits. This time, though, I have to admit I'm glad he "pulled an Owen." Otherwise, he wouldn't be here right now in my bedroom. . . .

We kissed. We kissed. We kissed. Now what?

"Yeah, well, it's worth it. Besides, I wanted to see what this Fourth of July celebration was all about. You've told me about it like a million times. Figured I should check it out for myself."

Eden comes home from her camping trip shortly after Owen's arrival, and we all sit down to pancakes. Owen pours an ungodly amount of syrup onto my plate. Eden smirks and tells us she and Leo finally made up.

Georgia starts clapping her hands with a glee that does not match her mood earlier this morning. "Oh, I'm so so so happy to hear this," she gushes.

"Okay, you can chill out now. It's not like we vowed true love. We just apologized for both being idiots when we were younger."

"That's all I meant!" Georgia says. "I'm glad that you put the past behind you."

"I don't know if it's *totally* behind me."

"It's not?" I ask.

Eden grins again. "I'm just saying, I wouldn't rule out the opportunity to spend more time with him. If it happens."

Georgia smiles. "Well, I'm happy for you, whatever you decide. But I'm done giving my opinions," she says, taking a perfectly cut bite of her pancake.

Eden and I look at each other with raised eyebrows, then burst out laughing.

"What?" Georgia says around her mouthful.

"So, Owen," Eden says, changing the subject. "You came all the way up here to see Daisy within, what, twenty-four hours of returning from Europe?"

I feel myself blushing. When she says it like that, it does seem . . . extreme. Romantic, even.

Owen shrugs. "Sixteen hours, technically."

Now it's Eden and Georgia's turn to share a look.

"He didn't want to miss the Fourth of July," I say in his defense. "It's a testament to my natural marketing skills."

"It's a testament to *something*," Eden says, her eyes glimmering with gleeful mischief.

"It's a testament," Owen announces, "to how I really feel about . . ." He looks at me and my breath freezes in my chest.

"Syrup." He grabs the bottle and drizzles a shocking amount onto his pile of three pancakes.

"The amount of syrup you're consuming is truly a health violation," I tell him, laughing off my brief moment of insanity—for one, flickering second I thought he was going to say my name.

"Oh really?" he says, pointing to my plate. "I believe this is an example of the pot calling the kettle . . . a description which similarly applies to itself."

"God, I hate it when the kitchen appliances accuse each other of the same crimes," I reply, and we both laugh while everyone else stares at us like we're nuts.

The conversation moves on, and soon we're all laughing. Owen is making jokes and telling stories, and I feel this sense of ease I haven't felt since we got to the lake. A sense of rightness and belonging.

We decide to carpool into town since it's going to be a crowded day. I throw on a clean pair of cutoffs and a tie-dyed shirt, and then Owen and I pile into the back seat of the car, with Georgia and Eden in the front.

Which is how it should be—the two older girls riding in front. Again, that sense of rightness returns. Riding around in the passenger seat next to Mateo, and even practicing driving myself—it was a rush, sure. But it was too fast, too soon. And now, as Georgia steers us down the road into town, a sense of calm washes over me. Already the past two weeks seem to fade like a summery dream.

And that's what it was, I realize: a fantasy. Yes, all those hours with Mateo were very real. But what they *meant* to me was the fantasy. All that time, he was mostly locked inside his own world, ruminating and doing the bare minimum to engage with me. It wasn't all in my head—but it also wasn't going anywhere. It was all so breathless and rushed that I couldn't see it for what it was, while I was still inside the bubble of it.

My heart still hurts. But it hurts a lot less.

Partly because the whole time I'm in the back seat next to Owen, and we're goofing around and shoving each other and laughing about dumb things, there's still this tiny voice in my head going: *We kissed. We kissed. We kissed. Now what?*

Obviously, the answer to that question, to the "now what," is . . . nothing. There's nothing to be done. Just let it go and be cool, be normal. Like Owen's being.

I've certainly learned my lesson about making things mean more than they really do.

It takes us nearly a half hour just to find a parking spot. Despite last night's rain, the sun is out and so are all the good people of Laurel, locals and summer vacationers alike. Main Street is blocked off from traffic and the whole town is decorated in red-white-and-blue banners and spangles. There's a band playing, several cotton candy machines, a bunch of carnival games, and even a Ferris wheel on the town green.

People with stands and tables along the sidewalk are giving away sparklers and Uncle Sam hats with the American flag pattern in glitter. I grab one for me and one for Owen, though his keeps falling off.

"I have a giant head," he laughs. "And besides, these aren't my colors. I look better in purple."

"I've never once seen you in purple," I reply skeptically.

"Oh, ye of little imagination," he says with a smirk.

I'm feeling even more myself after several hours of festival fun, plus approximately fifteen pounds of funnel cake. The four of us play the ring toss, balloon darts, and duck pond. We split up for a bit so Eden and Georgia can go shopping, and then we find them again and get ice cream. Dave and Mom show up, and Dave willingly puts himself in the dunk tank. I notice the glee with which Georgia aims the ball that sends him splashing into the tank, leaving his glasses floating nearby in the water.

The sun is high overhead by this point, and we're all sweating and happy. The smell of fried dough and kettle corn drifts through the air. The sounds of laughter, music, babies crying, kids screaming, and the occasional "I WON!" ricochet through the streets.

Eden and Georgia are in the midst of a competitive battle over whether rigged games counted as "fair wins."

"Oh my god, you *definitely* elbowed that twelve-year-old to get the prize," Eden is saying.

"She was *hogging the squirt gun*!" Georgia fires back, triumphantly holding up a giant stuffed banana in sunglasses.

I'm laughing along with them when, out of nowhere, Georgia's face changes, going paler than the stuffed banana.

I turn around to see Rhys and Mateo approaching, both of them looking perfect and handsome and, dare I say it, a little arrogant.

"Hey, ladies," Rhys says, sipping from a large soda cup. So casual.

Beside him, Mateo gives me a small nod, and I feel like I'm going to throw up.

Owen looks between me and Mateo, then back at me. "Is this the guy?"

I try to widen my eyes and subtly shake my head. The last thing I need is Owen making this weirder than it already is.

Rhys doesn't seem to notice any of this. "You guys wanna play duck hunt?"

"We already did," I blurt out.

At the same time, Eden takes Georgia's arm. "And we were just heading . . . over there," she says. "Away from, um, *here*. Sorry, boys!"

She pulls Georgia away, and I'm left staring at Mateo and Rhys like a gaping fish. "Um, this is Owen," I say awkwardly.

Mateo reaches out to shake hands, but Owen doesn't respond. He's just staring Mateo up and down like he's some sort of criminal. I can't say I blame him. He said he read my letter, and my letter didn't exactly hold back.

"If either of you do anything to hurt Georgia or Daisy again, just know, you have been warned," Owen practically growls.

"Whoa there!" I say, awkwardly laughing. "Yeah, sorry, we

have to go, too!" I drag Owen away before he can say anything more.

Once we're a safe distance, I face him. "What was that?"

He shrugs. "You're lucky I have no fighting skills whatsoever. That could've turned into a real street brawl."

I roll my eyes. "I highly doubt that. I don't think any one of the *three* of you even knows how to throw a punch."

But Owen doesn't laugh. "It just pisses me off, what some people think they can get away with."

"Hey, it's cool. You don't have to defend us girls. We're not, like, maidens in towers or whatever."

"Yeah, I know. Sorry. You could probably do a better job kicking that guy's ass than me."

"Violence is not how we resolve our problems, remember, Owen?"

He laughs, shaking his hand. "You sound like my mom."

"That was the aim. You're already going to be in enough trouble for taking the car. Your mom sounded pretty pissed when you called her."

"I would regret punching that kid in the face. But I do not regret driving up here in a stolen car. This is awesome," he says, his good mood returning.

"I'm glad you like it."

"I knew I would. What's not to love? Games I actually have a shot at winning, artery-destroying food, and getting to hang out with the Holliday girls? It's the best. I'm dying of thirst, though.

Let's get another lemonade. You want one?"

"Sure." I'm glad the awkwardness has passed, but I feel confused as we walk side by side to one of the lemonade stands. Why *did* Owen react like that? Is it possible he was not merely defending me and Georgia but actually a little . . . jealous? Or am I letting my imagination run wild? I think of what Eden said at breakfast. He *did* drive up here—risking the wrath of his parents—rather quickly. Come to think of it, he must've barely slept. I bet he didn't even unpack from his trip. All he had time to do was read my postcards and letter and set his alarm for early this morning.

Just like he must've set his alarm early the morning I left for the lake house, waking up with enough time to slip his first postcard to me onto our stoop so I'd find it before leaving.

I think of what Tre said at the club. *Is* that the kind of thing someone who is *just friends* would do?

We kissed. We kissed. We kissed. Now what?

I try to push the thoughts from my head as Owen takes a big slurp of lemonade. "I only got one since they're huge. We can share," he says, holding it out to me.

"Sure. It's not like we haven't swapped saliva before," I blurt out. I mean, we should probably put the kiss out in the open anyway, shouldn't we? Since I'm doing such a bad job of banishing it from my mind.

"True," he says slowly, and I feel this flash of relief—maybe he's going to take the bait and tell me what our kiss actually meant. But instead, he wags his eyebrows and adds, "Right before you started swapping saliva with that Mateo guy."

I swallow. "So?"

He shrugs. "So, nothing."

I take a giant sip of the lemonade. "Does it bother you? That I, you know. Kissed Mateo?" I feel embarrassed saying it out loud, but I already wrote it all in a letter. What do I have to hide now?

He shrugs again. "Should it?"

I stare at him. Owen, who I've been friends with for so long. How is he suddenly so slippery to pin down, so difficult to read? Was he always this way?

"I guess not," I finally answer.

I start walking, and he walks alongside me. Amiably. Like friends. "Good. Then it doesn't bother me," he says, taking the lemonade back.

"Good," I reply, though I don't feel good. I just feel . . . weird, and more confused than ever. "I . . ." I stop walking again and turn to look at him. "I've obviously made the mistake of making a kiss mean too much to me. And I felt really stupid about it. About *him*. So I thought . . . We should talk about it. About our, you know."

"Smooch? Kiss? Hot make-out sesh in Jenna's upstairs bathroom?" he teases.

I swat at him. "Owen, stop! I'm being serious!" I'm starting to regret trying to bring this up. I should've let it go.

"So what *did* it mean to you?" he asks. He puts this out there so casually, I'm taken aback. Because to be honest, I don't know the answer. All this time I've been trying to guess what it meant to *him*. What *did* it mean to me?

"I—I—I don't know, actually," I say.

Owen hands me back the lemonade. "I don't either."

"Really? Do you think it made things too complicated? Do you regret it?"

He thinks for a second. "No. I definitely don't."

"Oh," I say, relief flooding through me. "Okay, good. I don't either."

"You don't?"

I shake my head. "I mean, if we'd never tried it, we'd never have known what it was like. . . ."

"I guess everything's worth trying once, right?" he says. Which saps my relief away.

"So it was just a one-time thing?" I ask. "I'm just trying to, like, clear the air and everything."

"Right. Yeah. Totally. Just a one-time thing. I mean, so far." Owen squints into the distance. "Should we ride the Ferris wheel?"

"Are you trying to change the subject?" I tease.

"Why, yes, in fact, maybe I am," he says, and it's the first time I detect a slight blush. At least we're both embarrassed by the awkwardness this has created.

We get in line for the Ferris wheel, and it isn't until we're in the air that I realize this is even *more* awkward. Here we are, just the two of us, our legs swaying out over the crowds, riding one of the most romantic rides in the world. Another couple is literally kissing in the car ahead of us.

He nods toward them. "Jeez. Seems like everyone's making out these days."

I laugh. "Um, yeah. So annoying."

"*So* annoying." He turns to face me. "Should we be annoying, too? I mean, since they're already doing it."

Nervous butterflies burst through my stomach and chest. "Really?"

He shrugs. "Only if you want to see if we can out-annoy them."

"You make everything a competition."

"You know me so well." He smiles at me.

"Okay, fine," I say. "Let's do it."

He seems almost giddy now as he swivels to face me. "Here, you hold the lemonade," he says, handing it to me. Then he pushes my hair back from my face, and puts one hand on my waist, and pulls me closer to him.

And then we're doing it. We're kissing again.

And it's just as good as the first time. Maybe even better. Once again, we're both laughing a little, like we can't believe this is happening. But it's also too fun to stop. And his hand on my side is sending electric shivers through my whole body. And even though our entire kiss conversation felt completely awkward, somehow, this does not. This just feels . . . right.

When the ride finally comes to a stop and we're forced to get off the Ferris wheel, I feel lighter than air. My legs are a little wobbly. "Let's go sit down somewhere," I say, because I honestly don't know if I can keep standing without falling over.

"Sure." He lets me lead the way to a grassy area, shaded by a low tree. It's not completely private, given how crowded the fair is, but it's still set somewhat apart from the action.

"Owen," I say, taking a deep breath. "Here's the thing. I don't want to ruin our friendship."

He looks deflated. "That's cool, I get it."

"But on the other hand, I really like kissing you. Like a lot."

"Yeah?"

"I would like to keep doing it. But it scares me. I don't want to get carried away. I don't want to feel stupid again. I don't want to get hurt."

He takes my hand. "I wouldn't hurt you, Daisy."

"How do I know that?"

He shrugs. "I don't know, because I promise?"

"So you want to keep kissing, too?"

He smiles. "Obviously. I really like kissing you. I really, um . . . like you."

"As in *like* like? Or . . . like how much you like Milk Duds?"

He's bright red now. "Not the Milk Duds kind of like. Although they are *great*. I've probably had a crush on you for at least a year. I'm just used to acting very chill and aloof about it."

"Oh yeah, so chill, so aloof." I laugh.

"Shut up," he says, nudging me with his shoulder, and I can't keep the grin off my face. I can't believe this is really happening, and that everyone was right, that he *does* really like me.

"I'm sorry I didn't pick up on it sooner," I tell him. "But I could maybe have a crush on you, too." I squint at him, faux serious. "If I *really* tried."

He laughs. "You'd do that for me?"

"Anything for you, Owen."

And then I kiss him.

TWENTY

Georgia

I DON'T SEE BENNY all day at the fair, and part of me is glad. The feelings he's stirred up in me are powerful, and they've changed me so much, in such a short time. But it's been nice to just have this time with Eden and Daisy. We've all been so busy—and caught in our own romantic disasters—that I've been missing the coziness of the three of us hanging out.

We're all happy, tired, and full of festival food by the time we pile back into the car to go watch the fireworks on the beach. Eden cranks up the radio, singing along. When I glimpse back in the rearview mirror, I see Daisy and Owen holding hands, and I smile to myself.

But there's a pang in my chest, too; I always thought I was the sister who knew all about love. I was the one in the serious relationship that was going places. I'd found my "forever person." Or that's what I'd thought. That my love story with Rhys was just like Mom's love story with Dad.

Now it seems like maybe I never knew much about love at all.

And seeing how sweetly content Daisy looks right now makes me wonder if I should've let myself start making mistakes sooner. I think I have a lot of catching up to do.

We pull into the beach lot and snag one of the last remaining spots. Soon, people will be lining up along the street, leaving their cars on the side of the road and walking the rest of the way, blankets and picnic baskets in hand.

Mom and Dave are already here and have claimed a nice open area on the sand with a couple of blankets and beach chairs, a basket of sandwiches, and bottles of sparkling cider.

"You kids look sunburned!" Dave says by way of a greeting as Daisy, Eden, and Owen plop onto the extra chairs.

"I'm gonna get us some waters from the snack shack," I say, not ready to sit yet.

"I'll come with you," Mom says, standing up and brushing off her shorts.

We kick off our sandals and navigate the crowded beach barefoot, stepping carefully over the latticework of blankets and bags, shoes and outstretched legs. When we get to the snack shack line, snaking down practically to the lake's edge, we stand quietly for a minute.

"Georgia," Mom says, breaking our silence. "I want you to know how much I appreciate your help this summer. You've been handling everyone's schedules while I hole up in my writing studio. Dave and I have both been blissfully oblivious to the rest of the world, and you've made sure you and the girls get where you all need to go. I'm so lucky to have you."

I sigh. "It's— Yeah. No problem. How's the book coming along?"

My mom shrugs. "Really well, I think. You know, there's a lot of painful stuff that's come up for me, being back here. It's been good, though, to have a way to process it all."

I look at her in surprise. "The book is set at the lake?"

Mom nods. "Oh yeah, I didn't tell you that? It's based on my childhood, coming here every summer."

"Wow," I say, realizing I really had no idea—or even any curiosity about—what she was working on until now. "Sounds cathartic."

"It is," she says. "I think it's going to be a beautiful book. But it's difficult, too. As, you know, most beautiful things are."

I nod. "Have you . . ." I feel my voice getting tight in my throat. "Have you been thinking a lot about Dad while we've been up here? Or . . ."

"Oh, honey, of course I have. Every day. I think about him here, and at home. I don't believe that ever goes away."

I remember what Daisy said this morning. How it's possible to hold love and grief at the same time.

"Mom, I'm sorry I burst out of the house the other day. I'm . . . It's been hard to see how happy you are with Dave. I want that for you, but . . . are you sure you're ready?" I wipe a tear from the corner of my eye.

Mom wraps an arm around me. "I'm ready, Georgia. But it's okay if you aren't yet. You know, I was a little nervous to tell you."

"Really?"

Mom laughs. "It sounds silly, but I really wanted your blessing. With Nana and Gramps gone, all I've got is you girls. I knew Daisy would be fine with it, but it was your opinion I cared most about. You're so smart. You read people so well. And I know you're always looking out for us, for me."

"Mom," I say, trying not to cry. "I don't think I'm a very good judge of character after all." The tears come, despite my best efforts.

"Oh, Georgia." She hugs me. "Do you mean Rhys?"

I nod. "That and—everything?"

She sighs. "I don't think you judged him wrong. I think you loved him. I think he was right for you, these past few years. You needed him. And now, maybe you're just ready for something different."

It feels like such a relief to hear her say that. Like maybe my entire relationship wasn't a mistake, wasn't a lie. It was just—not meant to be forever.

Maybe we can't know what is.

We're up next in line, and Mom buys our water bottles. She hands one to me. "Here, you need to hydrate," she says. "You need water, and you need rest, and you know what, Georgia, honey? You need to give yourself a break now and again."

I nod, my throat still feeling tight. I unscrew the water cap and drink it gratefully. As its coolness rushes down my throat, I remember what it feels like to just give your body what it needs. Just that refreshing, calming reminder helps me feel centered again.

And that's when I see Benny.

"Mom," I tell her. "I'll meet you back at the blanket in a few minutes."

"Sounds good. Love you, Georgia."

"Love you, too. And Mom? I really am. Happy for you. For what it's worth, you do have my blessing."

She laughs, but her eyes glitter with emotion. "Thank you," she whispers.

Benny cocks his head and grins when he sees me walking toward him through the crowd—which makes me smile, too. He's standing in the wet sand, a few steps into the water, letting it lap around his bare ankles, and behind him, the sunset is making the lake a cotton-candy pink.

I stop when I reach the lip of the water, but he gestures for me to come in, and even though there's no swimming allowed during the fireworks, I walk in to meet him anyway. We're only like six inches deep. So what if we get in trouble? Maybe I'm okay with getting in trouble occasionally.

Sometimes it's worth it.

His smile grows—he can totally read me. He probably knows I'm debating the level of lakeside infraction we're committing.

He reaches up and gently touches my cheek with his thumb. "You got too much sun."

I shake my head. "I forgot to reapply."

"That's not like you," he says quietly, studying my face.

"I know," I say. "I was too focused on having fun."

He smiles even bigger, if that's possible. "I'm glad to hear that. I'm glad I found you. I wanted to see you earlier, but Lita hurt her hip and I've been helping her around the house. She wanted to come see the fireworks, but I thought walking on the sand might be too hard. So she's at home, watching from a window."

"I'm sorry to hear that," I say. "It's really sweet that you're here this summer to help take care of her, though." It occurs to me that I don't even know where his parents are, why he's spending this summer just with his grandmother.

There's so much I don't know about him. So much I want to learn.

And yet.

"Benny," I say. "I've been thinking about this. Us. I really like spending time with you."

"Me too," he whispers.

"But I need to take things slow. I'm not ready to get into anything serious right now. I need to figure out my whole life, my future. I think I should apply for a college transfer, see if I can switch schools next year or even spring semester. I want to think about where I'd actually want to go, if I hadn't based my decision on Rhys."

I was afraid Benny would be hurt, but he looks genuinely excited for me. "Georgia, that's great," he says. "I know you'll figure it all out in time. But it doesn't all have to be decided in the next few weeks, right?"

I laugh. "I guess not. But you know me. I like to get ahead on the planning."

"Yes," he laughs. "You certainly do. And listen. About us. Obviously, I still have a year of high school left. I don't expect anything beyond the summer. It's like I said on the dock the other night; I'm just happy to have this time with you. I'm happy to live in the present."

"Live in the present. That sounds really nice," I say. "A little terrifying, but really nice."

The sunset has deepened to a burning, fiery red, outlined in charcoal. Soon, the light will disappear behind the distant shore, and the fireworks will begin.

"Do you want to come sit with us to watch the fireworks?" I ask him. "Or do you need to get back to your grandma?"

His smile falters. "I should probably get back before it's totally dark. I want to make sure she's comfortable."

"Of course! Will I see you in the morning? Your training isn't complete, you know."

He laughs. "I'll be there."

He leans in and kisses my cheek. "I hope that didn't hurt your sunburn."

"It didn't," I whisper. I want nothing more than to pull him in and kiss him, but with all these people around, I'm too shy to do it. "See you tomorrow."

"Tomorrow," he whispers, close to my ear.

And then he walks out of the water, disappearing in the crowd.

It's almost entirely dark by the time I make my way back to our picnic spot.

"Don't knock over my sparkling cider," Daisy says. "It was the last pour!"

"You guys finished it all already?! I was gone for like ten minutes!" I say, stepping carefully across Daisy's chair to take a seat between her and Eden.

"You can have mine," Eden says, handing me her cup. "I already have to pee so bad it's a literal nightmare."

I laugh, accepting her cup. "When will you ever learn?"

She smiles at me in the darkness. "Probably never?"

"They're starting!" Daisy says.

And sure enough, as I look up, I see the first bursts of fireworks lighting up the sky in white and royal blue and gold, leaving a smoky halo.

Everyone starts oohing and aahing, just like you're supposed to, scrambling to take pictures. I watch a few more explosions of light, noticing the way the smoke curls in the air afterward. It's probably a terrible source of pollution, but it makes me think about how our lives are a little bit like the sky, full of the fading smoke of all the things that once lit us up but are now over. Life itself is fleeting. Love is fleeting. You never know what's going to last, what you're going to have forever, and what's going to fade and disappear.

I look at Daisy and then at Eden, their faces silhouetted in the changing colors lighting up the black sky. Two faces I know as well as my own. And I feel this swell of immense peace. I think about pulling out my phone to get a cute selfie of the three of us together—the Holliday girls on one of their favorite holidays—but decide I don't need to document this moment.

I'm going to just live in the present, and see what happens next.

EPILOGUE

Eden

"WATCH OUT!" I SCREAM, leaning across the console to grab Georgia's arm. "Truck!"

"Mauling me while I'm driving is not helping!" Georgia shouts back. She's trying to merge into the right lane on the FDR.

"Remind me to never get my driver's license," I say. "This is hellacious."

"You're the one who lives here! Just be thankful you have such a responsible—" But before Georgia can finish her sentence, it's cut off by a loud honk that causes both of us to nearly jump out of our seats.

I look over at her, and we both burst out laughing.

Daisy leans forward from the back seat. "Hey, can you two please keep us all alive? I want to enjoy my last weekend before you leave me for college and I never see you anymore!"

"Aw, Daisy. You'll see us on holidays," Georgia says.

"This weekend is going to be epic, don't worry," I tell Daisy. I have a full itinerary for us. Karaoke and my favorite sushi spot and the world's best outdoor vintage market. And maybe we'll bring a giant bottle of diet soda and ride the ferry around for hours, until my bladder explodes.

"I just can't believe the summer's almost over," Daisy says.

"I know, I can't either," says Georgia.

"No kidding," I say.

Luckily for us, Mateo decided to go back to Connecticut early so he could fly out to see his mom in Italy. Rhys then spent pretty much every weekend in the city. And Georgia spent a lot of her days with Benny. She seemed to be having a really good time, and it made me happy to see her softening, becoming more open to things not being perfect. They plan to keep in touch, but who knows what that will look like.

As for Owen, he had to leave after the Fourth of July, returning home to his worried parents, who grounded him for the rest of the summer. He and Daisy have continued sending each other postcards, though, which is just *so* old-fashioned and adorable. I'm pretty sure she's totally in love with him—and maybe was all along, but just didn't realize it. Ah, youth.

As for me . . . well, I woke up on the morning of the Fourth of July basically wrapped in Leo's arms. I felt him stirring awake, and I looked up. "I hope your arm's not dead from me sleeping on it all night," I said.

He smiled. "Eh. Who needs a working arm. This is much better."

But clearly his arm *was* working just fine, because he wrapped it around me tighter, then tilted my chin up so I was facing him. And without even waiting to find out if I had gross morning breath, he leaned down and kissed me.

With that kiss, it was like something deeply held inside both of us was finally freed. We were still in separate sleeping bags, but we quickly unzipped them and then laughed as I tried to untangle my legs (why am I so good at getting tangled in things???). And then we were tangled in each other, and we couldn't stop kissing. I kissed his whole face, him laughing. "I missed this so much," he said. "I really missed you, Eden."

"Me too," I said, realizing how true it was, despite everything I had told myself. Despite trying to believe I had moved on.

We lay like that, rolling around in the hot tent, making out until I could barely breathe, his hands finding their way up inside my loose T-shirt (*his* T-shirt, which I still have definitely *not* given back). I swear, we could have taken things a lot further—and I wanted to—but unsurprisingly, I had to pee. A night in the woods will do that.

So we packed up our gear and trudged back downhill, somehow finding the rest of the group without too much drama.

After Boundless Horizons ended, though, Leo had to return to the city. It was hard, finally making amends and realizing all those old feelings between us were still there, alive and well, only to say goodbye again. Especially since we're going to school on opposite ends of the earth. I'll be at USC, and he'll be at UPenn.

Which is why I'm extra excited to be coming home this weekend. I'll get to see him one last time before he packs up his car to drive down to Philadelphia. He's meeting us at karaoke tonight. I can't wait to make fun of his atrocious singing voice.

I can't wait to steal the mic all night.

I can't wait to tell him, again, like I've told him almost every night on the phone this summer, that I love him. And that I really believe now that everything happens for a reason.

But first—I can't wait to race around the city with Daisy and Georgia, my two favorite people in the world.

"Pull in over here," I say, pointing Georgia toward the parking garage. We rumble over some cobblestones on the side street and she makes a sharp left. "Wow, you've gotten better at this," I tell her.

"I'm a fast learner," she says.

"I'm starving," says Daisy.

"Here, have some more Sour Patch Kids," I say, handing a package back to her.

"Thanks. You're a lifesaver."

"Are you guys ready to have the best time of your lives?" I ask.

"I think we already did," Georgia says. "This whole summer was the best time of my life."

"Me too," Daisy says between chews.

"Me three," I tell them. "Best. Summer. Ever."

And then we dissolve into overlapping chatter, with me directing Georgia through the parking garage and Georgia saying she has nothing to wear tonight, and Daisy asking incessantly about what's for dinner—and in the chaos of us, I feel like the luckiest person alive.

THE HOLLIDAY GIRLS WILL BE BACK
FOR A MAGICAL WINTER BREAK . . .

READ ON FOR A SNEAK PEEK!

Eden

"WELL, I SHOULD PROBABLY let you pack, Eden," Leo says, and immediately my chest starts to tighten. It's weird, almost like I'm afraid to say goodbye, as if the whole saying-I-love-you thing is so temporary, it could wipe away like a message on the whiteboard on someone's dorm room door. Or, like, when you suck on a candy cane for five seconds and the stripes have vanished, leaving you with this slimy minty stick in your mouth . . .

"Leo, come in! Stay a minute!" my mom says, emerging from her bedroom with a fully loaded suitcase. "John, why are you eating a sandwich? We're having dinner when we get there!"

"It's a little snack," Dad says. Which is classic Dad—he eats like he's still a teenager and insists it's because of his height, and the fact that he still feels so young at heart. *If I'm as hungry as a teenager, I must have the metabolism of one!* But I know why Mom nags at him so much about food and exercise. Ever since my uncle Mitch, Dad's brother, died unexpectedly of a heart attack on one otherwise regular morning in October, it put us all on edge. It was a stark reminder how fragile our health can be. I mean,

Uncle Mitch was a paragon of athleticism. If it happened to him, it could happen to anyone. "What can I bring down to the car, hon?" Dad asks, diverting her attention.

"Oh, here, let me help, Nyla," Leo offers to my mom.

And soon, while I'm still throwing sparkly sweaters and my entire jewelry-making kit into my bag, my parents and Leo are running a tight ship, packing up last-minute items, adding bows to wrapped presents, wiping down counters, and moving bags and boxes up and down the elevator to the parking garage. (When we go "home" for the holidays, we go hard.)

"Honestly, Leo, thank you so much. I don't think we'd be getting out of here anywhere near on time if it weren't for your help," Mom says in the same voice she uses when we have a particularly cute waiter.

"Hello, Mom, am I invisible?" my brother, Jesse, asks, standing in the doorway of his dark bedroom, headphones down around his neck.

"By your own design," Mom replies.

Leo gives Jesse a fist bump. "Hey, man, cool shirt. Good to see you."

Jesse starts telling Leo about the significance of the phrase on his T-shirt—it's a reference to a video game I've never heard of—and I see my brother animated like he's awake and part of the world for once. I guess he, like my dad, can resemble a normal human sometimes.

Or maybe Leo just has this effect on people.

I can see Mom is noticing it, too. "It's such a shame you two have to say goodbye so soon," she says. "What are you doing for the rest of your winter break, Leo?"

He shrugs. "Sitting around my apartment waiting for Eden to get back."

"I doubt *that*," Dad says.

At the same time, Mom throws a hand to her heart like she's in some nineteenth-century novel. "We can't have that. Come with us!"

"What?" I ask.

"Seriously?" Leo asks.

"Cool," says Jesse.

"That's a *great* idea!" Dad says, coming up behind Mom and wrapping an arm around her back. "The Hollidays are a more-the-merrier family, trust me. We'd love to have you, and I'm sure Elena and Dave would, too."

Even though I spent the summer at the lake house with Aunt Elena and her boyfriend—now fiancé—Dave, I still sometimes startle, hearing them grouped together like an official unit.

"Are you sure?" I ask them.

I mean, I would *love* to spend more time with Leo, but . . . in a house absolutely *swarming* with Hollidays and our, well, many holiday traditions . . . that seems like it could be a lot to juggle. My time with my cousins is also important to me. Last time Leo and I were together, I really struggled to maintain friendships—I ended up putting all my energy into him. I don't want to make that same mistake again.

"Of course!" says Dad, oblivious to my hesitation.

"We won't take no for an answer!" says Mom.

"I don't have any of my things . . ." Leo says. "Though I just got in this morning. My bag is still packed. . . ."

"Won't your parents be bummed if we steal you?" I ask.

"We have to drive up the West Side Highway to head out of town anyway," Dad says over me.

"Let's call your parents and see what they say," Mom suggests.

This whole thing is becoming hugely embarrassing, but Leo seems to be enjoying all the positive attention. Mom gets him to put the Goldbaums on FaceTime and lots of mutual ravings are exchanged. I swear my parents are having a spontaneous love affair with Leo's. What is even happening?

"So, it's official," Mom says as Leo hangs up. "You're an honorary Holliday this season. Let's get into the car, then. You three will have to squeeze into the back," she says to me, Leo, and Jesse. "We'll swing by the Upper West to grab your bag!"

And that's how I find myself awkwardly straddling the middle seat bump, squished between my brother and my boyfriend for the three-hour ride to Rhode Island, the words *love* and *serious* still jostling in my gut like popping popcorn.

As the sun sets over the Hudson, flaring pink and gold against the city buildings, I wonder if this is going to be the best holiday ever or a complete disaster. He thinks he loves me—will he still think so when the Hollidays are through with him?